MVFOL

Sharon Sala

SHARON
SALA

COLD
HEARTS

MIRA®

ISBN-13: 978-0-7783-1830-9

Recycling programs
for this product may
not exist in your area.

Cold Hearts

Copyright © 2015 by Sharon Sala

All rights reserved. Except for use in any review, the reproduction or
utilization of this work in whole or in part in any form by any electronic,
mechanical or other means, now known or hereinafter invented, including
xerography, photocopying and recording, or in any information storage or
retrieval system, is forbidden without the written permission of the publisher,
MIRA Books, 225 Duncan Mill Road, Don Mills, Ontario M3B 3K9, Canada.

This is a work of fiction. Names, characters, places and incidents are
either the product of the author's imagination or are used fictitiously, and
any resemblance to actual persons, living or dead, business establishments,
events or locales is entirely coincidental.

® and TM are trademarks of Harlequin Enterprises Limited or its corporate
affiliates. Trademarks indicated with ® are registered in the United States Patent
and Trademark Office, the Canadian Intellectual Property Office and in other
countries.

For questions and comments about the quality of this book, please contact us at
CustomerService@Harlequin.com.

www.MIRABooks.com

Printed in U.S.A.

Compassion is the recipe for life. Take heed of kindness. Use liberally when necessary and omit judgment for others.

The coldest hearts beat in the bodies of those most wounded by life. It is not for us to judge a lifestyle when we are unaware of shattered dreams.

I dedicate this book to everyone who's walking a path they didn't see coming, with peace and grace to them for still finding their way.

COLD
HEARTS

One

It began with phone calls in the night.

The moment Melissa Sherman answered, the connection would be broken. After a time, the calls escalated to heavy breathing and ugly laughter. It wasn't until the caller began telling her in a slow husky whisper the disgusting things he was going to do to her that she finally broke, screaming obscenities in his ear, calling him an outright coward hiding behind walls and darkness, and hung up. Then she unplugged her landline and took comfort in the fact that he didn't know the number to her cell phone.

She had less than two weeks of peace and quiet before the stalking began.

Lissa's starfish night-light had seen her through most of elementary school, all of high school and a broken heart, four years of college and six years of teaching in Savannah, Georgia.

This past summer she and her night-light had returned to Mystic, West Virginia, to teach first grade. She'd never really thought about coming home to teach, but having her childhood home to live in free and clear had been too good to turn down. It was a hard trade-off, inheriting the house as she lost her last parent, but family memories were strong and vivid in every room.

Tonight the starfish was casting a faint yellow glow, lighting the way from her bedroom into the hall as she ran toward the living room, her footsteps making little *slap-slap* sounds on the hardwood floor.

It was after 2:00 a.m. and she'd already been up once, certain there was someone outside her house. The sound had been right beneath her bedroom window, a tapping sound, but nothing natural, because it had a very unnatural stop-and-go rhythm. It had taken all her nerve to look out, and then, when she did, she had seen nothing.

Uneasy, she'd gone back to bed and had just drifted off to sleep when she'd heard another sound that had had her on her feet in seconds. It was the sound of boots stomping heavily on the wooden surface of her front porch. Now she was running through the house in her old flannel pajamas. When she turned on the porch light to look out, she saw no one and nothing out of place. She thought about calling the police, but there was nothing to tell other than the fact she was scared out of her mind and the house that used to mean sanctuary now felt like a trap.

If her father was still alive he would have been sitting outside in the dark with a shotgun, waiting for the sucker to come back. And the longer she thought about that, the angrier she became, until she yanked the door open, letting it hit the wall with a bang as she stomped out onto the porch.

"You think this is funny?" she yelled. "You come

back here again and we'll see how hard you laugh with a load of buckshot in your ass."

Then she strode back in the house with her head up and blond curls bouncing, slamming the door behind her. Just to punctuate the promise, she turned on every light in the house and then went to bed.

Across the darkened street her stalker, a man named Reece Parsons, was crouched in an alley, grinning.

She was a feisty little bitch, but that was how he liked them. He could tell she would be fine in the sack, but she wasn't ready yet. He wanted her afraid for her life before he raped her because that, too, was how he rolled. As soon as she went back inside and closed the door, he slipped away.

The next time Lissa woke up it was 6:00 a.m. and her alarm was blaring. She rolled over and shut it off, facing the fact that it was not only time to get ready for work, but it was also raining.

She threw back the covers to get up, then winced as she stood. The floor was cold, and because of the rain, there would be no recess, which was a teacher's worst nightmare. This day couldn't get worse.

She headed for the bathroom to shower and paused at the sink to eye the knot of curls in her hair. Rainy days made her naturally curly hair go haywire, and today was no exception.

When her gaze landed on the little brown mole just above the right corner of her lips, she frowned. Mack Jackson, the boy from high school who'd broken her heart, used to kiss the mole for good luck before every football game. She had been trying to forget him for nearly ten years now but without much success. Such was life.

An hour later she was on her way out the door with hot coffee in one hand and a backpack full of games she would need for the indoor play periods, something they all had to get through before this miserable-ass day could come to an end.

But then the car wouldn't start and she realized she'd been wrong. The day had already gotten worse. She turned the key again and again, until the engine finally fired. Mumbling a grudging thank-you to the universe, she turned on the wipers and backed out of the driveway. But the moment she put the car in Drive, the engine began sputtering.

"No!" Lissa shouted, and stomped the gas with the assumption that too much gas was better than not enough.

The fact that she made it to the school parking lot without actually being late was a miracle. She didn't even care that she had to run through the rain with a broken umbrella to get into the building. She was on the job, and the time to worry about the car and the stalker was after school was over.

Both bays at Paul Jackson's garage and gas station were full, and his other mechanic was home sick with the flu. Paul had called in extra help to run the front while he worked on the repair jobs. He replaced a starter on the first car just before noon and sent the owner on his way. Now he was almost through putting new brake pads on a truck that reeked of marijuana. He wasn't the kind to pass judgment on his fellow man, but when the young guy came to pick it up, Paul intended to give him the same lecture he'd given his own son years earlier.

He paused a moment to wipe sweat off his brow and pop a couple of painkillers. His knees throbbed, his elbow was aching where he'd whacked it on the concrete and his knuckles were bloody—all part of a mechanic's job.

Just as he squatted back down, he heard a car pulling into the station and knew from the rough sound of the engine that something was wrong with it. He stood up, wiping his hands as he turned to meet the owner, and then smiled when he saw Lissa Sherman getting out.

She had been in the same class with his son, Mack, and they'd dated long enough that he'd wondered if one day she might become part of the family. Although that had never happened, he was still very fond of her. He noticed as she darted into the bay that she looked as exhausted as he felt.

"Hey, honey, it sounds like your fuel pump is starving the engine. It's running pretty rough."

She rolled her eyes. "Oh, Paul, this has been the day from hell. I didn't think the car was going to start this morning, and then, when it finally did, I headed straight for school. The rain kept the kids inside at recess, and they were wild and bored, so you can imagine how that went down."

Paul laughed. He had always enjoyed having her around the house. She was as unaware of her beauty as a woman could be and had a great personality.

"Yeah, I wouldn't trade your day for mine. At least I know how to fix cars. I couldn't wrangle a half dozen of those little rug rats, let alone a whole room full.

However, that's not why you're here. Tell me more about your car."

Lissa shrugged. "I don't know. When it finally started, it ran rough all the way to school. A friend helped me get it started again, and here I am in need of your help."

"Yeah, sure. Just leave the keys in it and I'll get to it first thing tomorrow."

"I don't suppose you have a loaner I could drive?" she asked.

Paul frowned. "No, I sure don't. Sorry."

Her shoulder slumped as she managed a smile.

"That's okay. How long do you think it will take you to fix it?"

"Might be the fuel pump. I can't really say until I take a look at it to see exactly what's wrong."

Lissa wiped a shaky hand across her face and tried not to let her disappointment show. Even though she lived in town, since her stalker had stepped up his game she felt insecure about being without transportation.

Paul eyed her closely. For some reason she seemed uneasy, even afraid. He didn't know what was going on with her, but he knew he would just spend another lonely night on his own when he went home. Or he could stay late and do his good deed for the day.

"Hey, how about I take a look at it this evening, and if it's not a big fix and I have the parts, I'll have it ready for you in the morning."

Her relief was evident, which told him he'd read her mood correctly.

"That would be super, and I sure do appreciate it," she said.

Paul glanced out at the downpour. "Do you have a ride home?"

She nodded, pointing to the car waiting at the curb.

"Okay, then. If I run into trouble, I'll call and let you know it might take longer to fix. Are you in the phone book?"

She thought of the landline she kept unplugged and wrote her cell phone down for him on a slip of paper.

"Call this number. It's my cell."

He smiled. "I should have known. Not a lot of people still have landlines anymore. There are lots of things changing in this world."

She thought of how calm her life had been before the harassment had begun.

"You are so right about things changing," she said. "So I'll see you tomorrow?"

He smiled. "Yes, tomorrow."

He watched until she made it to the curb, and then he pulled her car into the empty bay and hung the keys on the board by the phone.

Lissa was soaked by the time she got home. She changed into dry clothes before starting a load of laundry, then began making something for supper. Keeping her students inside today during the noon hour meant lunch hadn't happened for her. She wanted something filling but quick to make, which took her straight to eggs. Within a short time she had a cheese omelet and a couple of slices of buttered toast on a plate, and was ready to dig in. She settled in front of the television to eat, enjoying the food and grateful for the roof over her head because the rain was really coming down.

Once she finished eating, she cleaned up the

kitchen, switched the load of laundry from the washer to the dryer and took a cookie with her as she went back into the living room. She channel surfed for a couple of minutes until she happened on a country-music program highlighting hit songs from the past ten years. The moment she saw who was performing and heard the song he was singing, she froze.

Alan Jackson was singing "Remember When."

She closed her eyes, but it didn't stop the tears as the memory came flooding back.

Mack stood naked before her, his hand outstretched.

Lissa shivered once but took it without hesitation. They'd made love before, and she knew what it felt like to come apart in his arms.

He swung her off her feet and carried her toward the bed.

"I love you, Lissa. So much," he whispered, as he laid her down and then slid onto the bed beside her.

"I love you, too," she said, as she wrapped her arms around his neck.

The radio was playing softly in the next room, a song called "Remember When." She sighed as he began leaving a trail of kisses from the base of her throat all the way down to her belly. She would remember this moment long after they grew old together. She wanted him inside her so bad that she ached, but she knew Mack would take his sweet time. When his fingers slid between her legs, she moaned.

"Do you like that, baby?" he said softly.

"Yes, yes, yes."

His breath was warm against her ear, then her cheek, and then he kissed the little mole near her lips.

When he did, Lissa turned to capture the next kiss for herself, but instead of kissing her, he gently bit the edge of her lower lip and rolled her nipple between his fingers just hard enough to send a sharp ache of longing through her body.

He pushed a knee between her legs, asking her to let him in, and when she did, in one fluid motion he slid inside her so fast that she gasped, unprepared for the suddenness of his actions. She began moving beneath him, already chasing the climax to come. They moved in rhythm without speaking, lost in the sensation of making love.

She went from the heat of passion to a full-blown climax so fast she almost screamed. She was still coming down from the high when Mack shuddered. The blood-rush shot through his body in gut-wrenching waves as he collapsed on top of her and then kissed the hollow at the base of her throat before he pushed up on one elbow to look at her.

"We're so good together," he whispered. Then he kissed her again.

The song ended and so did the memory. She didn't want to remember how good they were together. She didn't want to remember how easily he could make her lose her mind. What she did remember was that six weeks later, when she'd found out she was pregnant, it had never occurred to her that Mack would let her down.

When she'd told him, the look on his face had been as panicked as she felt. But he'd immediately put his arms around her and told her that he loved her. It didn't help that she'd felt him shaking even as he'd said the word *marriage*. He wasn't the only one who was scared. Her future was changing, too.

And then she'd had the miscarriage. The fight they'd had afterward was almost bizarre. She'd never understood his anger or why they hadn't spoken since, and just thinking about it made her lose her appetite. Unwilling to go down that road again, she changed channels and tossed the cookie in the trash.

Wind blew rain against the window in a rat-a-tat pattern that gave her the shivers, but the evening passed without incident. It appeared the inclement weather was serving as a deterrent to her stalker. Even creeps hated getting wet and cold. She went to bed, assuming when morning came that Paul Jackson would have her car back in order.

It was ten minutes after eleven—almost the witching hour. Paul had Lissa's car on the hydraulic lift and was standing beneath it, finishing up the work. He'd replaced the faulty fuel pump but in the process had noticed an oil leak, and after a quick check he'd located a pinhole in the oil pan. After that he'd had to call Freddie Miller, the auto parts dealer, to open up so he could get a replacement and promise the dealer a mess of fresh catfish the next time he went fishing for his trouble. He hurried back to the garage so Lissa's car would be ready for her as he'd promised.

He was giving the bolts a last check to make sure they were tight when he heard the bell jingle on the front door. He frowned, thinking he'd locked it, then realized that when he'd come back from getting the oil pan, he'd probably left it undone. It was odd that anyone would come in, though, because all the lights were off except the one here in this bay, so he watched the doorway, a bit uneasy.

But when he saw who was walking into the garage, his uneasiness disappeared.

"You're out pretty late, aren't you?" Paul asked.

"So are you," the man said.

Paul glanced back up at the oil pan.

"Give me a second and I'll be right with you."

"Don't hurry on my account." The moment Paul turned his back, the man hit the control switch to the lift and dropped Melissa Sherman's car on top of Paul's head.

Paul was caught off guard by the initial blow and staggered a couple of steps back, unaware that the lift was still coming down. He didn't realize what was happening until the next point of impact cracked his skull. His legs buckled as the car came down on him, crushing the rest of his body.

The killer never flinched. The ease of the whole process reinforced his belief that this had had to be done to get where he needed to go.

The silence afterward was as gripping as it had been the day he'd hanged Dick Phillips. He hadn't planned on doing this tonight, but first driving by and seeing Jackson working late, then parking in the alley and finding the door unlocked, it had seemed as if fate had lent him a hand. The opportunity was too good to pass up. He was surprised by how easy this one turned out. He didn't even have to get his hands dirty. No muss. No fuss. No noise. Only one thing left to do. He wiped his prints from the lift release and the doorknobs, and made a quick exit as the blood began to run out from beneath the car.

* * *

Lissa hitched a ride to the station to pick up her car with fellow teacher Margaret Lewis. They were bemoaning how muddy the playground would be as Margaret pulled up to the station to let her out.

"Thanks for the lift, Margaret. I'll see you at school."

"I'll wait just to make sure Mr. Jackson is through. Otherwise you'll still need a ride. Leave your things here until you know for sure," Margaret said.

"Okay, give me a minute," Lissa said.

Margaret grinned to herself as she watched Lissa hurry toward the station. That girl never walked when she could run. She saw Lissa enter the station, then move through the door leading into the garage. A couple of moments passed as she lost sight of her, and then she saw her running back.

At first she thought Lissa was only coming back to get her things. It took a few moments for her to realize her friend was screaming. Margaret jumped out on the run.

"What happened? What's wrong?" she yelled, as Lissa came flying out of the station.

"He's dead! Mr. Jackson is dead. Oh, my God, my car fell on him! Call an ambulance! Call the police!"

Margaret gasped and ducked back in her car to get her phone, while Lissa sank to her knees and covered her face, too shaken to stand.

Police Chief Trey Jakes was already on his way into Mystic when he got a call on his cell. When he saw it was from the dispatcher, he wondered why he hadn't used the radio.

"Hey, Avery. What's up?" Trey said, as he topped the hill just outside town.

"You need to go straight to Jackson's gas station. A customer found him in the garage. Car fell on him. He's dead."

Now he understood the need to keep this news off the radio and as quiet as possible for the time being.

"Oh, hell. Who's on duty?" Trey muttered.

"Earl had just clocked out, but he's there now."

"Tell him to secure the scene and not to touch anything until I get there. Did you call the coroner?"

"Yes, sir. They said it will be a couple of hours."

Trey turned on the lights and siren. "I'll be there in five, maybe less. Keep radio traffic vague."

"Yes, sir."

Trey disconnected and accelerated. This was going to be one hell of a hard day. Paul's only son, Mack, was a friend. And with that thought came another that made the skin crawl on the back of his neck. Paul was his mother's old boyfriend and one of the survivors of a bad car crash his mom had been in when they were teens. The investigation into the death of Dick Phillips, who'd been in that same wreck, was still ongoing. First Dick, now Paul. Trey had been a cop too long to be a big believer in coincidence.

He hit the city limits of Mystic running hot. The early hour automatically ruled out excess traffic, but as he pulled up at the gas station, it appeared by the size of the gathering crowd that word was spreading anyway. He sighed. The joys of small-town living.

He saw Melissa Sherman sitting on the curb as he got out. She was crying so hard she was shaking, and he wondered what part she had in this hell. Then he saw his officer putting up crime-scene tape around the area, blocking off access to the gas pumps and the station, and headed for him.

"Earl?"

Earl was tight-lipped, his expression grim.

"Damn, Chief! It's an ugly sight. Looks like the lift failed. Blood is already drying, so it must have happened some hours back. Miss Sherman found him. She said he'd offered to work late on her car so she could have it first thing this morning. I took her statement. She's convinced it's her fault he's dead because it was her car that fell on him."

Trey felt sick. "Finish stringing up that tape and then disperse the crowd."

"Yes, sir," Earl said. He then turned to look as officers Carl and Lonnie Doyle drove up in their cruisers. "Carl and Lonnie are here, Chief."

"Good. You're clocked out, so as soon as you finish up, go home and get some sleep. I might need you again soon, and you need some rest."

Earl shuddered. "Oh, hell, Chief. I don't wanna sleep. All I'll see when I close my eyes is the body."

Trey sighed. "When you're through, go write up your report and go home anyway. I'll call if I need you."

Earl began tying off the crime-scene tape as Trey backtracked to where Lissa was sitting. When he touched her shoulder, she screamed, then leaped to her feet.

Trey sighed. "Sorry, I didn't mean to scare you."

Lissa's eyes were swollen from crying.

"My car… It fell. He stayed…should have said no. Oh, my God, it's my fault."

"No, it's not," Trey said. "Come sit in my car. I'll take you home later."

The suggestion seemed to shake her out of her hysteria. She began pulling herself together, wiping tears off her cheeks and pushing wayward curls from her forehead.

"No, no, I can't go home. I need to get to school."

"I don't think you're in any shape to—"

"I'll be okay." She shuddered, then drew a deep breath. "I don't want to go home. I need to think of something besides what I saw," she said, and dug a tissue out of her pocket and blew her nose.

"Then, for the time being, take a seat in my car."

"Yes, thank you," she said, before gathering up her things and moving toward the police cruiser on shaky legs as Trey headed back to the gas station. He went straight into the garage and then stopped, shocked to the core.

"Dear God," he muttered. He gritted his teeth and began looking at everything *but* the body.

At the outset, it seemed obvious the lift had failed. It happened. He would have to check on the whereabouts of the other mechanics who worked for Paul to see if they'd been with him earlier. After a quick survey of the garage, he was disappointed to find out there was no security camera on the premises. It would have helped to know if Paul had been alone. He would send his officers to check if any cameras from surrounding businesses had a view of the station. He met Carl and Lonnie on his way out.

"Carl, is that department camera still in your cruiser?"

"Yes, sir," Carl said.

"You know what to do. Get plenty of pictures from

every angle, and dust the control to the hydraulic lift and the front door for prints. Lonnie, you make sure and keep this scene clear. The coroner will be showing up in a couple of hours."

Lonnie's eyes widened. "Are you saying—"

"I'm just covering all the bases," Trey said.

"Yes, sir," Lonnie said, adding, "This just feels so weird. We don't have stuff like this happen here in Mystic, and now two of our locals are dead within a month, although Dick Phillips' death wasn't an accident."

"Yes, and we need to make damn sure this *was* an accident before we close this case, understand?"

Both officers nodded.

"You and Carl stay on the premises until the coroner is finished, and make sure this place is locked before you leave. Since the lift failed, you may need to call in the fire department to help the coroner remove the body."

"Yes, sir," Lonnie said.

One issue dealt with, Trey thought. Now he needed to talk to Lissa.

Two

Trey's phone rang as he was heading for his cruiser. He glanced at the caller ID and frowned as he answered.

"Hello, Mom. What's up?" he asked.

Betsy Jakes' voice was shaking. "Is it true Paul Jackson is dead?"

He paused near the back of his cruiser.

"Damn, bad news spreads fast in small towns. Yes, but I have yet to notify the next of kin, so I need to do that now before someone does it for me."

He heard his mother gasp, then begin moaning as if in great pain.

Trey frowned. "Mom?"

When the line went dead, he realized she'd hung up on him. His frown deepened. When Dick Phillips had died, she had scared him with her behavior, although he'd chalked up her reaction to being the one who'd found his body. Now she seemed on the verge of going down that road again. Damn it. He needed to be in three places at once. Then he thought of his fiancée, Dick Phillips' daughter, Dallas. She could go check on his mother.

He made a quick call home.

Dallas answered on the second ring. "Hey, honey, did you forget something?"

"No. Shit hit the fan early today. Paul Jackson is dead. Looks like the lift fell on him. Would you please go check on Mom, and if she's acting weird, stay with her for a little while until I can get over there? I need to talk to her, but I can't get over there for a while."

Dallas was horrified. With her father's murder still fresh in her mind, she immediately empathized.

"Yes, I'm on my way. I'm so sorry, sweetheart. I'll stay with her until you can get there."

"Thanks," he said, then pocketed his phone and got in the car with Lissa.

It appeared she'd been doing a repair job on her makeup. Her eyes were still red and slightly swollen, but she had reapplied some makeup and seemed calmer.

"Are you sure you want to go to work?" Trey asked.

"Yes, I'm sure," she said. "If I need to sign anything, just call the office and leave me a message. I can drop by the station after school."

"Earl said you already gave him your statement?" he said as he started the car and pulled away.

She nodded. "There wasn't much to tell. I went in to see if my car was ready and…" She swallowed around the lump in her throat, then took a deep breath. "I went in and saw what had happened. I ran back out crying. My friend Margaret Lewis called the police."

"Did she go inside?" Trey asked.

Her voice was shaking again. "Oh, no, no one else did except your officer."

"I'll ask you not to talk about the details, okay?"

She shuddered. "Of course."

A few moments later he turned the corner and pulled up to the front walk of the school building.

"So here you are. I still think you should have gone home."

She gave him a brief smile. "Thank you for the ride," she said, jumping out and fumbling with her things as she walked away.

Trey drove back to the station. He wanted the privacy of his office to call Paul's son and was dreading this call almost as much as the one he'd made to Dallas when Dick Phillips' body was discovered.

Inside, he sat down behind his desk, searched online for Jackson Lumber in Summerton and said a quick prayer.

Mack Jackson was outside in the breezeway of his lumberyard, watching one of his employees loading up an order. He eyed the short line of trucks and pickups behind it, four of which were also being loaded. After satisfying himself that all his customers were being helped, he headed back into the main building and then down the hall toward his office.

He was well liked by his employees and was one of Summerton's most eligible bachelors. He had no interest in changing that. He stayed friendly but kept everything casual when it came to feminine companions. His bookkeeper, a middle-aged woman named Bella Garfield, had told him that he looked like a dark-haired Daniel Craig, which always made him grin.

Being compared to the current James Bond wasn't a bad thing.

He paused in the hallway to get a can of Coke from the machine and had just popped the top when Bella stepped out into the hall and waved him down.

"Mack! Phone call for you on line four."

"Thanks," he said, lengthening his stride. He shut the door behind him and set the can on his desk as he picked up the call. "This is Mack. How can I help you?"

"Mack, this is Trey Jakes."

Mack smiled as he plopped down in his chair. "Well, hello, stranger. What can I do for you?"

"I'm afraid I have some bad news. Are you alone?"

Mack's smile disappeared. "Yes, I'm alone. What's happened?"

"I'm so sorry to have to tell you, but your father was found dead in his shop this morning."

Trying to make sense of what he'd been told, Mack reeled as if he'd been slapped.

"What? No! Oh, God, no! Was it a heart attack? Did—"

"No, Mack. No heart attack." Trey braced himself for the rest. "He was working on a car late last night, and it appears the lift failed and crushed him beneath it."

When Mack went silent, Trey didn't know what to think. "Mack? *Mack?*"

Mack's voice was shaking, and his eyes were so full of tears he couldn't see his desk. "I'm on my way."

"Look, Mack, the coroner isn't here yet and—"

"Are you telling me he's still there? Under the car?"

"It's procedure in an unattended death. The coroner has to see the scene intact."

"Are you implying it wasn't an accident?" Mack asked.

"No, I'm not implying anything, but it's my job not to assume anything, either."

"I hear you—now you hear me. I'll be there."

"No, man, you don't want—"

The line went dead in Trey's ear. He sighed. This was the second time that morning someone had hung up on him. He left the police station through the back door and returned to the scene of the accident.

It took Mack less than thirty minutes to put the lumberyard into his sympathetic manager's hands and go home and pack. He'd made the drive from Summerton to Mystic countless times, but never like this. This time he was scared to go home.

Once, when he was six, he got mad because he couldn't go to his grandparents' house and ran away. He didn't get far before he realized he didn't know how to get there, so he stopped, then was scared to go home because he was afraid of the consequences. He felt like that now, afraid to go home because of the consequences awaiting him.

He was also bothered by how his father had died. He had been such a stickler for safety in the garage that this scenario seemed improbable. Of course hydraulic lifts could fail, but he'd never imagined them dropping so fast a man couldn't escape. The horror-filled image in his head kept getting worse with each passing mile. Had his dad cried out for help and no one had heard? Had he suffered?

He didn't know he was crying until his vision finally blurred to the point that he couldn't see the road.

He pulled over onto the shoulder, slammed his SUV into Park and then laid his head down on the steering wheel and sobbed. One image after another swept through his mind from when he was a child. All the nights when he was little and his dad had read him a story to put him to sleep. The countless holidays spent together with his parents. The year the front porch had collapsed from a heavy snow and they couldn't use the front door for two months. Losing his mother when he was only ten. Mack and his father had become inseparable afterward. Now the thought of his father dying alone in excruciating pain was horrifying. His dad had been there for him when he'd needed him most, but in Paul's darkest moment, he'd died alone.

Overwhelmed with grief and guilt, Mack lost track of time.

It wasn't until a semi rolled past him so fast it shook his car that he pulled himself together and resumed his journey. He had always thought the worst thing that could ever happen to him had been when he'd found out Melissa Sherman, the girl he'd loved more than life, had aborted their baby, but he had been wrong. Today was, without question, even worse.

Trey was at the garage with his officers, absorbing the implications of what they'd just told him, when Mack Jackson arrived. Trey could tell he was in shock as he got out of his car, and his hesitant steps bore witness to how much he dreaded going into the garage, yet he kept moving forward.

Trey went to meet him. "Mack. I'm so sorry."

Mack couldn't look at the sympathy on Trey's face

without breaking down again, so he nodded without meeting his friend's gaze.

When he started into the garage, Trey stopped him. "I'm telling you again, you don't want to go in there."

Mack looked up then, with anger in his eyes. "Hell no, I don't want to go in there, but he's alone, damn it! He's alone! That's not right. It's just not right."

Trey stepped back. "Then, I have to go with you. You can't move anything. You can't touch anything."

"I know," Mack said.

Mack kept his eyes on the back of Trey's head until they were inside the garage, and then he looked down.

He saw the car, then the pool of drying blood, and then he saw a work boot, and that was enough. He turned away, and his voice was trembling with shock and emotion when he spoke.

"I see and still don't believe. He was all about safety measures. He was careful, so damn careful," he whispered. And then he looked up at Trey, unaware that he was crying again. "I need to stay with him. Show me where I can stand."

Trey sighed. "Just stay where you are. The less we move around, the less likely we'll disturb anything vital."

"I won't move," Mack said, taking a stance not unlike a soldier standing guard at his post.

Trey kept his distance, giving Mack the space he obviously needed to keep his emotions contained, but at the same time he was worried. He hadn't heard back from Dallas, so he didn't know if his mother was okay or if she had flipped out like she had before. He didn't know if his sister, Trina, had left for work or if she was still at the house, too. Something was up with the two men dying so close together. He could feel it.

Mack kept his gaze fixed on a dirty spot on one of the windows directly across from where he was standing and didn't look away. He'd spent countless hours in this place growing up. It used to be his favorite place to spend time with his dad, but once they took his father's body away, there would be little need to come back other than to tie up loose ends.

He and Trey stood without talking while the world went on around them. Through the window he could see cars driving past, people on their way to somewhere else. A kid rode by on his bicycle. A couple of men parked a few doors down and went into a used furniture store. Mack didn't understand how life could be so ordinary out there and a living nightmare in here.

Trey kept an eye out for the coroner's vehicle. When a blue car wheeled in and parked, and a black van with a county logo on the doors pulled in beside it, Trey pointed. "They're here."

Mack blinked.

"I'll be right back," Trey said as he strode out.

Mack watched the men getting out of their vehicles. When they opened up the back of the van, a chill swept through him. He could almost feel his father's presence.

"They're here, Dad. Just hang on a little longer and we'll get you free."

Moments later Trey came back, accompanied by a trio of men, one of whom Mack recognized as Pryor Addison, the county coroner.

Addison knew the Jacksons and was disturbed to

learn what had happened to Paul, but he frowned when he saw Mack. "You shouldn't be here," he said.

"And he shouldn't be under that car," Mack said.

Addison sighed. "You need to step outside, son."

"No, sir, with respect."

Addison shrugged and went to work directing his crew as to which pictures he wanted and from what angles, and then circled the car several times trying to decide which side they needed to jack up to remove the body. Until it was out from under the car, there was nothing definitive to see. "So the lift failed?" he said.

"So we assume," Trey said. "We haven't moved or touched anything since the body was discovered."

Addison looked around for the lift controls and had pictures taken of that, too. "Okay, we need to get this car off the body without causing further damage."

Trey couldn't get the thought out of his mind that this wasn't an accident. Carl had already told him there were no prints on the lift control, which made no sense. There should be prints galore. Every time it went up or down someone had to use the control. Now was a good time to test it.

"Do you have a problem with me trying out the lift?" Trey asked.

Mack looked at Trey as if he'd lost his mind. "What are you saying?" he asked.

"I'm not saying anything," Trey said. "I just need to make sure the lift is inoperable before I call in the fire department to help remove the car."

Addison shrugged. "I have no problem with that. Either it will work or it won't, right?"

"Yes, sir," Trey said, and reached for the control.

The hydraulics kicked in, and the lift began moving up without a hitch.

Mack caught a glimpse of his father's body and turned his back. Trey had been right. He didn't want this sight burned into his memory.

The coroner frowned, and then glanced up at Trey. "What made you think to do that?" he asked.

"My officers dusted for prints. There weren't any," Trey said.

Mack picked up that something was wrong. "What the hell is going on here?"

Trey held up a hand. "Come outside with me... please."

Mack left without looking back, but as soon as they got outside, he stopped.

"Talk to me, damn it. That's my father. I have a right to know what's happening."

"Get in my car, Mack. I don't intend to advertise this, and I expect you to keep quiet about it, too."

Mack got in the police cruiser, and as soon as Trey slid behind the steering wheel, despite the state Mack was in, he started questioning him.

"What do you know about the wreck your dad was in the night he graduated from high school?"

Mack was struggling with the notion that his father's death wasn't an accident and was clearly unprepared for such a seemingly random question.

"What the hell does that have to do with—"

"I don't know," Trey snapped. "Can you answer the question or not?"

Mack shoved a shaky hand through his hair. "Sorry. I...I know it happened. I don't know much of anything else."

"Do you know the other people who were in it with him?"

Mack was trying to focus on this conversation when his thoughts were on what was going on inside the garage.

"No, I don't remember. I think there were a couple more, but I don't know if I ever knew who they were."

"You know Dick Phillips was murdered recently," Trey said.

"Yes, Dad told me. He was really upset and—" Mack stopped. All of a sudden the questioning clicked. "Was he one of the kids in the car with Dad?"

"Yes, along with their girlfriends. Dick's girlfriend, Connie, died that night. She was the driver. The other girl was your dad's girlfriend, Betsy. The same Betsy who's now my mom."

Mack's eyes widened in disbelief.

"Your mom? Your mom was my dad's old girl-friend?"

Trey nodded.

"What does she say about all this?" Mack asked.

"Nothing. You may or may not know that the survivors were injured so severely that none of them had a single memory of what happened after the actual graduation ceremony."

"Are you saying someone is after the three of them?" Mack asked.

Trey shrugged. "I can't say that the wreck has anything to do with why Dick died, but I'm a cop, and having one man murdered who was in that wreck is one thing. Having two dead within the same month feels like more than coincidence to me."

Mack was stunned.

"Will the coroner be able to tell if my dad was murdered?"

"I don't know. But if we can ascertain there's no mechanical fault with the lift, we'll have to assume someone lowered it on him."

"I know the company Dad used to maintain it. The information is in his office at the house. I'll get it to you," Mack said.

"I'd appreciate that," Trey said. "When you go through your dad's things, if you see anything like a journal or a diary, I need to see it."

"I'll go through his things, but honestly I don't expect to find anything. We got real close after Mom died, and I'd swear on a Bible there were no secrets between us."

Trey nodded.

"I understand, but just keep it in mind, and remember, I don't want a word of this repeated. If these deaths are related to that wreck, the last thing we want is for the killer to be forewarned that we've figured out the connection."

Mack was shaken to the core. Here he'd thought the worst thing to happen was that his father had died, but to think he might have been murdered seemed worse, almost obscene.

"Understood," he muttered.

"So I guess you'll be around the rest of the day?" Trey asked.

"I'll be staying in Mystic for sure until after Dad's services," Mack said.

Trey frowned. "I don't know when the coroner will release the body."

"I understand." Mack glanced out the window at

the crowd gathered on the other side of the street. "I never did get the need to witness other people's grief."

"Some thrive on being the first with the latest news, true or not," Trey said.

It was the word *first* that made Mack wonder who'd actually found his dad.

"Who discovered the body?"

"Melissa Sherman. That's her car on that lift, and she took it really hard. She's blaming herself because your dad offered to work overtime on it last night so she could have it this morning."

Mack was in shock. He saw her face in his mind, the way she'd looked when they made love, the way she'd laughed, the way that little mole at the corner of her mouth had always drawn his gaze to the supple curves of her lips, and then the way they'd parted. It hadn't been pretty, and he still held a serious grudge. It was inevitable that he would now be forced to see her whether he wanted to or not. How bizarre that they would be thrown together again like this.

"I didn't know she'd moved back to town," he said.

Trey nodded. "Just this year. She inherited the house she grew up in when her mother died. She's teaching first grade at the elementary school."

Mack hunched his shoulders against the sudden ache in his chest. He didn't want to care about her, but he kept thinking how awful it must have been for her to be the one who found the body. She had always loved his dad, and now she was blaming herself. He couldn't let that go.

"Will you talk to her about the lift?" Mack asked.

"At this point I'm not saying anything more until it's been checked out, and you can't say anything about what we talked about, either. Not even to make her feel better. We'll know the truth soon enough."

Mack nodded. "I understand, but I don't think it's fair for someone to be living with misplaced guilt, that's all."

"You can talk to her all you want, but not about this," Trey said. "Again, I'm very sorry for your loss. I'll make sure the coroner's office has your contact information. They'll notify you when they release the body. Here's my card. Use either number if you need me."

"Thanks," Mack said, and quickly entered the information in his phone. He slipped a card out of his pocket and handed it to Trey. "This has my cell number in case you need to reach me."

They looked up just as the coroner exited the building, followed by two men carrying a body bag. Once they put it into the van they slammed the doors and drove away.

Mack's voice was shaking. "I guess I need to lock up."

"Do you have keys?" Trey asked.

Mack nodded. "I assume you want everything left as is?"

"Yes, at least until after I get the lift inspected," Trey said.

"I'll text you the info after I get home."

"I'll seal the entrances after you lock up," Trey said. "Tell your dad's employees to stay off the premises until I give the all clear."

Mack got out with his keys in hand, went straight to the front door and locked up, then circled the building, making sure the back entrances were locked, as well. When he returned to the front of the station, seeing the yellow crime-scene tape across the doorway seemed surreal. He felt the stares from the crowd across the street but never looked up as he got in his car and drove away.

Marcus Silver was pale and shaken as he came to the breakfast table. He dropped into his chair, and then waved away the maid and the plate of food she was carrying.

"Just coffee, please," he said.

She set the plate on the sideboard and then quickly filled his cup before leaving the room.

His son, T.J., swallowed a bite of waffle then frowned. "What's wrong?"

"I just got some bad news," Marcus said. "Paul Jackson is dead."

T.J. laid down his fork. "What happened? Heart attack?"

Marcus shook his head. "No, he was crushed beneath a car he was working on."

T.J. gasped. "God, dying is a hell of a way to begin the day!"

Marcus looked up. "Oh. No, it didn't happen this morning. They think he was working late on a car when the lift failed. The car belonged to Melissa Sherman. She's the one who found him this morning."

T.J.'s heart skipped. Lissa! How odd that she was mixed up in such an ugly death. They had shared a few dates right after she'd first come home, but then she'd refused further invitations. He'd stopped asking, but it still rankled that she'd quit him. He liked to be the one to call the shots.

"That's terrible about Mr. Jackson. I'm sorry to hear that. He was one of your classmates, right?"

Marcus nodded.

T.J. reached across the table. "Is there anything I can—"

His father stood abruptly. "Excuse me," he said, and left the dining room like a man on a mission.

T.J. stood as if to follow him and then paused. He didn't know what he could have said to make this better, so he sat back down. He couldn't help but think how fragile life was, and he was grateful his father was still with him; then he thought of Lissa and wondered how he could turn this to his advantage.

Three

Will Porter was finishing breakfast and preparing for an early meeting at school. His wife, Rita, was sitting at the other end of the breakfast table nursing a cup of coffee spiked with a shot of the bourbon she'd gotten drunk on last night. It was all he could do to look at her these days. She was such a disappointment and hardly the wife he needed if he was going to get himself elected state superintendent of schools. His dreams were big, but Rita's daily hangovers were bigger. He still wasn't sure what he was going to do about her, but he wasn't going to let anything derail his aspirations to get out of this one-horse town.

When his cell phone rang, he was actually relieved. It saved him from having to tell her goodbye. Instead, he just waved at her as he stood up and walked away, talking as he went.

"This is Porter. Yes, Suzette. I'm on my way. What? Heard what?" He paused in the hall. "Really! That's terrible. So is everyone there? Good, tell them I'm on my way."

He dropped his phone in his pocket and reached for

his briefcase just as Rita picked it up and handed it to him, tilting her cheek in a flirtatious manner.

"You almost forgot my goodbye kiss."

"I didn't forget anything," Will said as he took the briefcase out of her hands.

She grabbed his coat sleeve. "Who was that on the phone? I heard you say something was terrible. What happened?"

"It was Suzette. She called to tell me the parents I'm supposed to meet with this morning are waiting on me, so turn loose of my sleeve, I need to go."

Rita frowned. "What's so terrible about that?"

"Oh, that. She said Paul Jackson was dead. Crushed by a car he was working on."

Rita shrieked. "Oh, my God! That's terrible! And he was such a sweet man."

Will frowned. "Really? Did you fuck him when you were in school like you did Dick Phillips? Are you going to throw *that* in my face, too?"

Rita slapped his face.

He returned the slap and sent her reeling.

"There, now, if you needed an excuse to get shit-faced drunk again today, I just gave it to you."

He walked out, slamming the door behind him.

Rita was still screaming obscenities as he drove away.

Gregory Standish was on his way to the bank when his cell phone rang. He glanced down at caller ID and frowned. He'd just sat through a silent breakfast with his wife and daughter, and now his wife wanted to talk. He gave a long-suffering sigh and answered.

"What is it, Gloria?"

"Gregory! I just heard the most terrible news," she said. "Paul Jackson is dead. They found him crushed beneath a car this morning. There will be a funeral for sure, and I don't have a thing to wear. Carly and I are going shopping in Summerton, so I won't be home for lunch. You'll have to pick something up in town."

His heart skipped a beat. Those two were going to bankrupt him yet, and a bankrupt banker would never be mayor of Mystic. It was a small dream in comparison to some, but it was his, and every day his family's spending habits drew him further away from realizing his goal.

"Don't spend money, Gloria. I told you—we're already strapped as it is."

"Don't be silly, Gregory. You're president of the bank. You have plenty of money."

He groaned as the line went dead in his ear.

"Son of a bitch," he muttered, dropping the phone back in his pocket.

Now his stomach was in knots. Jackson's death had given his wife had a new excuse for a shopping spree. He hadn't seen that coming.

Mack pulled into the driveway and stopped beneath the carport, taking care to leave room for his dad's truck, and the moment he thought that, he groaned. His dad wasn't coming home. The knot in his belly grew tighter as he killed the engine. He grabbed his suitcase and headed for the house in slow, hesitant strides, reluctant to go inside. Today he'd been robbed of all he held dear.

When he unlocked the door and walked in, he was struck by the quiet familiarity of the house. How dare the world keep spinning when he was in free fall? He closed his eyes, and when he took a deep breath, he knew by the lingering scent of stale coffee and bacon grease what his dad had eaten for breakfast the day before. He dropped the suitcase by the door and turned the lock before going into the kitchen.

It was just as he suspected. An unwashed skillet was still on the stove, the bottom covered with congealed bacon grease, and the carafe in the coffeemaker was half-full. His dad would have reheated it last night and finished it off with his supper as he cleaned up, only last night he hadn't gone home. He'd stayed to do a customer a favor, just as he'd done countless times before, but this time something had gone tragically wrong.

His hands were shaking as he poured the coffee down the sink and refilled the carafe. Once the coffee began to brew, he took his suitcase back to his room, tossed it on the bed and then turned around to hang up his jacket. As he did, his gaze went straight past the open door of his room to the one across the hall. How many times had he awakened at night as a kid and taken comfort from that open door, knowing his dad was so close? He had been convinced nothing could hurt him then because Dad would protect him from nighttime monsters. He'd known that as surely as he'd known his own name. And yet he couldn't shake the feeling that a real monster had come and taken his father's life.

As soon as he hung up his clothes, he went straight to the desk, found the name and phone number of the company that serviced the hydraulic lift, then texted it to Trey.

Next order of business was to call the employees.

There were only two, and he was sorry for their circumstances, but as of today they were out of a job. The best he could do, if they wanted to move or make the daily drive to Summerton, was to offer them a job at his lumberyard. If not, they were on their own.

Betsy Jakes was making bread, and with her daughter, Trina, already at work, she had the house to herself. Kneading the dough was good therapy. The dough was a physical thing she could hold on to, which was vital for a woman losing her grip on reality. It was bad enough learning yet another of her friends was gone, but something else was happening that caused her concern.

She was losing track of time, and it had happened again this morning.

She had no memory of hanging up the phone or going to the kitchen after talking to Trey, no memory of gathering up the ingredients to bake, and yet here she was, making bread. There was a sick feeling in the pit of her stomach, along with the bitter taste of bile. She was on the verge of throwing up but afraid if she gave in to the feeling something terrible would happen, so she kept working the dough with slow, rhythmic movements, pushing out air bubbles with each downward thrust from the heel of her hand.

She was elbow-deep in flour and yeast, the radio playing loudly enough in the background that she didn't hear Dallas's car as she pulled up outside.

Dallas drove around to the back of the house. After Trey's concern about his mother's state of mind, she was anxious as to what she might find. She got out on the run, peered through the window in the back door and saw Betsy at the cabinet. Relieved that she seemed to be doing okay, Dallas tried the door. It was unlocked. Instead of knocking, she opened it.

"Knock, knock," she said, standing on the threshold holding a carton of eggs and waiting for an invitation.

Betsy was smiling as she turned around. "Come in, sugar! It's good to see you!" Flour flew in every direction as Betsy lifted her hand to wave, and they both laughed when some of it settled back on her face. "I guess I should qualify that. Come in, but don't get too close. I seem to be making a bigger mess than usual this morning."

Betsy seemed just fine. Dallas breathed a sigh of relief. "My little hens are laying up a storm. I brought you some fresh eggs," she said.

She put the eggs in the refrigerator, hung her jacket on the back of a chair, then gave Betsy a hello kiss.

"Thank you for the eggs," Betsy said. "Coffee is fresh. Help yourself."

"Thanks. So I see you're making bread. That will be yummy."

"Yes. With that nip in the air, it seemed like a good thing to do today," Betsy said.

"I haven't made yeast bread in ages," Dallas said as she brushed the flour from Betsy's cheeks and then poured herself a cup of coffee.

Betsy's smile widened. She was beyond happy that Trey and Dallas were back together. She thought it was a ridiculous waste of life when people who loved each other as they did couldn't find a way to work out their differences so they could be together.

"Oatmeal-raisin cookies are in the cookie jar if you want one with your coffee," Betsy said.

"I never turn down any of your cooking," Dallas said. She grabbed a cookie, and then pulled up a kitchen stool and sat down.

"I suppose Trey sent you to check on me," Betsy said. "It's terrible about Paul, isn't it? The news took me aback, I can tell you. Such a horrible thing to have happened. I've been thinking about Mack ever since I heard."

Dallas ignored the twinge of sadness she felt. Her dad's murder had been such a shock, and it was still unsolved. She could empathize with what Mack must be feeling.

"Trey did suggest I stop by to make sure you were okay."

"Losing people we love, no matter how it happens, is a terrible thing," Betsy said, and then paused in her kneading to give Dallas a long look.

"Are you doing okay? I mean, are you finding ways to stay busy and happy since you decided to move back home? I know you had an exciting life in Charleston."

Dallas took a sip of coffee, and then set the cookie and the cup aside.

"I had a busy life, but it quit being exciting years ago. I just didn't know it until I was forced to face what I'd given up to get it. Trey and I are fine. Don't worry any about us, okay?"

Betsy gave the dough one last flip on the bread board and then covered it with a clean white cloth so it could rise.

"I'm not worried about any of my kids," she said. She washed her hands and poured herself a cup of coffee. "Let's go sit where I can put my feet up. I'm feeling my age today."

Dallas followed her into the living room without comment, although there was something about the unfamiliar stoop to Betsy's shoulders and the dragging steps that gave her some concern. When she saw the way Betsy eased herself down in the chair, she knew something was off.

"Are you in pain?"

Betsy stifled a sigh. "No, honey. I just haven't been sleeping well."

Dallas frowned. "But you're not in pain?"

"Oh, no! Not a bit. Just tired. I'll take a nap this afternoon and be good to go. Now, tell me, how's the egg business?"

Dallas smiled. "Not slacking off, that's for sure."

Betsy leaned back and momentarily closed her eyes, and as she did, everything went black. She heard the sound of screeching brakes and someone praying, and jumped out of her seat so fast she knocked the mug off the table. It broke, splashing hot coffee all over the legs of her pants and the hardwood floor.

"Oh, good grief!" she said. "I am so clumsy."

"I'll get a rag to clean it up," Dallas said, as she ran to the kitchen.

Betsy got down on her knees to pick up the broken pieces of the cup, and all of a sudden she was on her hands and knees in the floorboard of a car and flying down the road so fast she could feel the vibration beneath her fingers. The scent of vomit was up her nose and burning the back of her throat, and someone was screaming. She didn't realize that it was her making all the noise until Dallas dropped down to the floor beside her, calling her name.

"Betsy! Betsy! What's wrong? Are you hurt? Did you fall?"

Betsy rocked back on her heels. Her hands were shaking, and she kept brushing at her face and the front of her shirt, expecting it to be covered in vomit. She looked down at the broken cup and spilled coffee, and shivered.

"I don't know," Betsy mumbled. "I don't know what's happening."

Dallas was scared. The way Betsy was acting, it was almost as if she had suffered some kind of seizure.

"You have coffee all over your pants. Let me help you to your room. You can change and then lie down for a while. I'll stay and finish off your bread, okay?"

"I have to clean up the car," Betsy muttered, pointing down at the floor. "I threw up, and I have to clean it up."

Dallas's heart skipped a beat. *Clean up the car? Because she threw up in it?*

"It's okay, honey. I'll clean it," Dallas said, and she all but pushed Betsy down the hall to her room.

It took a few minutes for Dallas to get Betsy into clean clothes, but as soon as she did, Betsy crawled up onto her bed and rolled over. She closed her eyes so fast it gave Dallas the impression that she was seeing something she couldn't face and wanted it all to go away.

Dallas took a quilt from the quilt rack and covered Betsy up to her chin, then hurried back into the living room to clean up the floor. As soon as she was through, she picked up her phone to call Trey, and then stopped. He was certain to have his hands full right now, and he couldn't do anything for his mother that she wasn't already doing. He would call when he got time, and she would talk to him then.

The killer stood with the crowd of onlookers across the street from the garage, nursing a cup of coffee and listening to the gossip mill creating a whole set of rumors out of thin air. He smirked, thinking what tiny minds they had and small worlds they lived in, and how easy it had been to erase past errors. Only one more to go and then the future would be secure.

Lissa was struggling at school and finally gave in to the fact that she couldn't maintain a sane thought for more than a few seconds. She kept seeing that foot and the pool of blood, and all she wanted was to take yesterday back. Then she would never have gone along with Paul's offer to work late on her car. She would have assured him it wasn't necessary and that she could easily get a ride to work. But she couldn't revise the past, and now a good man was dead. She wasn't sure how she was going to live with that and ever be happy again.

Added to that, her first-graders were getting on her last nerve. She knew from experience that children sensed when the adults in their lives were troubled and acted out accordingly. Today it was taking all her concentration to keep them occupied. Tears welled constantly, but she kept blinking them away. Every time she looked out at the red clay of the muddy playground, the red water in the puddles made her think of the blood that had run out from under her car. She had an overwhelming urge to throw up.

Finally it was lunchtime, which meant the day was half over. She marched her students from the classroom to the cafeteria, and then went about the business of getting them settled down to eat. Some brought lunches and went through the line just to get a carton of milk, while others juggled trays filled with food from the cafeteria.

Every day during lunch, at least one child dropped a tray. She just hoped today it wasn't one of hers. If anyone cried around her today she was likely to join them.

She was standing beside the cooler, putting a carton of milk on every tray and congratulating herself on hiding her emotions when she accidentally dropped a carton, and then another and another. That was when she realized her hands were shaking to the point that she couldn't maintain her grip. She glanced around to make sure no one noticed and began using both hands to do her job.

But she'd been mistaken. All her coworkers knew what had happened. They knew why she'd been late getting to school and were sympathetic. When someone said her name and then tapped her on the shoulder, she found herself face-to-face with her principal.

"Mr. Wilson! Would you like a carton of milk?"

Wilson calmly took the milk out of her hand and put it on the tray of the waiting student, then cupped her elbow.

"No. I came to tell you we have a substitute for your class for the rest of the day. You need some time at home."

Lissa's eyes welled. "I'm fine, really."

"No, you're not, and I wouldn't be, either. Go get

your things and meet Louis at the office. He volunteered to take you home."

One of the aides took over milk duty as she and the principal walked out of the cafeteria. Now that the decision had been taken out of her hands, she felt the walls she'd put up beginning to crumble. She hurried to gather up her things, left her lesson plans out on the desk for the substitute teacher and headed for the office.

Louis Parsons, the school custodian, was already there with keys in hand. He was a stocky thirtysomething man who wore his hair in a ponytail and was so shy around women that he looked down at their feet instead of their faces when he spoke.

"I can carry that bag for you," he said. He slipped the big tote from her shoulder as he escorted her to the parking lot.

The drive home was completely silent.

Lissa was teary eyed and still trembling when Louis pulled up to her house. When he started to get out, she stopped him.

"You don't need to get out, and thank you the ride."

He kept his gaze fixed on the hood of his car. "I'm sure sorry about what happened to Mr. Jackson."

"So am I, Louis. Thank you again for the ride."

He ducked his head as she gathered up her things and got out, the house key in her hand. Her steps were dragging as she heard Louis drive away. She made it up the steps and was fumbling with the key, trying to get it in the lock, when she heard a car pull up behind her.

She wouldn't turn around. She didn't want to talk to anyone, but she couldn't get the key in the lock fast enough to make an escape. All of a sudden there were footsteps coming up the walk, and then someone was calling out her name.

"Lissa! Lissa! Wait up!"

Her shoulders slumped.

Oh, perfect. It's T.J.

She wasn't in the mood to talk. They'd said all they needed to say to each other a couple of months earlier, when she'd quit accepting his invitations to dinner, but before she could think of a way to head him off he had bounded up the steps and slipped a hand beneath her elbow.

"Let me help you inside," he said, as he took the keys from her hand and quickly opened the door.

Lissa entered reluctantly. Once he was inside, he was difficult to get out.

"I'm not up to visitors today, T.J."

He ran a finger down the side of her cheek as his voice softened.

"I know, Liss. I heard what happened. I'm so sorry you were the one who found the body. It must have been awful for you."

Lissa pushed his hand aside. She hated the nickname he persisted in using and didn't intend to talk about what had happened with anyone, especially him.

"I don't want to talk about it. Please go, T.J. I just need to be alone."

T. J. Silver wasn't used to women refusing his attentions, and this only reminded him how pissed he was that she had ended their very new, very tenuous relationship after just a handful of dinner dates.

"I understand how you feel, but I just want to help. I assume your car is going to be unavailable for a while. Could I give you a ride to school tomorrow?"

The last thing she wanted was to owe him any favors.

"No, I have that covered," she said. She then went to the door and stepped aside, waiting for him to leave. "Thank you for checking on me. It was very kind."

T.J.'s eyes narrowed angrily, but he managed a smile as he slid a hand beneath her hair and cupped the back of her neck.

"I didn't do it to be kind, Liss. I did it because I care about you."

She stiffened beneath the familiarity, and she knew he felt it.

"So you have my number," he said. "Call if you need anything, okay?"

"Thank you again," she said.

He gave in and walked out, and the moment he crossed the threshold she shut the door and turned the lock.

His fingers curled into fists when he heard that click, but he kept on walking.

Lissa leaned against the door until she heard him drive away. Only then did she abandon her post and go to her room to change.

Being around women made Louis Parsons nervous. He would never have volunteered to take Melissa Sherman home on his own, but the principal was his boss, and he'd asked if Louis would take her home, so he had.

He kept glancing at the floorboard and the seat of his truck as he drove away, making sure she hadn't left anything behind. His identical twin brother, Reece, used the truck at night, and he made a big deal of keeping it clean, which Louis thought was stupid because

Reece's dog, Bobo, shed like crazy and Reece was always taking Bobo for a ride.

He got back to school and slipped right into the routine as if he'd never been gone, hauling the oversize trash cans from the school cafeteria to the Dumpsters and sweeping up the floor after the last lunch shift had ended. He stayed busy all afternoon and then went to work cleaning up the rooms after school was out, thinking all the time of the comfort waiting for him back home. Even though he and his brother shared a house, they didn't share their lives. Louis worked days, his brother worked nights and, even though they shared a vehicle and sometimes the dog, their paths rarely crossed.

His steps were dragging as he locked up the building and headed to the parking lot. It was almost supper time, but he was going home to take a nap. He'd always taken a nap after school when he was little and he did the same thing now because routines and schedules were how Louis Parsons rolled.

The house he and Reece rented was on the far side of the park in the old part of Mystic. The houses weren't shacks, but they were a little run-down, most of them in need of a coat or two of paint or minor repairs. Louis had fixed the front steps when they'd moved in, and painted the porch so the outside looked neat. The interior was a work in progress. He liked to stay busy during the day, even on weekends, but that meant quiet projects because Reece slept days.

He unlocked the door and entered quietly, wrinkling his nose at the doggy smell of the house as he headed for the kitchen with his to-go coffee mug. He rinsed it out to refill tomorrow, wrote a note to Reece telling him what food was available in the refrigerator for his nighttime meals and headed down the hall to his room.

He took off his work clothes without looking at his body, and slipped between the sheets and closed his eyes. Silence engulfed him as he fell asleep.

Four

Trey finished writing up the report, and then printed it out and filed it. It was almost noon before he got the schedules rearranged and his officers back on duty. And he still hadn't checked in with Dallas. He went back into his office and shut the door, then dropped into his chair and made the call.

Betsy was still sleeping when Dallas's cell phone signaled a call. She'd put it on vibrate so it wouldn't disturb Betsy and was relieved to see that it was Trey.

"Hi, honey," she said, careful to keep her voice low.

"Hello, sweetheart. How are things going? Was Mom all right?"

Dallas looked over her shoulder to make sure she was still alone.

"I thought so at first. She was making bread when I got here, but she looked so tired…almost old. I've never thought of your mother as old before. We went into the living room to sit down. She leaned back and closed her eyes, then for no obvious reason jumped up so fast she knocked her coffee off the table. The mug broke and coffee went everywhere. I went to get something to clean it up, and she started screaming. I ran back and found her on her knees in the middle of the spilled coffee. It was the most frightening sound I've ever heard."

Trey's heart skipped a beat. "Oh, my God, did she fall?"

"No, I don't think so," Dallas said. "But she acted like she didn't know where she was. I tried to get her up to go change her clothes, and she kept looking down at the floor telling me she couldn't leave yet because she'd just thrown up in the floorboard of the car and she had to clean it up."

The hair stood up on the back of his neck.

"The floorboard of a car? She said she threw up in the floorboard of a car?"

"Yes. It makes no sense," Dallas said. "I was afraid she'd had some kind of seizure, because she went right to sleep after I got her cleaned up."

Trey frowned. "I'm coming out. Don't leave, I'll be there soon."

"Oh, I'm not leaving. I have to bake the bread dough she has rising. Have you talked to Trina?"

"Not yet. As for Mom, don't tell her I'm coming," Trey said.

Dallas felt sick. Would this turmoil never end?

Trina Jakes was taking inventory on the number of radiator hoses they had in stock and comparing it to the computer readout of stock on hand to make sure the numbers matched.

Freddie Miller, her boss at Miller Auto Parts, was beginning to suspect someone was selling inventory at a cut rate to certain customers and pocketing the money because he kept coming up short on parts when the computer said they were still in stock.

There were only three other employees besides her who could be doing it: Tony, Elton or George, and she had to guess that since she was the bookkeeper and never waited on customers, Freddie didn't suspect her. That and the fact that he'd asked her not to mention what she was doing made his suspicions fairly obvious.

She was down on her knees in the aisle when someone tapped her on the shoulder. She looked up.

"Hey, Red, what are you doing?"

She frowned. Not only did she not like that Elton called her Red, but she'd just been confronted, something she'd hoped wouldn't happen. She had to come up with an explanation fast.

"Oh, I'm checking some stock numbers against an invoice I got the other day. They don't match, and I can't cut a check to pay until I know for sure we got the right merchandise."

"I can help," Elton offered.

"Thanks, but I already have the numbers I'm looking for in my head, and it would take longer for me to make you a list than for me to just do it."

"Whatever," he said. He grinned, and then gave a lock of her hair a little tug. "So when are you gonna dump that Daniels dude and let a real man show you a good time?"

Trina stood up. It was a defensive move she'd used on the men before because she was taller than all three of them.

"I already have a real man, and quit calling me

Red," she drawled. She then strolled up the aisle and back into her office.

The phone was ringing as she walked in the door, and she hurried to answer.

"Miller Auto Parts. This is Trina."

"Hey, sis, it's me."

Trina had already heard about Paul Jackson's death, so she guessed why he was calling.

"Hi, Trey. Sorry about Mr. Jackson. You guys caught a bad one this morning, didn't you?"

"Have you talked to Mom?"

She frowned. "Not since I left for work. Has something happened?"

"She freaked out again when she heard about Paul's death, just like she did when she found Dick Phillips' body. Dallas is with her, but I wondered if you could give me your opinion of how she's been acting recently."

All of a sudden Trina felt anxious. "Secretive, weepy, a little frantic at times, and then most of the time she's Mom. What's going on?"

"Not sure. I'm going out to check on her shortly. If you feel worried about her at any time, night or day, call me, okay?"

Tears suddenly blurred Trina's vision. "You're scaring me, Trey."

"Yeah, well, *she's* scaring *me*, so that makes two of us. Listen, I've got to go. Remember, call if you need me."

"Do you think we should call Sam?" she asked.

Trey thought of their oldest brother, an ex-military, hard-core private investigator and the last member of their family to put up with bullshit from anyone.

"Not unless we need someone to put out a fire or start a war," he drawled.

Trina giggled. "Yes, you're right. Don't worry. I'll keep an eye on Mom."

"Good deal. Talk to you later."

The click in her ear signaled the end of the conversation, but it had just begun a whole new set of worries. This stuff scared her. She needed to talk to Lee. She was having dinner with him tonight. He was the rational one in their relationship. He would make everything all right.

Betsy woke up to silence and for a few moments wondered why she was in bed, and then she remembered. She threw back the quilt and sat up on the side of the bed, absently rubbing the scar along her hairline. She distinctly remembered throwing up, but the bitter aftertaste was absent. And she'd been screaming. They were going too fast. That was it—they were going too fast! But that made no sense because she'd just woken up in bed, so had she dreamed it?

"Betsy?"

Startled by the sound of another voice, Betsy stood up as Dallas entered the bedroom.

"Dallas? Oh, yes, you were here, right? How rude of me to go to sleep."

Dallas wanted to hug her, but there was something about the way Betsy was standing that told Dallas not to push her.

"It's actually time to work your bread. I was going to do it, but since you're up I thought you might want to do it yourself."

Betsy blinked, and just like that she was back. She

smoothed the hair away from her face and slipped into her shoes.

"Yes, the bread! I love that first rising when you go to punch it down, don't you? It's like popping a big rubber balloon! Let's get that bread in the baking tins and then make something for lunch, okay? You can stay, right?"

Dallas smiled. "I'd love to have lunch with you."

Betsy patted Dallas's cheek as she sailed past her on her way back to the kitchen. She knew what to do now. She had purpose.

A short while later Betsy had the dough in the pans and was covering them up for the last rising. Dallas was heating up some soup Betsy had taken out of the freezer when they heard the front door open.

"It's me!" Trey yelled.

"We're in here," Betsy called. Then she looked at Dallas and smiled. "Good thing we got the big carton out to reheat. Trey loves beef-and-barley soup."

Dallas smiled and kept stirring. When Trey walked into the kitchen he went straight to her.

"Hey, honey, thanks for coming over," he said softly, and kissed the back of her neck.

Dallas nodded and then glanced toward Betsy, who was already getting out the ingredients to make grilled cheese sandwiches to go with the soup.

"Something sure smells good," Trey said. "I hope you made enough for me."

"Always," Betsy said. "One sandwich or two?"

Trey kissed her cheek and smiled. "One is enough, thanks. What can I do to help?"

"You can set the table. You know where everything is, right?"

"Sure," Trey said. He began getting plates and bowls from the cabinet, and flatware from a drawer.

"Can you talk about the case?" Dallas asked.

Trey shrugged. "Not much to tell right now. It was a bad scene. Mack is in about the same shape you were when I called you."

Dallas sighed. "I am so sorry. This is just a horrible thing to have happened."

Trey glanced at his mother. She was far too cheerful. "Mom?"

Betsy flipped the two sandwiches on the grill and then looked up. "What, honey?"

Trey stopped what he was doing and walked over to the stove, took the spatula from her hand and then wiped away the tears running down her face.

"Come sit. I'll do the last sandwich," he said.

Betsy complied without comment.

Dallas turned off the heat under the soup.

"Should I dish up the soup or wait?" she asked.

"Wait until I get the last sandwich grilled," Trey said as he took the finished sandwiches off the grill and put on the last one.

"Betsy, honey, would you like a cup of coffee?" Dallas asked.

Betsy wrapped her arms around herself and began rocking in her chair.

"Does it feel cold in here to you? For some reason I'm freezing," she said.

"I'll turn up the heat," Dallas said, and headed for the thermostat in the hall.

Trey glanced toward the table. His mom had lost all color in her face.

"Mom?"

Betsy looked up. "Hmm?"

"What's happening?"

She shivered again. "I don't know, Trey, but I think I'm losing my mind."

Trey flipped the sandwich and turned off the grill, then handed Dallas the spatula as she walked back into the kitchen.

She moved to the grill as Trey sat down beside his mother and took her hands. Her skin was clammy, and he could feel the tremor in her muscles.

"Talk to me, Mama. You told Dallas you threw up in the floorboard of a car."

Betsy touched the scar again. "I just dreamed that, didn't I?"

Trey shrugged. "I don't know. Was it a dream, or were you remembering something that already happened?"

Betsy pulled her hands away and covered her face. "I don't know. I just don't know."

He'd never seen her like this, but she seemed so fragile, he was afraid to push her.

"Don't worry about it. We'll figure it out together, okay?"

Betsy swiped the tears off her cheeks, took a tissue from her pocket and blew her nose as she stood. "It's time to put the bread in the oven."

"And lunch is ready," Dallas said as she carried the sandwiches to the table.

"I'll pour the coffee," Trey said.

"I'll dish up the soup," Dallas added. She headed back to the stove while Betsy set the timer for the bread.

"That bread is going to smell so good," Betsy said.

Trey watched her turn back into the mother he knew and felt a chill run up his spine. He didn't know what had happened the night she graduated, but he would bet his retirement that they'd either been a part of something illegal or they'd witnessed something bad. What he couldn't figure out was why they were being eliminated now. What was happening that made getting rid of them so important? If his theory about these deaths was correct, she would be next, and he couldn't let that happen. He needed to find that old accident report. Maybe there was something in it that would help him make sense of all this.

Mack had gone through the desk, the computer files, the old lockbox his dad kept in the back of the closet, the shoe boxes full of old income tax papers and every place he could think of looking for anything resembling a journal or a diary. If there was nothing wrong with the lift, then they needed answers to this nightmare, but he couldn't find a thing.

He sat down on the corner of his dad's bed and closed his eyes. The faint scent of diesel, probably from an old pair of his dad's work shoes, coupled with some manly aftershave, was so reminiscent of his father that he kept thinking the man was going to walk in at any moment. Mack took a deep breath, choking back tears, but before he could gather his thoughts, someone was knocking at the front door.

He got up with a heavy heart, and when he saw one of the ladies from his dad's church on the porch holding a covered dish, he sighed.

Feeding the grief stricken had begun.

* * *

Lissa, standing in the hall outside her bedroom, was bordering on what felt like a full-blown panic attack. The thunder of her heartbeat was so loud in her ears that at first she didn't hear her cell phone ringing. By the time it dawned on her what was happening the call had gone to voice mail. Since she didn't want to talk to anyone, she didn't bother checking to see who it had been.

The only person she needed to talk to was God. She mouthed the proper words, and then cried until her eyes were so swollen it hurt to blink before she dropped to her knees. Despair was heavy, weighing her down as she stared at the floor in disbelief.

Why had this happened?

She felt like she was being punished, and yet Paul Jackson was the one who had died. So was it his punishment and she'd just become the tool, or was it hers and his life was gone because of it?

Sick at heart and too exhausted to get up, she slid forward, stretching out facedown on the cold hardwood floor, and closed her eyes, wishing she could disappear forever.

Along about 6:00 p.m. Jim Farley, the pastor from Paul Jackson's church, stopped by to express his condolences. By Mack's count he was visitor number seven, and when this one left, Mack was leaving, too. He couldn't take any more well-wishers and didn't want anyone else to pray for him. He didn't want prayers. He wanted answers.

Mack took a deep breath, bracing himself for yet

another painful conversation. "Pastor Farley, thank you for coming," he said.

The little man smiled, which made the scar across his upper lip—the result of a hockey puck gone wild during his youth—pull sideways just the tiniest bit.

"Good afternoon, Mack. I came without calling. I hope that's all right," Farley said.

"Of course it's all right. No one stands on ceremony here," Mack said, as he led the way to the living room.

The pastor took a seat in the recliner as Mack said, "I have coffee. Would you like a cup?"

"That would be wonderful. It's a bit chilly outside today. As for the coffee, I take mine black," the pastor added.

"I'll be right back," Mack said and headed for the kitchen. He came back a couple of minutes later carrying two mugs.

Pastor Farley took his mug, then cupped it in his hands to warm them as he took the first sip.

Mack set his aside and waited.

The pastor was just as off balance as Mack. The horrific nature of Paul Jackson's death was the elephant in the room. He took a second sip of the coffee and then set his cup aside, too.

"Of course I came to offer my condolences," the pastor said. "The news of your father's death is heartbreaking. I am so very sorry for your loss."

Mack swallowed past the lump in his throat. "Thank you."

"Is there anything I can do?" Farley asked.

Mack shrugged. "I appreciate the offer. Of course I'll have a memorial service, but I can't think about that just yet."

"Of course, of course," Farley said. "You just let me know your wishes and we'll make it happen for you." He took another sip of coffee and then leaned forward. "Know that prayers are being said for you, son. Know that we weep with you. Your father was my friend."

Mack tried to swallow past that lump again, but it didn't happen. He put his head down as tears welled once more. He heard the pastor saying a prayer, but he wished that Farley would just leave. He wanted this to be a terrible nightmare, so that all he needed to do was wake up.

Fifteen minutes later Pastor Farley was gone and Mack was on his way out the door. He wasn't exactly running away from home. He just needed distance from the pain of being here without his dad. He had no destination in mind when he got in his SUV and drove away, but it didn't take long to realize he was retracing the paths of his youth, from the park where his mother used to take him to play, then past the elementary school where he'd lost his first tooth and broken his arm two years later when he'd bailed out of a swing.

He turned down the street that led to the baseball field, parked behind home plate, and then stared past second base to center field and the fence beyond.

The sun appeared to be hovering atop the trees, setting them ablaze with the color of late fall. His hands were shaking as he gripped the steering wheel. Once again, he felt his dad's presence.

"I lived half my childhood in this dirt, didn't I, Dad? And you sat on the third row of the bleachers watching it happen. I don't know if I ever said thank-you, but I'm saying it now."

Tears blurred his vision as he closed his eyes and

leaned back against the seat. He sat until the sunlight was fading and the fire was gone from the sky before he started the car and drove away, heading north out of Mystic. He didn't care where he went, as long as it was out of there.

Reece Parsons woke with a hard-on and a rumble in his empty belly. He thrust muscular arms over his head, stretching like a big cat and arching his back just enough that the covers pushed against his erection. He thought about jacking off for the pleasure of it, then remembered a prior commitment with Melissa Sherman and decided to save the good stuff for her.

He got out of bed and peed off his erection, then walked naked through the darkened house with Bobo at his heels, irked that Louis always left all the lights off. Just once he could at least leave the one on in the kitchen. Then he shrugged. Louis was just like Mama. She was as tight as a bowstring and had gone behind them turning out lights when they were growing up, like wasting a second of electricity was going to put them in the poorhouse when they were already there.

He let the dog out in the backyard and then glanced at the windows, making sure the blinds were pulled and the curtains drawn before he turned on the lights. He liked being naked, but he didn't want to call attention to himself. He'd come to learn as he grew up that flying under the radar was far safer.

He read Louis's note, then dug out a couple of covered dishes from the refrigerator and stood at the counter, eating the food cold with a fork. He covered up what he didn't eat and put the dishes back, and then popped the top on a longneck beer and drank it standing at the sink.

Bobo scratched at the door, and Reece opened it just enough for the little terrier to squeeze in, then locked it behind him, tossed the bottle in the trash, burped, farted and went to get dressed. He thought about logging on to the computer and checking the NASDAQ or maybe seeing how his international investments were doing but changed his mind. He didn't want to keep the little lady waiting.

It was just after midnight, and Lissa still couldn't sleep. Her heart was so heavy that even taking a deep breath seemed impossible. The weight of her guilt was more than she could bear.

And she kept thinking about Mack.

He would come home, if he wasn't already here. Sometime she would have to face him, if for no other reason than to get her car before she could get rid of it. Their lives had been so intertwined and then shattered in a way she would never have expected. Now, knowing she would most likely see him again as the owner of the instrument of his father's death seemed the height of all irony.

She gave up trying to sleep and sat in the dark with the TV remote in her hand, watching a sci-fi classic with the sound on mute.

Even after she began hearing footsteps on the porch, she was so numb she didn't react. If it was the stalker who'd been bothering her, she was going to pretend she wasn't home.

But then she heard a knock at the door. She glanced at the clock and threw back the covers. Her heart was pounding as she moved barefoot through the house. Surely this wasn't a real visitor—not at this time of night. It had to be her stalker! Didn't he know what had happened? Wasn't there a rule in the universe that if one really bad thing was happening to you, then you were no longer fair game for anything else? If there wasn't, there should be.

The house was bathed in shadows of varying shades of darkness, broken only by the faint glow of the street-lights showing through the blinds. When she got to the living room she peeked out, but there was no one in sight. She turned on the porch light and peered through the small window in the door, but the yard was empty. Hesitantly, she turned the dead bolt and then opened the door.

Still focused on looking for some*one*, she stared intently into the shadows beyond the yard before she happened to look down. Breath caught in the back of her throat as she saw a stream of blood seeping out from under the overturned rattrap. When she realized the feet of the dead rat were still twitching, the world tilted. She began to scream and was still screaming when she slammed the door and ran for the phone.

When Mack left Mystic, he drove straight back to Summerton and holed up at his home. He'd spent years remodeling the old two-story house into the showpiece it was now, and it represented everything he loved about architecture.

The interior was also a reflection of the things that made him comfortable: oversize sofas with accents of dark wood and rich oxblood leather upholstery, heavy damask draperies hanging floor to ceiling. He had a

king-size bed, large walk-in closets and wide plank
hardwood flooring in a warm walnut stain.

It was not only a source of great pride that it was his,
but he'd come back to it because it was his safe place
to fall. Only, once he got here, nothing had changed.
There was nowhere to go to get away from the fact
that his father was dead. The last time he'd felt this
sad and empty was the day he'd found out Melissa
had aborted their child. And knowing he would have
to see her again at some time during this nightmare
didn't make him feel any better. He had lost all faith
in women after that day. But he knew his heart and,
while she'd shattered it completely, after the years in
which they'd loved without boundaries, she was still
under his skin.

Now that he was home, he changed clothes, brought
in the mail and began going through some phone messages regarding work before he dug through the refrigerator for something to eat. He wasn't really hungry,
but he felt empty and it was all he could think to do
to fill up the space.

When he began looking at his options, his stomach turned. There was a refrigerator full of food at his
dad's house, but he didn't want any of that, either. He
wound up eating a piece of leftover cake and emptying the entire pot of coffee he'd made.

As time continued to pass, the urge to stay here
was overwhelming, but the last thing he could do for
his dad was stay strong and see this through. So he
cleaned up the mess he'd made, locked up the house
and headed back.

It was past midnight when he drove into Mystic. The
sky was overcast, and the moon that had been high in

the sky hours earlier was hidden somewhere behind gathering clouds. He was wondering if Chief Jakes had been in contact yet with the people who serviced the lift down at the garage when he braked suddenly for a cop car. It went flying through an intersection with lights flashing and the siren screaming. The sound made the hairs rise on the back of his neck.

Someone was in trouble.

He started to accelerate through the intersection when another police car appeared at the far end of the street and took a sharp left, obviously heading to the same location. He frowned. It wasn't his practice to be a siren chaser, but since this was where he'd grown up and he knew almost everyone in town, he turned and followed the disappearing lights.

Five

Lissa was standing in her living room in the dark with her arms wrapped around her waist, still struggling with the urge to scream. Her bare feet were cold on the hardwood floors, her eyes wide and fixed on the front door. She had locked onto the faint sound of approaching sirens as if they were her lifeline, and when the lights from the first cop car appeared in the driveway and swept across the wall behind her, her knees buckled.

They were here. Thank God, thank God. She was no longer alone. Without hesitation, she stumbled to the front door and then opened it wide.

The two police cruisers arrived at the house within seconds of each other just as Mack turned the corner at the far end of the block. He watched the officers emerge from the patrol cars and immediately recognized the Doyle brothers. Now he was even more curious as to what was going on.

When it dawned on him that they were at the old Sherman house and he remembered Melissa was living there again, he tapped the brakes, slowing even more. Then he saw the front door open, and when he saw the blonde with a familiar tangle of curls appear in the doorway, he felt like he'd been sucker punched. He thought about driving away—letting her business be hers—but something held him here, so he stopped in the middle of the street to watch.

The officers were all the way up on the porch by the time Mack noticed the porch light highlighting the terror on her face. He would never be able to drive away without finding out what was wrong, so he shifted the car into Park and headed for her house.

Lonnie Doyle arrived in his patrol car only seconds ahead of his brother Carl and was all the way up on the porch before he saw what was on her doorstep. He stopped, startled by the sight.

"What the hell?"

"What's wrong?" Carl asked, as he came up the steps behind his brother. When he saw the rat beneath that overturned trap, the first thing he thought of was Paul Jackson beneath that lift. Some sick son of a bitch was messing with her big-time.

"Someone was just here," Lissa sobbed. "I didn't see who it was, but he's been harassing me for weeks, and tonight he left this."

Mack was walking toward the house, pulled toward her presence like a moth to the flame, when he heard the words and the fear in her voice. He was shocked that a stalker was at work in Mystic. And then he reminded himself there was already an open murder investigation and the possibility that his father's death might somehow be connected. A stalker only added to his disillusionment. He didn't know how to feel about seeing her again, but the look of pure terror on her face wasn't okay. He didn't see the rat until he was on the steps, and then he almost stumbled. The reference was impossible to miss. Who the hell would do something this cold?

Both officers heard the footsteps behind them, and their hands were on their weapons as they turned, but when they recognized who it was, they relaxed.

Before they could ask what he was doing there, Mack walked between them and stopped just shy of the rat, his gaze fixed on Lissa's face.

"Melissa."

She stared, too stunned to answer.

"Are you okay?" he asked.

She was already in shock from what had just happened, but after his father's death, she had known this moment was coming and dreaded it. She swayed on her feet as the world began to spin.

Mack leaped over the bloody trap and caught her before she fell.

Lissa grabbed hold of his forearms to steady herself, then hid her face against his chest, too rattled by his appearance to think.

Lonnie glanced at his brother. "Carl, get a couple of pictures."

Carl arched an eyebrow. "You talkin' about the rat or the lovebirds?"

Lonnie glared.

Carl grinned as he pulled out his cell phone and went to work.

Mack looked down at the little pink pigs on her white flannel pajamas and sighed. Who knew that it would be an old girlfriend in pink-pig pajamas who would settle a tiny part of the ache in his heart?

"Are you hurt? Did he harm you in any way?" he asked.

She came to her senses just as his hand cupped the side of her face, and she stepped back and away from him so fast she stumbled.

"I'm not hurt," she said, scrubbing the palm of her hand against the side of her face, trying to remove the sensation of him from her skin.

Lonnie interrupted, anxious to get this dealt with. "Miss Sherman, I need to take your statement, but it's a little chilly and your feet are bare. How about we go inside?"

Lissa turned on the living room light and then led the way back into the house. Mack followed the sway of her hips all the way to the sofa, with Lonnie behind him, leaving Carl to bag the evidence and search the area for the perpetrator or any clues to his identity.

Lissa sat down with her chin up and her eyes brimming with unshed tears, then pulled an afghan over her legs and absently tucked it beneath her feet.

Mack sat down in a chair with a clear view of her face without being invited to stay. He'd already inserted himself into the ongoing drama without asking, and he wasn't about to follow protocol now.

Lonnie pulled out his phone, laying it on the coffee table near her as he settled at the other end of the sofa.

"I'll record and transcribe your statement, and you can sign it later," he said.

Lissa sighed. Hyperconscious of Mack's presence and the lingering fear of the stalker in her life, all she could think was *I can't believe this is happening.*

Lonnie hit Record and then asked the first question.

"I gather from what you said earlier that this isn't the first time you've been harassed. Am I right?"

She nodded, and then realized that wouldn't translate to a recorder and answered, "Yes, that's right."

"Do you know who's doing it?"

She clutched the afghan as if it was body armor, unaware she was crying.

"No. I have no idea."

Lonnie kept firing questions. "How long has this been going on?"

She shivered. "Almost a month."

"Can you elaborate on what's happened?"

She did, telling him about the progression of phone calls, the frightening innuendos that had turned into stalking, ending with what happened tonight.

"I wasn't asleep," she added. "Today has been a nightmare, and I couldn't close my eyes without—"

She stopped in midsentence, remembering who else was in the room. She might resent him for the way they had parted company years ago, but she knew he was hurting for what he'd lost, and it was all her fault. She couldn't face him and see the accusation in his eyes.

Lonnie inserted a quick question to shift the focus.

"Have you been having problems with any of your students?" he asked.

Lissa was startled by the question, and for the first time reacted without thinking.

"No, of course not! My students are six-year-old children. Whoever's been calling me is a grown man."

Lonnie tried another angle. "What about parents? Have you had any run-ins with them?"

Lissa shook her head. "No. My life was fine, unexciting, but fine until the phone calls began. And now this." She pointed toward the porch. "How do I take that? Is this a direct threat aimed at me, or just an ugly reminder that I caused a man's death?"

At that point, Mack could remain silent no longer.

"That's bullshit, Lissa. You didn't cause anything. That could have been anyone's car. It happened. You didn't have a damn thing to do with it."

"But it *wasn't* anyone's car. It was mine," she said, and then began to sob.

Mack had never been able to hear her cry, and now he got up and walked toward the kitchen to keep from taking her in his arms. He hurt for what she was going through, and for himself. And he knew something she didn't. His dad's death might turn out to have been a murder, which should free her conscience of any culpability.

Lonnie could see she was too upset to continue and stopped the recording before slipping the phone back in his pocket.

"I'm sorry this is happening, and while we don't have much to go on, maybe we'll get lucky and pull a print from the…evidence," he said. "In the meantime, I would suggest you put up some security cameras. That might be the fastest way to identify your stalker. And remember, we're only a phone call away. In the meantime, I'll let myself out."

And then they were alone.

Lissa began wiping at her tear-streaked face as Mack walked back into the room. She didn't want him to see her tears, so she looked at the floor between his feet.

The past ten years looked damn good on her, Mack

thought. She wasn't any taller, but the wide-eyed innocence of childhood was gone from her face, leaving her with a sultry pout to her lips and those sleepy green bedroom eyes. The flannel pig pajamas were more tease than cover, her bare feet a reminder of the bare body he'd once known as well as his own.

"How does this work?" he asked.

The question surprised her. The last time she'd seen him, nearly ten years ago, he'd been so enraged she didn't think he would even want to be in the same room with her, let alone act as if nothing was wrong.

"It doesn't," she said.

"Will you let me help with the security system?"

She shrugged. "If you mean you know someone who can install it, I would appreciate a name."

She'd shut down, and he felt it. Even more, he got it and knew it had nothing to do with his father's death.

"Then, I'll be in touch. I am sorry about what's happening to you."

Lissa strode to the front door with as much confidence as she could muster, then opened the door and stepped aside.

"And I am so very sorry for your loss," she said softly.

Mack sighed. She was staring at the floor, refusing to meet his gaze. He got the message. He walked outside and was off the porch before he heard the lock turn. He didn't belong here any more than that dead rat.

Reece Parsons was dancing with excitement, waiting for the reaction to his latest little love note. He hadn't been certain of his next move tonight until he'd found out about Paul Jackson's death, and then he'd known immediately what came next.

It had taken a good five hours to find and catch a live rat before he could even go to her place, and then it was a matter of getting everything on her porch and waiting for the sound of her footsteps before he dropped the trigger on the rat and left it in its death throes on her doorstep.

The moment he dropped the trap, he bolted into the shadows between her neighbors' house and hers, then slipped down the first alley he came to and kept running. He was breathing hard when he finally reached the truck and unlocked the door. Everything was fine, just as he'd left it. His little dog was asleep in the seat, but he wasn't through with Melissa Sherman. He clipped the leash on to the dog's collar and dragged him out.

"Come on, Bobo, let's take a walk."

Bobo's legs were short but his attitude was big, and the word *walk* was always welcome.

Even though the night was chilly, sweat was drying on Reece's forehead as he walked Bobo through the park, purposefully taking a shortcut that would take him within two blocks of Melissa Sherman's house. He'd heard the sirens and guessed she'd finally called the cops. He wanted to see what was happening. It was a different kind of high to know she was that kind of scared.

The wire-haired terrier was nosing beneath every bush and sniffing trails left by nocturnal creatures but Reece had other business and all but dragged Bobo back toward her house. They exited the park at a side street and immediately headed for the sidewalk. The moment he saw two cop cars at her place, he grinned. There was another vehicle at the curb and he wondered who it belonged to, but this was no time to get too curious. He decided he would just walk Bobo by the house and maybe get a peek at what was going on as they passed.

Then, as if on cue, a stray cat slunk out from beneath the SUV parked at the curb and took off across the street. Bobo leaped forward so fast the leash slipped from Reece's hands and he took off running after it. All of a sudden Melissa Sherman's welfare was playing second fiddle to recovering his dog.

Carl took the pictures, then bagged up the dead rat and trap, securing everything inside his vehicle before he began to check out the neighborhood.

The lights had been off in every house when they'd arrived, so he doubted there would be any witnesses, but it was his job to ask.

He began with the house north of where Melissa lived and asked them if they'd seen anyone running away from her place earlier. He got a play-by-play of where the residents had been sleeping and what they'd had for supper before going to bed, but no one had seen anything.

He went down the block, knocking on doors and asking the same question without getting a useful answer. He had just started back up the block on the other side of the street when he heard a small dog begin to bark. He turned around to look just as a man came running out of the shadows.

Reece was a little panicked. He loved Bobo and didn't want to lose him, but this was not how he'd intended to revisit the scene of the crime. Not only was the dog outrunning him, but Reece was running out of energy.

"Bobo! Bobo! Come back here! Heel, Bobo, heel!" he yelled, and then groaned when he saw an officer come off the porch of the house across the street.

When the cop began running toward him, his heart skipped a beat. But when the officer made a little side step and grabbed the trailing leash and caught Bobo, he relaxed.

Bobo's escape ended with a yelp as the leash tightened and pulled him up short.

The grateful cat disappeared into the shadows.

Reece approached the cop, winded and gasping with every step, and smiled as the officer handed over the leash.

"This is pretty late at night to be walking a dog," Carl said.

Reece pretended disgust as he picked Bobo up in his arms. "Tell that to Bobo. He's the one with the nervous bladder."

Carl chuckled as he reached over and patted the terrier's head.

"You're the man, Bobo," he said, and then he glanced up. "By any chance, have you seen anyone else on foot in this area in the past thirty minutes or so?"

Reece's heart skipped a beat. He was actually being questioned as a witness to his own crime. This couldn't get much better.

"Why? I see patrol cars at Miss Sherman's house. Did something happen to her?"

"No, she's fine. Just a prank gone wrong," Carl said. "So did you see anything or anyone suspicious?"

Reece thought about pointing the finger at someone else and then at the last minute didn't.

"No, sir, I did not. Bobo and I were originally in the park. I just wound up here trying to catch him."

Carl nodded. "Okay. Just be on the lookout as you go back."

"Are we in any danger?" Reece asked, holding Bobo a little tighter.

"I don't think so, but just be aware."

"Yes, yes, we will," Reece said, and hurried away.

It wasn't until he was back in the park that he began to grin. This had turned into a most interesting night. He gave the little dog a quick hug and kiss.

"Good boy, Bobo, good boy."

Bobo yipped once.

Reece was still smiling as he reached his vehicle. He put Bobo safely inside, then scooted in beside him and started the engine. It was time to get home and do a little work. Sunrise would be here before he knew it.

Six

Mack walked into the house on autopilot, moving through the rooms without turning on lights. He was still reeling from the unexpected meeting with Melissa. He wanted to hate her, but time and maturity had taken the edge off his rage, and the fear on her face had done a number on his heart.

When he got to his room, he shucked off his clothes, giving them a toss into the corner of the room before crawling into bed. He couldn't remember the last time he'd slept in this house—most likely it had been years because he lived so close the need had never been there.

He didn't know if the chief had already contacted the company that serviced the lift, but whenever they came out to test it, he wanted to be there. His dad deserved his full attention, regardless of the outcome.

He rolled over onto his back, pulled up the covers and closed his eyes and, as he did, the image of Lissa standing in the doorway with an expression of total horror on her face immediately flashed on. He tried to get her out of his mind but instead fell asleep dreaming of the past.

* * *

The hot sun was coming in through the skylight at Jackson's Garage and down onto the back of Mack's shoulders. He'd come into his own in this, his eighteenth year. His shoulders had widened, and the muscles in his body were toned to a fault from working in his father's garage for so many years. He knew he was changing outwardly, but what the world had yet to find out was that he was changing inwardly, as well. He had already come to terms with giving up the idea of college and was planning to go to work full-time here as soon as they told their parents about the baby. It wasn't how he'd planned his future, but the baby was part of their love and he did love Melissa Sherman. And he would be heartily glad when he was through fixing this flat.

He ran his fingers along the side of the tire and then let it bounce once as he dropped it to the floor. As he did, he heard laughing and looked up just as Kelly Pryor and Jessica Shayne, two girls from his graduating class, ran past the open breezeway toward their public restroom.

People in Mystic often used the restroom during working hours because they kept it unlocked, and he thought nothing of it as he rolled the tire over to the car. He squatted down beside the jack, making sure it was still stable before he lifted the tire into place and began replacing the lug nuts.

He had done this so many times in his life that he could have done it blindfolded and had only one lug nut left to put on when the automatic air compressor behind him suddenly kicked off. The abrupt silence was startling, and when he realized he could hear the two girls talking, he glanced over his shoulder, trying to locate the sound.

All he could see was an air vent, and he guessed it must link to the bathroom, which was weird. He made a mental note to say something to his dad, then blocked out their chatter until he heard them say Melissa's name. He stopped to listen. She was the most important person in his life, and they were facing a life-changing decision.

They'd been struggling to find new footing with each other ever since they'd found out about the baby. It had changed everything they'd planned, from college to career goals. He didn't know how to talk to her without feeling guilty. She'd cried when she told him she was pregnant, and even though he took just as much blame as she did, they were struggling. But now someone was talking about her, and he felt the need to make sure what they were saying was okay. He leaned forward, listening to the conversation.

"Are you sure?" Kelly asked. "She never seemed like that kind of girl to me."

Jessica laughed, and he could practically see her roll her eyes. "Oh, come on. She and Mack have been a thing for years. You know they've been doing it. I heard from a really good source that she was preggers and all freaked out. You know how uptight her parents are. They would probably kill her."

"So she's pregnant. They both graduated. They'll figure it out," Kelly said.

"That's where it gets good," Jessica hissed. "I heard she already got rid of it. Easy come, easy go."

Mack reeled as if he'd been punched. He couldn't believe it, *wouldn't* believe it. Granted they were fac-

ing a tough situation, but she would never kill their
baby. Never. He was still shaking when his dad walked
into the garage.

"Mack! Are you through with that tire?"

He knelt back down to put the last lug nut on the
wheel and then stood.

"All done," he said, brushing the dust off his hands.
"Hey, Dad, I'm gonna take my lunch break now. I'll
be back around two, okay?"

"Yeah, sure," he said.

Mack took off out the front door on the run. He
jumped in his truck and drove straight to the Sherman
house, knowing Lissa's parents wouldn't be home until
evening. He drove without caution, too numb to think,
and took the turn into her driveway in a skid. His hands
were shaking when he knocked on the door, and then
Lissa was standing in the doorway and he could tell
by the look on her face something was wrong.

"We need to talk," he said, and walked in when she
stepped aside.

"Do you want a Coke?" she asked, as she shut the
front door.

Mack was so rattled, he said everything wrong.

"No, I do not want a Coke. I want to know if you're
still pregnant."

When she paled and then began to cry, his heart
sank.

"You're not, are you?" he yelled.

She flinched as the tears fell harder. "No, I'm not,
I had a—"

He slapped the wall beside her head.

"Don't say it! Don't fucking say it, Lissa. I thought
I knew you. I thought I *loved* you. I don't ever want

to see your face again!" he yelled as he left the house, slamming the door as he went.

Mack woke up with a start and realized he was crying. He groaned and threw back the covers, and even though it was at least two hours before dawn, he got up.

For him, sleep was over.

Lissa's sleep was fretful. She dreamed about dead rats and bloody feet and people knocking on her door. From there, the dream morphed into the day she'd lost the baby.

The windshield wipers were fighting a useless battle against the downpour. This trip to Summerton was to be Lissa's first appointment with an obstetrician, and she was wishing that she had stayed home and gone another day.

From the moment she'd found out she was pregnant, it had turned something on inside her that she hadn't even known was there. In a way, she felt like an explorer. Everything from this moment on would be uncharted territory for her, but she would be the one in control. Before, her life had been dominated by being Mr. and Mrs. Sherman's daughter and, for the past four years, being everything Mack Jackson needed her to be. She loved her parents and she loved Mack, but she'd almost lost herself in the process. Finding out about the baby had changed everything. Her plans for the future were changing along with her body. Although her parents didn't know it, college was on hold. Already her breasts were a bit swollen and tender, and she imagined the tiny being growing inside her, wondered whether it would be a boy or a girl, wondered if it would have her blond hair or be dark like Mack.

A shaft of lightning struck somewhere off to her right, momentarily making her lose concentration. As she did, the rear end of the car fishtailed and began sliding sideways. She was bordering on panic when she remembered her father's words: *steer into a skid*. Once she did that, the car was back in the proper lane and her panic subsided.

The rain was still coming down when she finally drove into Summerton, and with no small amount of relief. The sooner this appointment was behind her, the better, because she needed to be home before her parents got off work. Her stomach was in knots as she took a turn, and then she groaned when she realized she'd turned a block too early. By the time she back-tracked, located the medical building and found a place to park, she was shaking.

Secrets made her feel guilty, and this wasn't the way she'd been raised. She and Mack had talked, and as soon as a doctor officially verified her pregnancy they were going to tell their parents. She glanced in the rearview mirror, made a face at her reflection and grabbed her umbrella. The rain was still coming down as she headed toward the building on the run.

She was halfway across the parking lot when she slipped. She felt herself falling, and then her feet went out from under her as she went down, landing hard enough that she was momentarily dazed. When she came to, she was flat on her back and faceup in the downpour, in so much pain she was afraid to move.

Out of nowhere, two men in hard hats appeared, staring down at her in dual dismay.

"Miss! Are you all right? We saw you fall. Where do you hurt? Can you move?"

Lissa groaned. "Oh, my God...I hurt everywhere. Give me a minute. I think I can get up."

"Maybe we should call an ambulance," one of them offered.

"No, no ambulance!" Lissa cried, and began trying to move.

The two men helped her up, then steadied her until she got her bearings. She was drenched but upright. Her ears were ringing, but she could move. It was going to be okay.

"Thanks, guys, I've got this," she said.

"Here's your umbrella," one man said.

She took it gladly, grateful to get the rain out of her face, and held it over her head as she walked into the building. The shelter was welcome as she paused in the lobby to check the roster, looking for the location of the doctor's office.

By the time she got on the elevator she was miserable. Her clothes were sticking to her skin, her shoes were full of water and every muscle in her body was beginning to throb. When she caught a glimpse of herself in the mirrored walls of the elevator she groaned. What a mess! The moment the elevator stopped, she got off and began looking for a bathroom to clean herself up.

She found one nearby, and when she walked in and saw the hand dryer on the wall she headed for it. After setting her purse and umbrella down, she hit the start button and bent over so that the hot air could dry her hair. She couldn't do much about her wet clothes but she did take her shoes off and dry the insides with paper towels, then thrust them under the dryer, as well.

When she'd done all she could do, she hurried down the hall to the doctor's office to check in. As she sat down to fill out the new patient forms, her aches and pains increased. Sore muscles began to tighten, and wet clothes exacerbated the misery. To add to her discomfort, she recognized one of the women in the waiting room as the mother of one of her classmates, and she was giving Lissa a very cool, very judgmental stare.

"Why, hello, Melissa. You're a ways from home," the woman said.

"Hello, Mrs. Shayne. Yes, ma'am, I guess we both are. Terrible weather, isn't it?"

Beverly Shayne nodded politely and, to Lissa's relief, returned her attention to the magazine she was reading.

Seeing someone she knew made Lissa even more nervous. Would Bev Shayne go back to Mystic telling everyone where she'd seen Lissa Sherman? Then she reminded herself that women of all ages went to gynecologists, and she was a woman—a young one, but a woman nonetheless. On the surface this would not be of any consequence.

But the longer she sat, the worse she felt. When her belly began to cramp she was in so much pain she couldn't determine where she hurt the most. By the time they called her back, the pain was so bad she was shaking.

The nurse eyed Lissa as she led her to the examining room, looking past the wet clothes and damp curls to the muscle jerking at the side of her jaw. Lissa moaned as she crawled up onto the table then rolled over onto her side and curled up in a ball, which increased the nurse's concern.

"Melissa Sherman?"

"Yes, ma'am."

"Are you in pain?"

"Yes, ma'am. I fell in the parking lot, and the longer I sat, the more I began to hurt."

The nurse moved to the table and took Lissa's pulse, then made a note before reaching for the blood pressure cuff.

"So you are here for a prenatal exam?"

Lissa moaned. "Yes."

"Where do you hurt the most?" the nurse asked.

"It was just my back and hips, but I think my belly hurts worse now."

"Your stomach? How so?"

"Oh, my God," Lissa said, and then gritted her teeth as a spasm rolled across her belly. "That's the worst cramp I ever had in my life."

"Lissa, I need you to take off all your clothes and put this gown on. Can you stand up to do that?"

Lissa nodded, and then took the gown and slid off the table.

"I'll be right back," the nurse said.

Undressing was more difficult than Lissa had expected because the wet clothes stuck to her skin, and by the time she got her jeans down she was shaking. The wet denim was in a puddle around her feet, but she didn't see the blood running down the inside of her leg until she bent down to pick them up.

"No!" she cried, and grabbed at the blood with both hands, as if she could stop what was happening. Her heart began to hammer as the room started to spin. She looked up as the door opened, then held out her hands. "Help me."

Betsy Jakes was sitting cross-legged in the bed with her journal in her lap, her glasses persistently sliding down her nose no matter how many times she pushed them up. She was desperate to get everything on paper before she forgot the dream. There was a horrible knot in her stomach, and her head was spinning. She felt like she was losing her mind. She paused, looking back at what she'd just written.

Someone died. I think we saw it happen. I don't think it was an accident. I keep seeing it in my dreams but I cannot see a face.

Then she added, "I have to remember or they'll kill me, too."

Suddenly there was a knock at her door. She slapped the journal shut and shoved it in a drawer in her bedside table.

"Yes? Come in," she called.

Trina opened the door and peeked in.

"Mama, are you all right? I got up to go to the bathroom and saw the light under your door."

Betsy made herself smile.

"Oh, sure, I'm fine. I just got up to take some pain meds. I woke up with a headache, and now it's keeping me awake." Then Betsy reached over and turned off the lamp, and crawled back beneath the covers.

"Okay," Trina said, but she didn't buy the story.

Something was going on with her mother, something frightening.

They were all worried about her, but none of them knew what to do. Trina went to the bathroom and then back to her own bed, but she couldn't sleep, so she lay awake, waiting for daybreak.

In her own room, Betsy went back to writing in the journal.

As Reece was scrolling through the latest NASDAQ figures, he was also mulling over what to do next with Melissa Sherman. The little game he'd been playing was taking on a life of its own, and he was at a cross-roads. Now that she'd called the police, the danger of being caught had increased exponentially, so where did he go from here? Did he quit while he was ahead and let everything cool off for a few months, or up the ante? For him, the next logical progression was always getting inside the house. If he did get that far, would scaring the shit out of her be enough, or did he want to fuck her? And if he did that, then he had to have the balls to kill her, because he wasn't about to take a chance on being identified and sent to jail.

When he'd targeted girls before, he hadn't always fucked them. Some of them just needed killing. But he was entranced with this one and wanted a taste of what she was like before he killed her.

It was nearing 4:00 a.m. when he decided to sleep on it. He shut down the computer, then went to bed. He was still sleeping like a baby with Bobo curled up on top of the covers at his feet when he heard Louis's alarm go off. He roused momentarily as Bobo jumped off the bed, then rolled over and went back to sleep. The alarm was Louis's problem, not his.

Louis got up and shut off the alarm, then listened to tell if Reece's dog was awake. He always let him out in the backyard to do his business before he left for school. When he got up, Bobo came trotting in from the hall, his ears up, his tail wagging.

"Hi, Bobo," Louis said. "Wanna go outside?"

Bobo made a dash for the kitchen. Louis hurried along behind and let him out in the fenced-in backyard, and then proceeded to make coffee and fix a lunch to take to school.

As he was working, his cell phone signaled a text. He stopped and walked over to the charging station, saw that the text was from their mother, in Florida, and winced. Mama never wanted to talk to him. She always wanted to talk to Reece, but Reece was asleep, so she must have decided he would have to do.

He picked up the phone and read the text. Call me. It's important.

Now he was worried. Should he wake Reece up anyway? No. Reece would be pissed. He'd better find out what was wrong before he made a decision about that, so he called her back. She answered on the second ring.

"Reece? Honey, I'm so glad I caught you at home."

"Reece is still asleep, Mama. It's me, Louis. What's wrong?"

There was a moment of silence and then a sigh.

"Really? I thought I called Reece's cell. Just put him on the phone and let me get this over with."

Louis frowned. "No, Mama. He gets mad if I wake

him up. You tell me and I'll write him a note. He can call you back later."

"Oh, for the love of God!" Pinky Parsons shrieked.

"If you're gonna be mad at me, I'm hanging up," Louis said.

"No, no, don't do that! I'm sorry," Pinky said. "Do you swear you'll write the note?"

"Yes. Don't I always? Doesn't he always call back?"

"I guess."

"So what's wrong?"

"The company that owns my apartment building sold it. The new company is raising the rent, and I can't afford it. I'm gonna have to move."

"Well, I'm real sorry to hear that, Mama," Louis said. "But you'll find a new place, maybe better than that one. It's a dump anyway."

Pinky cursed beneath her breath. "That's just the problem. Dumps are all I can afford. This was the cheapest one in town. I can't afford anything else here, so I need to stay with you until I can get on my feet again."

Louis stifled a gasp. They'd only just moved to Mystic this past summer. He had been lucky to get the job at the school, and he didn't want his routine messed up, which would happen anyway because eventually either his brother or his mother messed shit up. That was just how it was.

"We don't have much room," he said, hoping to dissuade her.

"I don't mind. It won't be for very long."

"Reece still has Bobo, and you don't like dogs."

"I can put up with it for a while," Pinky said. "I have your address. I'm taking the bus to Mystic. I'll be there about tomorrow afternoon. You be sure and tell Reece. You know he doesn't like surprises."

"I know. I'll tell him," Louis said, defeated and trying not to panic.

"Okay, son. So, uh…I'll see you tomorrow."

The click in his ear was as definite as the fact that their mother was actually going to be living with them. He couldn't imagine anything much worse. Reece was going to have a fit. Bobo would bark and snap at her because she kicked at him when no one was looking, and there would be hell to pay on all fronts.

Why, why, why did stuff like this have to happen just when he was settling in? Then he heard Bobo scratching at the back door and went to let him in.

"Well, furball, you better enjoy yourself today. Mama is coming to visit."

Bobo sat down, waiting for his food dish to be filled.

Louis shrugged. "Don't say I didn't warn you," he muttered, as he got a scoop of dry dog food and dumped it in the dish, and then gave the dog fresh water.

The silence in the room was broken only by the crunch of kibble and the sounds Louis made as he ate his cereal.

When he was through, he wrote the note to Reece, then finished getting ready and took himself and his lunch to work, leaving Bobo and the bad news behind.

Lissa woke up with a gasp and threw back the covers, certain she would be covered in blood. But the pink pigs on the old white flannel pajamas were unstained and the bedclothes pristine. She combed her fingers through her hair in frustration, knowing she had Mack Jackson to thank for the resurrection of that nightmare.

It was less than an hour before daybreak, soon enough to quit the bed and get ready for the day ahead. School was her safe place to be. It wasn't just a job to her. It was her calling. The children kept her connected to the things that mattered, and today of all days she needed her work to help keep her mind off the current hell of her life.

Since she was still without a car, she decided to rent one.

She put on a pot of coffee, made herself a peanut-butter-and-jelly sandwich, and then got her laptop and searched online for car rentals in her area. When she realized one of the rental agencies was owned by a man she'd gone to school with, she began to breathe a little easier. She was going to take a chance and wake somebody up, hoping he would help her make this happen.

By the time the coffee was done, she was agreeing to the final details over the phone. The car would be delivered to her within the next forty-five minutes—plenty of time to sign off on it and get to school.

An hour later Lissa was in the rental car on her way to school, dressed warmly for playground duty in an all-weather coat, brown corduroy slacks and a blue turtleneck sweater. She'd made herself a ham-and-cheese sandwich for lunch and had a Hershey's candy bar stashed for her planning period. Life felt almost normal as she drove into the parking lot. She grabbed her things and started toward the building, determined to get through this day with her emotions in check.

With regards to her stalker, she had to admit she

felt an odd sense of relief now that she'd turned things over to the police. If she was lucky, maybe that would be the deterrent he needed to cool him down.

As for Mack Jackson walking back into her life, it had certainly resurrected all her old feelings, including the lingering resentment she carried for how they'd parted ways. Last night's bad dream had only exacerbated her mood.

And then she entered the building, and the distant sound of children's voices down in the cafeteria made her smile. They were getting their bellies filled, and later she was going to fill their heads with knowledge. It was her perfect world.

The principal turned and smiled at her as she walked into the teachers' lounge for a cup of coffee to take to her room.

"Good morning, Melissa."

"Good morning, Mr. Wilson, and thank you for yesterday."

"Certainly. I trust you had a good night's sleep?"

She blinked. "It was fine." Then she grabbed her cup, filled it and left the lounge before he could ask her any more questions.

The janitor was down on his knees in the hall cleaning up a spill when she passed.

"Good morning, Louis. I see someone has already made a mess for you to clean up."

"It's okay," he said softly, and kept wiping.

She stopped. "Thank you for taking me home yesterday. You were very kind to volunteer."

He shrugged slightly. "I didn't mind."

Lissa smiled. Louis was just being Louis, which

today was welcome. The more things that stayed normal, the better off she would be.

She hurried down the hall to her room to unload her stuff, took a quick sip of coffee and then got to work. When the first bell rang and the chatter of children's voices filled the hall and then moved into her room, the last bit of anxiety she'd come with was gone.

Mack was dressed early but hoping for a little peace and quiet so he could finish going through the house. He didn't really expect any revelations, but he'd promised Trey Jakes that he would look. An hour passed, and he was about to call it quits when he opened a drawer and saw his mother's old jewelry box. She'd been gone so many years that he assumed his dad had kept it for sentimental reasons, but for as long as he could remember it had been on a corner shelf near the bedroom window.

Now it was in a drawer? Why?

Only one way to find out.

He opened it slowly, taking care not to break a loose hinge, and at first saw nothing except bits and pieces of outdated costume jewelry. It wasn't until he began poking through the necklaces on the second level that he found the key. He knew immediately what kind of key it was, and he was shocked.

He actually stopped and sat down on the corner of the bed, palming the key to a safety deposit box he'd never known about while trying to wrap his head around why his father had kept it a secret.

"Okay, Dad. You always told me everything. I know your lawyer has a copy of your will. I knew every time your doctor changed your meds. I even remember you telling me one time how you wanted your funeral to play out. I know you expected me to sell the garage one day because I wasn't going to live here, and I know you trusted me implicitly, but I never knew about this. Why did I not know about this?"

Unfortunately, Paul wasn't there to explain himself, and Mack was an impatient man. The only way to get answers was to go to the source. He glanced at the clock. The bank would be open in five minutes. It was time to take a look at his father's secrets.

But his trip to the bank became more involved than he'd imagined. Because Paul Jackson was deceased, and because he was the only one on the signature card and his estate would have to go through probate, the box had to be opened in front of witnesses, including his dad's lawyer, Adrian Emerson.

So he made a quick call. The phone rang once, twice, and then a woman's no-nonsense voice was in his ear.

"Emerson Law."

"LaDelle, this is Mack Jackson. Is Mr. Emerson in?"

"Oh, Mack, I am so sorry about your father. One moment while I connect you."

Mack stood up and turned his back to the lobby as he walked toward the plate-glass windows. The sky was an odd shade of blue-gray. He hadn't listened to the weather since he'd been here, but it looked like it might rain.

He saw Trey Jakes drive by in his patrol car and wondered if he'd heard from the lift company. There was a knot in his gut that kept getting tighter. He needed to know the truth about his father's death. Had it truly been just a horrible accident, or had he been murdered?

"Adrian Emerson speaking."

Mack jumped. He'd almost forgotten he was on hold for the lawyer.

"Mr. Emerson, this is Mack Jackson. I found a safety deposit key at my dad's house. I'm at the bank, but they have to open the box in front of witnesses, including Dad's lawyer, so I was wondering if you were free."

"Mack, my condolences for sure, and I'm glad you called. I have about an hour before my next appointment. I'll be right there," Emerson said before he hung up in Mack's ear.

At that moment Mack saw Trey Jakes go back by and realized it might be wise if he was present, too. He got out the card Trey had given him and made a quick call, explaining what was going on. Trey made a U-turn and beat the lawyer to the bank.

By the time the group assembled inside the vault, there were five people present: Gregory Standish, the president of the bank; his secretary, who would record the event; Adrian Emerson; Trey Jakes; and Mack himself.

He eyed the wall of safety deposit boxes with a mixture of curiosity and dread.

"What are you thinking?" Trey asked, as they waited for the secretary to get the recording equipment set up.

Mack shrugged. "That this might not amount to a thing, and that it might have been something he and Mom had together and he just forgot about it."

"He wouldn't forget," Gregory Standish said. "Everyone gets billed annually for the rent, and he must have paid it every year or the box wouldn't still be in his name."

Mack gave up trying to figure out why it was here. They would find out soon enough.

"Okay, here we go," the secretary said.

She took the bank key and Mack's key, opened the door and removed the box without fanfare, then promptly pulled out a large manila envelope with Paul Jackson's name on the front and handed it to the lawyer.

Emerson opened the flap and tilted the envelope, letting the contents slide out onto the table. The first thing he picked up was a piece of paper. He read it, frowning.

"It appears to be a list of the items in the envelope. The heading reads, 'Property of eighteen-year-old Paul Jackson of Mystic, West Virginia, removed from his person in ER during triage.'"

Trey Jakes' heart skipped a beat as he glanced at Mack. That damn wreck *was* going to tie the deaths together after all. He could feel it.

Mack frowned at the odd assortment of items as they were being listed.

An old wallet containing a five-dollar bill, a condom still in a wrapper and a school picture of Trey's mother, Betsy.

A stained tassel from a graduation cap.

A folded-up program from graduation night.

A handful of coins totaling a dollar and twenty-three cents.

"I believe that's all," Emerson said, then absently checked the inside of the envelope. "Oh, wait! There's something else."

He pulled out a smaller envelope.

"It has Mack's name on it," Emerson said, handing it to him.

Seven

Mack didn't know what to expect, but he wasted no time opening the envelope. His eyes widened as he scanned the text, then he took a deep breath and handed it to Trey.

"I think this is something you're going to want to read."

"Please read it aloud for the record," Emerson said, as Trey took the letter.

Trey nodded.

"Mack, if you're reading this and you are questioning my death in any way, there's something you need to tell Trey Jakes. The tassel in the envelope does not belong to anyone from the wreck. The night of our graduation, before we ever left town, we gave our caps and gowns to our parents. I was told the tassel was in the pocket of my pants. I have no idea how it got there, but it was bloody, as was everything else I'd been wearing, so they thought nothing of it. I don't remember the wreck or what we'd been doing before it happened, but after Dick died, I began having dreams, and one of them had to do with that tassel. I kept seeing a boy's body on the ground, holding a tassel soaked in blood, so maybe it was already bloody when I put it in my pocket. Maybe they can get DNA off it. Maybe it will help figure this mess out. I don't know what happened, but I think the four of us were a part of something bad. I can't bring myself to believe we caused it, but we were so drunk when we had the wreck there's no telling what might have happened beforehand. I want to think we witnessed it. I want to think we were on the way back to Mystic to get help when the wreck happened. I want to think that, but I'm not sure. All I know is that I've had a feeling in my gut ever since Dick's murder that either Betsy or I could be next. You know how much I love you. You know how proud I am of all you've accomplished. Live your life. Don't waste it. Go make peace with Melissa. I know you still care.

Dad."

The silence in the vault was telling. The banker, Gregory Standish, was pale and shaking as he stared down at the rusty-looking tassel in disbelief.

"So that's not dirt on there," he muttered.

Trey pulled an evidence bag out of the inner pocket of his jacket, and bagged and tagged it in front of them, then pocketed the letter.

"I need to get this to the state lab," he said, patting the pocket where he'd put the letter. "I'll make sure you get this back."

Mack shook his head. "I don't want it. I know he loved me. That message was for you."

Trey glanced at his watch.

"The serviceman is coming to the garage to look at the lift in about a half hour. I need to be there to let them in. Do you have the keys to the garage on you, Mack?"

Mack nodded. "I'll follow you there."

Trey pointed to the banker and his secretary.

"Everything you heard in here is confidential because it's directly connected to an ongoing murder investigation, so I don't expect to hear any gossip around town, understand?"

Standish and his secretary both nodded.

Satisfied he'd done all that was needed, Trey headed out, leaving the others behind in the vault.

Mack was shaken as he glanced over at the lawyer.

"Mr. Emerson, I don't suppose you need me anymore. The box has been opened and the contents recorded, right?"

"Right. An inventory of the contents will be included in the papers when his estate goes into probate."

Mack nodded, then shook hands with the banker. "Thank you for your assistance and consideration."

Gregory Standish turned on the charm. "You're entirely welcome, Mr. Jackson, and on behalf of all of us here at the bank, please accept our condolences on the loss of your father."

Mack left then, his mind already on the next facet of the investigation. If that lift was truly faulty, then there was no way to back up what his father had written, but if the lift was fine, the letter was added proof that his father had been murdered. He wasn't sure how he felt because either way, his father was still dead.

Mack saw Trey leaning against the hood of his cruiser and talking on the phone when he pulled up to the gas station. He walked past Trey and overheard just enough of the conversation to know that Trey was talking to his mother about having lunch with her later, and he guessed she was going to be the next person to be interviewed regarding what was happening. He didn't envy Trey the job of having to interview his own mother. By the time he got to the station and unlocked the doors, Trey was right behind him.

"What are you thinking?" Mack asked.

Trey wasn't in the habit of talking police business with a civilian, but this case was different.

"My mom hasn't been the same since finding Dick Phillips' body. Now, since your dad left that letter, it leaves me wondering if maybe the murder triggered some blocked memories from that wreck for her, too. However, that's all supposition until the lift is examined."

"Is Lissa Sherman's car still on the lift?" Mack asked.

Trey nodded. "Until I figure out if this is a crime scene or the scene of an accident, it's still part of an ongoing case."

Mack turned around and jammed his hands in his pockets, wondering at the whimsy of fate that had thrown them back together again after all these years. The wind was chilly, and he hunched his shoulders, wishing he'd put on a heavier jacket before leaving the house. When he saw a long blue van pulling up to the stoplight down the street he shifted nervously from one foot to the other. The service company was here.

"Hey, Trey, here they come," he said, pointing.

"Good. Maybe we'll get a definitive answer soon."

After the van pulled up beside Mack's SUV and parked, he recognized the two men who got out.

The older man came straight toward him with his hand outstretched.

"Mack, Junior and I were sure sorry to hear about what happened to your dad. He was a fine man."

"Thanks, Eldridge. This is Chief Jakes."

"Chief, this is Eldridge Warren and his son, Junior."

The men nodded at each other, Trey thanked them for coming and then led the way inside, explaining what he needed to know.

"This is the same car that was on the lift. It went up fine when we removed the body, and then we let it down for safety's sake. However, I need to know what caused the lift to fail."

"Yes, sir," Eldridge said. He walked over to the control and pressed it. He looked surprised when the lift went up without a hitch. He pressed the control again, and the lift lowered without a bobble. He frowned. "I'll need to get down into the trap to check everything out," he said.

"I'll do it, Pop," Junior Warren said, and then glanced at Trey. "He hurt his back a couple of months ago."

Mack raised the door in the floor that led down into the space beneath that held the equipment that powered the lift.

"The light is just to your right as you go down," Mack said.

"Right," Junior said, and they watched the lights come on as he descended.

They heard him banging around, and then there was silence.

Eldridge frowned. "What's going on?" he yelled.

"Nothing," Junior said, then walked to the foot of the stairs and looked up at the three men staring down at him. "If the hydraulics had failed, there would be hydraulic fluid all over, but everything is dry."

"I'm gonna hit the control again. You watch the gauges for fluctuations," Eldridge said. Then he shook his head. "No, I'm coming down to see for myself. You handle the control, Mack."

Mack got into position. "Yell when you're ready," he said, watching as Eldridge slowly descended.

He heard father and son talking but couldn't make out what they were saying, and then Eldridge yelled, "Now, Mack! Hit the control."

Mack's heart was pounding as the car rose on the lift without issue.

"Is it all the way up?" Eldridge called.

"It's up," Trey said.

"Now let it down," Eldridge said.

The lift went down as easily as it had gone up, and Mack's heart began to pound. He glanced at the expression on Trey's face but couldn't get a read on what he was thinking, and then Trey turned toward him.

"Do it again, up, then down."

Mack complied, and as it was going down, Junior and Eldridge climbed up, turned out the light below and lowered the door.

"There isn't anything wrong with that lift," Eldridge said. "The pressure is perfect on every gauge, and the equipment is dry. If the lift was faulty, the hydraulic fluid would have leaked out all over everything."

Trey took off his hat and shoved a hand through his hair in frustration.

"So you're saying that the only way the lift could have come down on Paul Jackson was if someone hit the control?"

Eldridge blinked. He hadn't taken the thought to its logical conclusion. "Well, I guess…yes, that's what I'm saying."

"Will you need anything more from us?" Junior asked.

"No, and thank you for coming so promptly," Trey said.

"Just send the bill to the garage, as always," Mack said. "I'll make sure you get paid."

Eldridge shook his head.

"No, there won't be any charge on this trip," he said gruffly. Then he walked out with his son behind him, leaving Mack and Trey alone. The silence between them was telling.

Finally it was Mack who spoke, his voice rough with emotion. "Damn it, just say what we're both thinking."

Trey turned his head and their gazes locked. "Your father's death is going to be ruled a homicide."

Mack grunted, then looked down at the floor. The bloodstains were still there, trailing out from beneath Lissa's car.

"Is this going to be public knowledge?" he asked.

"As of this moment, yes. Why?"

Mack shrugged. "Lissa blamed herself, so when school is out today I'm going to tell her what happened. It should relieve her conscience."

Trey picked up on the tension between them and vaguely remembered that they'd dated years back. He thought of the message Paul Jackson had sent to his son about renewing the relationship and decided to give him a little help.

"Feel free to give her the news," Trey said. "I've got to go talk to my mom. Her life is in danger. Meanwhile, this is officially a murder scene. We need to lock the place back up."

Mack followed Trey out and locked the door, then turned around and gazed at the scene before him. Mystic was home, and home had suddenly taken on a very dark visage.

It was midmorning and Lissa was wiping tears and snot off six-year-old Jolie Wade's face while giving Roger Lee Westfall her best serious expression.

Roger Lee was looking nervous. He didn't know exactly what he'd done wrong. All he'd done was tell the truth after Jolie went and told Aaron that Roger Lee was her boyfriend. He'd told Aaron she wasn't, and now Jolie was crying and he couldn't tell for sure if Miss Sherman was mad at him or not. Having two people upset at him would be daunting, especially when he didn't know why.

Lissa wanted to laugh, but of course she couldn't. Little Miss Jolie was going to break a thousand hearts before she grew up and found her man, but it appeared Roger Lee wasn't going to be the first to fall. She admired the little guy for his honesty, and for not being swayed by blond hair and blue eyes.

Meanwhile, Jolie was a six-year-old wreck. She had already decided she wasn't going to like that Roger Lee ever again, but she didn't have the skills to gracefully end the fit she was throwing.

Lissa handed Jolie a handful of tissues. "Go wash your face and blow your nose, then hurry back. It's almost time for snack."

Jolie took the tissues and walked out of the room with her jaw set.

Lissa motioned for the little boy to come to her desk. He approached reluctantly, his voice shaking and his eyes welling with tears,

"Am I in trouble, Miss Sherman?"

"Do you think you should be in trouble?" she asked.

Roger Lee shook his head. "No, ma'am."

"Why not?" she asked.

"'Cause I told the truth. Jolie isn't my girlfriend. I don't like girls all that much."

Lissa offered him a handful of tissues, too.

"Then, that's that," she said. "And no more talk of boyfriends and girlfriends in my class. We have important things to learn, right?"

He took the tissues, and before she could stop him, he blew his nose, then wiped his eyes.

Lissa stifled a groan. "Next time wipe your eyes first and then blow your nose."

"Yes, ma'am," Roger Lee said, handing her the tissues and going back to his chair.

Lissa looked down at the snotty tissues, rolled her eyes as she dropped them in the trash and pumped a squirt of hand sanitizer into her palm.

She was handing out fruit snacks when Jolie came back into the room and sat down in her chair with a dramatic thump. Her eyelashes were still wet with tears as she shoved the half banana aside and tore into her little box of raisins. By the time she'd had her first bite, she was already trying to trade her banana for the raisins belonging to the girl beside her. It was obvious Jolie's stronger personality was about to win out, and Lissa promptly stepped in.

"Jolie, we're not trading snacks today," Lissa said.

"But I don't like nanners," Jolie shrieked.

"Then, you don't have to eat it. When you finish your raisins, you may go sit in the reading circle."

"Then, I won't have two snacks!" Jolie yelled, ready to cry again because her world was momentarily out of orbit.

"Use your inside voice, please," Lissa said calmly as she continued passing out snacks.

Jolie scooted her chair back and forth just enough to make the wooden legs squeak against the tile flooring, but to Lissa's relief, she stopped without further orders.

Lissa understood Jolie's need to be pissed. She knew all too well how it felt to be rejected, but this was unacceptable behavior in her classroom.

When snack was over, they cleared their tables and hurried over to the reading circle.

Lissa eyed Jolie, who was now orchestrating who she wanted to sit with, and then glanced over at Roger Lee. He didn't appear to care where he sat as long as it wasn't by Jolie Wade.

This was the first time in her teaching career that she'd had a child as boy crazy as the little blonde. It wasn't until after school when she was relating the drama to some of her fellow teachers that she found out why.

"Oh, I can tell you exactly why Jolie is boy crazy,"

Margaret Lewis said. "She has two teenage sisters. It's probably all she hears."

Lissa chuckled. "Ah...that explains everything."

Margaret began gathering up her things. "Need a ride home this evening?"

"No, I rented a car, but thanks for the offer," Lissa said. "I'll see you tomorrow."

She left the teachers' lounge, headed for the exit and waved at Louis, who was emptying trash cans.

"Have a nice evening, Louis."

"Yes, ma'am, you, too," he said absently, as he rolled the trash bin toward the next room.

The sun was out, but it didn't feel all that warm. The north wind was fairly stiff and had a chill to it, a reminder that winter would be here all too soon.

Lissa hurried to the car and got in, grateful to be out of that wind, then noticed the grocery list she'd left in the console this morning so she wouldn't forget to go by the supermarket after school. As badly as she wanted to get home, this had to be done first.

She drove to the supermarket and parked, then grabbed the list as she exited the car. Her mind was already on the job ahead when she heard someone calling her name and turned around.

Well, great. Jessica. My nemesis in high school wants to continue her reign.

"Lissa! Oh, my dear!" Jessica York cried as she threw her arms around Lissa's neck. "I heard about what happened at the garage. How awful! Was it really your car that killed Mr. Jackson?"

Lissa blinked, felt the blood rushing to her head as she unwound herself from Jessica's grasp and headed back to her car.

Jessica kept calling out behind her, "What's wrong? Where are you going? Was it something I said?"

Lissa laid the grocery list in the cup holder and started the car. She wouldn't look at the bitch for fear the woman would be smiling. If she was, then she would have to get back out of the car and whip her ass, and that might get her fired. A teacher's morals and behavior had to be above reproach.

So she wouldn't have cream in her coffee and she wouldn't eat cereal tomorrow morning, she thought as she drove to the exit. It wasn't the end of the world.

The light turned green.

She drove through the intersection, suddenly anxious to get home. And then she thought of the stalker and her heart skipped a beat. Would he be back again, now that she'd called the police? The peace she'd found during the day with her students was coming undone.

Why is this happening? What did I do wrong? Dear God, what did I do wrong?

By the time she pulled into the driveway and parked, she was once again in tears. She was getting her things out of the passenger seat when she heard the sound of a car slowing down. She turned around just as Mack pulled into her driveway and parked behind her. She knew there were tears on her face, but her hands were full, and right now she didn't much care what he thought.

Mack had been dreading this moment for a lot of reasons, but none of them had involved seeing those tears—at least not at first. The frightening thing was the urge he felt to hurt whoever had made her cry.

"I see I've come at a bad time. I should have called."

Lissa rolled her eyes and headed for the door. He could follow or he could leave. Either way, she didn't much care.

Her silence took Mack aback, and then he hurried forward and followed her up the steps. When she began fumbling with the key he took it from her trembling fingers and let her in, then stood aside.

Lissa walked past him, dumped the stuff she was carrying on the sofa and then turned around.

"What do you want, Mack?"

"I need to talk to you."

That seemed like the last thing she wanted to endure.

"I don't much want to talk to *you*," she said. Then she shrugged. "I'm sure you understand."

He wasn't going to pretend that didn't hurt, but she needed to know about the lift, so he crossed the threshold and closed the door behind him.

Lissa rolled her eyes. "Oh, well! Do come in."

Mack felt raw enough without getting into a fight and began to explain.

"This won't take long, but you need to know that my dad's death wasn't an accident. There was nothing wrong with the lift. Someone killed him. Trey thinks it's connected to Dick Phillips' murder, too. I wanted you to know so you would stop blaming yourself."

It was the last thing she'd expected to hear, and the relief that washed through her was immediately negated by the lost expression on his face.

"Oh, Mack! I… Uh, you…" She sighed and wiped the tears off her cheeks. "I'm so sorry I was rude, and while I *am* grateful for this news, it doesn't change your loss. Forgive me."

He shrugged. "As I said, you had nothing to do with it. You needed to know."

"Thank you so much. As you can imagine, it's a huge relief."

He eyed the shadows beneath her eyes. He knew why she hadn't been sleeping—because of her stalker—but he couldn't let go of the tears on her face. "Can I ask you something?"

"You can ask."

He got the message. Just because she agreed to listen didn't mean she would answer.

"Why were you crying?"

She sighed. "It was stupid." Her face was a mirror of what she was feeling as she threw up her hands and started talking.

"Jessica York. She's the one person from our class who never grew out of being a bitch, and I obviously haven't grown up enough to ignore her."

Mack frowned. "Jessica York?"

"Oh, you know…Jessica Shayne. She married some guy from Savannah and lived there for years. She divorced and moved back to Mystic a month before Mom died. I saw her at the funeral."

The skin crawled on the back of his neck, remembering Jessica was the one who'd inadvertently told him about the abortion. He couldn't think of one thing to say that would be proper. Lissa was still talking, and it took all he had to focus on what she was saying.

"I shouldn't let her get to me, but after all these years she still gets her kicks spreading gossip, most of which isn't true. She even started that rumor years ago that I'd had an abortion, when her mother knew good and well about the miscarriage because it happened in the doctor's office while she was there."

There was a roaring in Mack's ears, and for a couple of seconds he thought he was going to pass out. He could still see Lissa's lips moving but he couldn't hear what she was saying. He was sick to his stomach, and his heart felt like it might burst.

What had he done?

What the hell had he done?

He staggered toward an easy chair and sat down hard.

Lissa knew by the look on his face that something was wrong and immediately attributed it to finding out his father had been murdered. She was ashamed of herself for not taking his feelings into consideration and moved toward him, intent on nothing more than offering a comforting word, but he clasped her hand, and before she could react he pulled her into his lap and hid his face in the curve of her neck.

At first she was too startled to move. Then she was on the verge of getting angry when she realized he was crying.

"Mack?"

"I'm sorry," he said, and held her tighter.

Now her heart was breaking for his sadness. She couldn't imagine the horror of knowing someone you loved had been murdered.

"You don't have to apologize for crying about your father being murdered. Anyone would be devastated."

He took a deep breath and then lifted his head. He'd wronged her. She deserved the apology face-to-face.

"That's not what's wrong," he said.

"Then, what?"

"I didn't know about the miscarriage."

An old ache tugged at her heart. "Yes, you did, remember? You came to the house and asked me if I was still pregnant, and I told you no. You freaked out. Yelled at me and stormed out. I never saw you again."

He swallowed around the lump in his throat.

"Because I thought you'd had an abortion."

"No!" she screamed. She tore free from his arms and jumped up, so shocked she was shaking. "Who told you that? Why would you believe it?"

Mack stood. "I overheard Jessica and another girl laughing about it. I didn't want to believe it. I kept telling myself you couldn't do that. I drove all the way to your house, so numb I couldn't think."

Lissa moaned, and when he reached for her again, she moved back.

He felt sick. The look of disbelief on her face was as painful for him now as the day he'd thought she was admitting she'd killed their child.

"I asked you if you were still pregnant. You said no so quickly, I thought—"

"But Mom and Dad called you the night it was happening. You knew! You already knew!"

He stood there for a moment, absorbing the words that had just come out her mouth and trying to find a way to answer without damning people she loved, but there was no way to make that happen.

"No, Lissa, I didn't get any phone call about you. Not from them or anyone else."

Lissa was screaming inside, but her voice was devoid of emotion.

"It was my first prenatal appointment. It rained all the way to Summerton. It was raining so hard that

I took a really bad fall in the doctor's parking lot. I started bleeding in his office. They carried me out on a stretcher and took me to the hospital. That's how Mom and Dad found out. That's how Mrs. Shayne even knew I'd been pregnant, and then her bitch of a daughter spread the word and twisted the knife with the lie."

"Why didn't *you* call me?" he asked.

The question angered her. "I was in labor, delivering what would have been our baby. Mom and Dad were furious that I was pregnant, even though they knew I was losing the baby. I was crying for you. I asked them to call you. I thought they did. I stayed overnight in the hospital wondering why you didn't come. It never occurred to me they didn't tell you. They brought me home the next day, and then you showed up a couple of hours later and put an end to what was left of us."

The emotional knife drove deep into his heart. Could he die from this much pain? He wanted to hold her, but she'd made it plain she didn't want him to touch her.

"I'm sorry. I was a stupid kid, and I'm so sorry," he said.

Lissa lifted her chin. "We stopped being kids when we made a baby."

He took the criticism with his head up and tears on his face. "You're right. I can't imagine how abandoned you must have felt, and I will be sorry until the day I die that I wasn't there for you. I'm even sorrier about how I behaved. You didn't deserve that, but you were my world, and in an instant I believed I'd lost the girl I thought you were and the chance to be a father. I went crazy. That's my only excuse. Forgive me, Lissa. Forgive me for hurting you that way."

He walked out of the house, and she didn't try to stop him, but her head was spinning.

Her parents had lied—to both of them.

Eight

The killer found out that Jackson's death had been ruled a homicide while he was having lunch at Charlie's Burgers. He was smiling at the waitress who was topping off his glass of sweet tea when he keyed in on the conversation in the booth behind him.

"…said it was murder. No, they don't have any leads. Who would want to kill him? Paul Jackson was an upright guy."

The waitress glanced down at him and smiled. "Do you want dessert? Our pies are great. We have lemon, chocolate, coconut cream and peach."

He patted his stomach as he leaned back. "I think I'll pass today, but thanks."

She left the tab on the table and moved on as he pulled a handful of bills from his wallet, making sure to leave her a big tip. He had no qualms about the outcome of his handiwork. He'd known they would figure it out once they discovered the lift hadn't failed, and he left with a confident stride. He had no reason to assume he would ever be found out.

* * *

Betsy Jakes was sitting across the table from Trey, watching him finish off a piece of pie. When he reached for his coffee cup, she jumped up and refilled it before he could ask. She was anxious. She might even say nervous. He had yet to mention one thing about why he'd showed up in the middle of a workday and stayed to eat lunch with her. She was always happy to see him, but something felt off. She gave his shoulder a quick pat as she topped off his coffee.

He looked up, the smile gone from his face. "We need to talk," he said.

Her heart skipped a beat. Her instincts had been right. Something was wrong.

"Well, sure, honey. You can always talk to me about anything. Is everything all right with you and Dallas?"

"We're fine, Mom. I need to tell you something, and then I need you to hear me out afterward, okay?"

"Okay, I'm listening," Betsy said.

Trey saw the smile on her face, but it never reached her eyes, and her hands were shaking.

"Paul Jackson's death has officially been ruled a homicide."

"I guessed as much," she mumbled.

He was surprised she was so forthcoming. "Why would you think that?"

She reached up to push a wayward curl from her forehead and then started to cry. "It's connected to Dick's murder, isn't it? It's about that wreck, right?"

Trey reached for her hands, but she pulled them back. He hated to push, but he had to ask.

"Do you remember anything about that wreck, Mom?"

Her fingers went straight to the scar along her hairline. "No. Not really. At least I don't think so."

"What do you mean, 'not really'?" Trey asked. "Please. If you remember anything, even if you're not sure it pertains to the wreck, you need to tell me."

"I've been having dreams about stuff, but none of it makes any sense," she said.

"Tell me," he said.

Betsy flinched. The hard edge in his voice surprised her. "It's just stuff that's all mixed up," she said.

Trey reached for her hands again, and this time he caught them and wouldn't let go.

"Look at me, damn it! Do I look like I'm kidding? Two people are dead, Mom! Three counting the girl who died the night of the wreck, and you're the only one still breathing. I'd like to keep it that way."

Betsy moaned. "I'm going to be sick," she whispered, and she got up and ran out.

Trey silently cursed the situation and followed her, stopping outside the bathroom door. She came out a few minutes later, pale and shaken.

"Mom?"

She walked into his arms and laid her cheek against his chest. The hopelessness she exhibited was scaring him, like she'd already given in to the inevitable.

"I'm sorry, Mom. I'm sorry I upset you, but I have two dead men, no suspects and a gut feeling that you're the next target. I'm trying to help you, not scare you."

Her voice was faint and shaky, but her hold on him was fierce. "I know, son. You didn't scare me. I'm scaring myself. I dream and see blood. I dream I'm back in that car and I think we're being chased. That's all I know. I swear."

Trey rocked her where they stood, wondering how their calm and ordinary lives had so quickly been turned upside down.

"I don't want you staying out here by yourself," he said.

All of a sudden the mother he knew was back as she pushed out of his arms with an angry frown on her face.

"And where would you have me go? Trina is here with me every night, so I'm not by myself."

"You *are* here alone every day, and expecting Trina to be your safety net at night is only putting both of you in danger."

"Then, she can go stay with you and Dallas. You don't even have a suspect, so if I went somewhere and hid, there's no way to say when I could come back. I won't be run out of my home! Do you hear me, Trey? This is *my* life. *My* choice. I'll keep the rifle loaded and nearby. That is my only concession."

Trey heard anger in her voice but knew it wasn't directed at him. She was angry with the situation and how it was messing with her life. She'd never abided change well, and now was no exception.

"I hear your words, now hear mine," he said. "Before this day is out, someone will be here to install a security system, and I expect you to use it. If I ever come out here and am able to walk into this house without setting off an alarm, I will physically move you into my home with me and Dallas, whether you like it or not. Understood?"

She glared.

He glared back.

"Fine," she muttered.

"I'm going back to work. I love you dearly."

Betsy sighed. "I love you, too. You really are your father's son."

Trey sighed. If she was talking about Dad, she was giving in.

"I have one thing to ask of you," he said.

"What?"

"If you think of anything else, promise you'll tell me immediately. Finding this killer fast is crucial. Since we don't actually know his agenda, there could be others besides you, understand?"

Her shoulders slumped. "Understood."

"Thank you for lunch," Trey said, and then he was gone.

Betsy watched him driving away and then went through the house locking every door and window, something she hadn't done since the month after she'd buried her husband, Beau. She got the rifle out of the closet and loaded it, then carried it to the kitchen and put it in the corner close to where she was working.

By the time Trina came home from work, Trey had already briefed her on what was happening, so when she saw a van from a security company parked in the yard, she wasn't surprised.

She walked in just as the tech was finishing the last of the installation. He gave Trina and Betsy instructions as to how the system worked, and showed them how to install an app on their phones that would arm it or turn it off no matter where they were. Then he gave them his card as he left.

Betsy looked at the keypad like it was a bomb and walked off without comment.

Trina armed the system and went to change clothes.

Reece Parsons woke up with a headache and found the note from Louis about their mother's imminent arrival, which made his headache even worse. Even after taking pain pills, he wasn't able to go back to sleep. He was aware when Louis came home from work, and got up to confront him about their mother's plans. That caused an argument, after which Louis made himself scarce.

Reece thought of his brother's constant retreat from life as hiding and was thankful he wasn't made that way. He went after what he wanted with no apologies to anyone. Right now he was standing at his bedroom window watching sundown with a hard-on. It was a sign that he'd made his decision. Melissa Sherman was under his skin and he wanted more. But right now Bobo was dancing around his feet, ready for their evening walk. He sighed. First things first.

"Come on, buddy, let's get this over with. Daddy has a date tonight."

He noticed Louis had picked up a bucket of fried chicken, and he grabbed a drumstick as he left the house with Bobo prancing around his heels. He ate as they walked, anticipating new adventures. Tonight he was getting inside her house and then inside her pants, but not until he was sure she was asleep. He knew the layout of the house from prior visits, when he'd scouted the perimeter. All he needed was some cooperation from the weather, and from the looks of the gathering clouds hiding the half-moon, that just might happen.

* * *

Lissa had been glad to get home from school that afternoon, but the moment she'd walked into the house her thoughts had gone immediately to what her parents had done to her relationship with Mack. She'd been trying to think back to what all they'd said and done that night. She remembered them coming into the ER angry. They weren't sorry she was losing the baby and kept saying it was God's way of fixing what had happened. She remembered her mom and dad fighting, and her mother saying it was all Mack's fault and this was her chance to start over.

She'd been in so much pain and so scared, and hearing them talk like that had been shocking. All the years they'd been dating, she'd never once heard them say anything bad about him, and now they were acting like he'd turned into the devil. At one point she had stopped her dad in the middle of his rant and told him to shut up, that Mack hadn't forced her to do anything, and that she'd been as willing a participant as he was. After that, they had moved her into a room in the birthing wing of the hospital, and while her mother had gone with her, her dad had never come back to see her there.

Despite all that, it was still staggering to her that they'd purposefully lied. The only possible reason was that they'd wanted to make sure she and Mack didn't resume their relationship and, thanks to misunderstandings and gossip, it had worked.

She felt guilty it was her parents who'd done this, but at the same time she was still a little pissed off that Mack had *ever* thought she wouldn't want their child.

With great effort, she pushed the mess to the back

of her mind and began working on lesson plans for the week while keeping an eye on the weather report.

As the afternoon faded into darkness and it began to rain again, she sighed. It meant another recess indoors tomorrow. Even if the storm passed on before morning, the ground would be too muddy for kids to play outside. She had some craft supplies on hand, and a couple of DVDs to pass the time.

Something rattled outside the window, which made her jump, but when she looked out all she saw was the for-sale sign from the house next door blowing down the street.

Reece Parsons was standing up against the back wall of the storage shed next door, taking shelter from the wind and rain. It had come up unexpectedly, and he was damn cold. He wished now that he'd gone into Louis's closet and borrowed his parka, but then Louis would have gotten all wound up about not getting it dirty. Louis was a pain in the ass and had more hangups than a 911 operator, but he *was* his identical twin, even though DNA was all they had in common.

Louis worked with an entire school building of women and was scared of them all, while Reece was obsessed with the opposite sex and how many ways he could hurt or scare them, which was how he got off. He didn't know why he was like that, but it was what made his dick get hard, and that was all that mattered.

He heard a dog begin to bark, but the property where he was lurking was unoccupied, and the oncoming storm had darkened the night sky, making him confident of his hiding place.

He was waiting for Melissa Sherman to go to bed,

and as soon as the lights went out and he was certain she was asleep, he was going in. After that she was his for as long as he wanted, then he would slit her throat. It was a swift and silent way to get rid of a witness.

Mack was numb. It was after midnight, and he still couldn't sleep.

Inadvertently, he'd hurt the only girl he'd ever loved and didn't know how to fix it. He understood why Lissa would hate him. He pretty much hated himself. All these years he'd lived with unjust anger and wasted the years they could have been together.

He sat within the silence of his dad's house, going over and over the sequence of events before something finally broke through his fog of self-directed anger and a thought occurred to him. If her parents had called him like she'd asked when she was in labor, none of the rest of this hell would have happened.

And then he got angry all over again. Why had they done that? They'd known that he loved her. The hospital could have called him, too. But then, as fast as his rage rose, it died. The hospital had done exactly what it was required to do by law and notified the next of kin, which meant her parents. Just because he'd gotten her pregnant, that hadn't given him any legal rights. They hadn't been married. That meant when it had come to the girl he loved and the baby they'd made, the hospital hadn't owed him anything.

But Mack kept struggling with the truth.

Why the hell had her parents been so furious that they hadn't even told him what was going on?

He and Lissa had been inseparable through all four years of high school and had made plans to go to college together. They must have known he would stand by her.

Why hadn't they called him as she'd asked?

Were they punishing her or him, or both of them?

It wasn't until the wind and rain began that he remembered he'd promised Lissa to help her set up security for her house. In the middle of the revelation about his father's murder and learning about her miscarriage, he'd forgotten all about it.

He walked out on the front porch, looking up and down the street through the downpour, and thought about calling to make sure she was okay, but when he glanced at his watch and saw the time, he knew it was far too late to call. And there was no way he would ever get to sleep knowing that if anything happened to her tonight, he would not only have let her down again but put her life in danger.

He walked back into the house, got his all-weather coat and his car keys, got in the car and started back toward her house. He wasn't sure what he would do once he got there, so he would play it by ear.

The thunder and lightning mingled with the noise Reece made as he broke the glass in the kitchen door. He was dripping wet as he thrust his arm through the opening in the broken glass and felt around until he found the dead bolt.

The glass crunched beneath his shoes as he let himself in and moved across the kitchen floor, leaving muddy prints as he went. Confident that the storm would continue to shield him from discovery, he didn't even bother trying to mute his footsteps.

Lissa was sound asleep when she heard the sound

of breaking glass. She sat up in bed, listening to the wind and the rain on the roof, and thinking a branch had fallen and broken a window. She jumped out of bed and quickly put on her house shoes in case there was glass on the floor. She was on her way out of her room when she heard footsteps, and then the distinct crunch of glass beneath them.

Her heartbeat skipped and then began to pound as panic followed. It had to be her stalker! The fact that he was inside the house sent her into flight mode.

She turned the lock on her bedroom door just as he entered the living room. She could hear his footsteps clearly on the wood, and when they became muffled, she knew he'd just crossed the Oriental rug.

Oh, my God, oh, my God.

Her hands were shaking as she grabbed her cell phone and headed for the window. Within seconds she was kicking out the screen and crawling out into the downpour, calling 911 as she went.

Reece knew which side of the house Lissa's bedroom was on, and when he started down the hall, he was so excited he was shaking. He turned the doorknob to her room and was surprised to find it locked. Anticipation turned to anger as he kicked the door open and ran into the room. Moments later a flash of lightning revealed the empty bed. The open window and blowing curtains were a shock.

He let out a roar of rage and ran toward the window just in time to see her running through her front yard toward the street. Through the downpour he saw something bright in her hand and realized it was her cell phone. She had already called the cops.

"Son of a holy bitch!" he shouted, and began grabbing stuff and throwing it against the walls, taking pleasure in the sound of breaking glass and destroying what was hers.

Mack turned the corner toward Lissa's house just as a flash of lightning lit up the sky. The rain was really coming down, dimming the faint glow of the streetlights, so when he caught a glimpse of someone running through her yard, his first thought was of the stalker and he quickly accelerated. But it wasn't until the runner passed in front of his headlights that he realized it was Lissa. He stopped the car, then jumped out in the rain, yelling her name.

Lissa was still in flight mode when she saw the headlights, and when she heard the squeal of brakes and someone shouting her name, she stumbled and fell. Her cell phone went flying, and her hands were already burning from abrasions when she recognized Mack's voice, and then she was in his arms. The relief of knowing she was safe was overwhelming.

"Lissa! What's wrong?" he asked.

"He's in my house! I think he came in the backdoor. I heard breaking glass and then footsteps. I went out my bedroom window, and I've already called the police."

Mack pushed her toward his car. "Get inside and lock the doors!" he shouted, and took off running.

"Mack, don't! Wait for the police!" she screamed, but he wouldn't stop.

She turned around to look for her phone then grabbed it and bolted toward his SUV. She leaped into the seat and quickly locked herself inside. The engine was still running, so the interior was warm, but she was dripping water everywhere and still shaking as the horror of what was happening sank in.

This was far more than phone calls and knocking at the window. He'd come into her house—come after her—to do God knew what. And now Mack was in there with him.

Lord, please keep him safe.

The faint sound of sirens was encouraging, but would they arrive in time?

Reece's fit of rage ended abruptly when he heard the faint sound of sirens and realized how much time he'd wasted tearing up Melissa's room. He turned, running blindly through the house toward the back door, so intent on escape that he didn't hear any footsteps but his own until he went from the living room into the kitchen, and then it was too late.

Mack circled the house on the run, confident the stalker had gained entry through the back door. He saw the broken pane and leaped up the steps, pausing inside the kitchen in the darkness and listening to see if the stalker was still inside. When he heard running footsteps coming up the hall, he tensed, muscles tightening. The bastard was still here and in the act of escape.

He braced himself for impact.

Reece rounded the corner into the kitchen, caught a glimpse of movement and panicked. He'd indulged his disappointment a little too long and had only moments to pull his knife as the man came toward him.

Mack caught a flash of metal and threw up his arm

just in time to deflect th

It missed, but cut through

caught his arm instead. The

but it didn't stop him. Mack took the i

flying tackle. They hit the floor hard,

from Mack's wound as he rolled to e

knife slash; then he grabbed his atta

began slamming it against the floor

make him drop the knife. Their life-a

was eerily silent except for an occasion

Mack landed two hard blows to the s

nent's face, and the other man began pounding his fist against the wound on Mack's arm in retaliation. The pain was intense, and in an effort to free his wounded arm, Mack inadvertently loosened his grasp.

Reece grinned in the dark when he felt the change in the other man's grip. It was just enough to let him get his knife hand free.

In one last frantic move to escape, he jammed the knife deep into the back of his enemy's shoulder. The man went down with a groan, and just like that, Reece was free!

He scrambled to his feet, pulling out the knife without care for the blood that gushed in its wake, then bolted out the back door, running into the rain as the sirens' screaming grew closer.

Nine

Lissa was wet and scared and couldn't stop shaking. Once she'd heard the police sirens she'd had the good sense to pull Mack's car out of the middle of the street where he'd stopped, and now she was parked beside the curb. She was staring out the window, watching the dim glow of her neighbor's outdoor security light, when she saw a faint figure of a man come from her backyard, cross the space between her house and the empty one next door and disappear into the night.

She scooted forward on the seat, waiting and waiting for Mack to run into view as he gave chase, but saw nothing. Her heart dropped. Something was horribly wrong.

The police were close. She could clearly hear the sirens now, but she couldn't wait. Without thinking about her own safety, she did exactly what he'd told her not to do. She grabbed the keys from the ignition and got out of the SUV on the run, clearing the distance from Mack's car to her house in record time.

The back door was open, and she turned on the light as she ran in, then froze. Mack was belly down on the floor in a pool of blood, and he wasn't moving. It was a moment of déjà vu, seeing him as motionless as she'd found his father. A lifetime of loving him and hating him shot through her so fast she couldn't think, and then a gust of wind broke the silence, banging the door shut behind her. She screamed Mack's name as she tossed the keys onto the countertop and dropped to her knees beside him, praying as she felt for a pulse in his neck that he wasn't dead.

There was so much blood she couldn't find one, but she wasn't about to quit on him and bolted toward the cabinets for clean towels. She grabbed a handful, ran back to Mack's side and began applying pressure to his wounds in a desperate effort to stop the bleeding.

When he suddenly groaned she began to cry. He wasn't dead! God had given them a second chance.

Mack was regaining consciousness just as the police cars pulled up at her house, but by then Lissa was almost as bloody as he was.

When Trey and Earl came running into the kitchen with their weapons drawn, they were shocked by the sight of so much blood.

"Call an ambulance!" Lissa cried. "Mack has been stabbed."

Earl made the call as Trey rushed to her side.

"Are you hurt?"

"No, this is all his," she said.

"Did you see him?"

"No, I heard him coming through the house and went out my bedroom window. I was running across the street when Mack drove up. He put me in his car and ran into the house. I caught a glimpse of the intruder leaving my house. When Mack didn't come out, I got scared. I came in and found him like this."

Mack groaned and tried to roll over.

Trey dropped to his knees to help Lissa restrain him. "Mack!" he ordered. "Don't move. An ambulance is on the way."

"Had a knife…would have killed her," Mack whispered.

Lissa looked up at Trey in disbelief. "Why is this happening?"

"I don't know," he said, helpless to explain.

Mack was about to pass out again, but when he heard Lissa's voice, he reached for her.

Lissa grabbed his hand, wanting him to know she was still there, but he was unconscious again.

Trey stood up and began issuing orders. "Earl, I need you to call the precinct and tell the dispatcher to get all deputies to this location and start a house-by-house search. He could be hiding out. He might be injured. We won't find a blood trail thanks to this rain, but we might find *him*."

Earl ran out, relaying the chief's orders to Dispatch as he pulled his flashlight and took off toward the house next door.

"Can I go with him in the ambulance?" Lissa asked.

"No, but you can be with him in the ER," Trey said.

It wasn't what she wanted to hear, but she would take it.

She grabbed another clean towel to use as a compress because the first two were blood soaked.

"He's losing so much blood," she said. Then she heard a siren whoop twice outside her house before it stopped.

"The ambulance is here," Trey said.

"Thank God," Lissa said. Then she bent down and whispered in Mack's ear, "Help is here. Hang on. I need you to be okay."

Seconds later a pair of EMTs came up the steps ahead of a team of firefighters. Trey began filling them in on what had happened as Lissa moved away to allow them full access.

She stood for a few seconds watching them work before one of them saw the blood on her.

"Ma'am, are you hurt?" he asked.

"No, it's all his," she said, and ran to the kitchen sink and began scrubbing the blood off her hands and arms as the EMTs quickly inserted an IV into Mack's arm.

When Lissa heard them talking about the possibility of a blood transfusion, she quickly interrupted.

"His blood type is O negative."

The EMT looked up. "Are you sure?"

"Absolutely certain. Mine is O positive. His is O negative. Unless he's changed his habit, there will be a card in his wallet attesting to that fact."

Trey dug through Mack's hip pocket, pulled out his wallet and then found the card.

"She's right," he said, and laid the wallet on Mack's belly as they slid him onto a gurney and strapped him down. "Insurance cards and other info are in the wallet, too," he told the other EMT. "Don't lose it."

They covered Mack with a waterproof blanket and then moved him out through the rain to the ambulance.

"I'll stay here while you go change," Trey said to Lissa, indicating her bloodstained clothing. Then he took out his phone to call the county sheriff for help. He needed this scene processed and didn't want to call any of his deputies off the search to do it.

Lissa didn't hesitate. She could only imagine what she looked like, but it didn't matter. She just needed Mack to be okay. She needed to tell him something— something she'd just realized when she'd thought for one awful moment that he was dead.

She bolted down the hall toward her room, turning on lights as she went, but the moment she reached her door, she stopped and screamed.

Trey was just about to make the call when he heard her and ran through the house, fearing the perp had doubled back and waited for her. The relief of finding her in one piece was dimmed by what he saw.

"He destroyed it," Lissa whispered.

Trey put a hand on her shoulder. "Close the window. It's raining in."

She walked across the room and pulled the window down, then locked it, although the effort was moot. The devil had already come and gone.

"Can you find enough clothes to get dressed?" Trey asked.

Lissa was shaking as she looked at the chaos. The starfish night-light, the last link to her childhood, was on the floor in pieces. The closet door was open, and clothes were strewn all over, and everything that had been in the dresser was now on the floor.

"I think so."

"Well, find enough to last you for several days, because you're not coming back here until this man is behind bars. What he did to this room is a sign of what he would have done to you when he was through. This isn't just some Peeping Tom. This man is dangerous, and I would bet my retirement you aren't the first to catch his eye."

The pain in Reece's jaw was making his whole head throb, and his eye was swelling. He was rattled by how quickly his simple plan had gone awry. By the time he got home he knew he had two options—either get out of town before daylight, or stay hidden here until all his bruising had faded. He didn't know whether he'd killed the guy and didn't much care. What pissed him off most was that Melissa Sherman had outsmarted him and gotten away.

He glanced at the clock. It was already tomorrow. Since their mother was due here later in the afternoon and the only vehicle belonged to Louis, if he took it and left town he wouldn't put it past Louis to claim it was stolen, which would make the mess he was in that much worse.

His best bet was to just stay here and stay out of sight. No one in Mystic knew him. He'd made sure of that. And since he didn't work for anyone but himself, it wasn't like he would be missed at any job.

Bobo came trotting into the kitchen and yipped once.

Reece groaned.

"I suppose you want to go out, but you're not getting any farther than the backyard. It's raining cats and dogs out there." And then he laughed. "Cats and dogs, Bobo. You're a dog. Get it?"

But all the dog had heard was the word *out*, and he was already headed for the door at a trot.

Reece let him out, then turned on the back porch

light as he closed the door and headed for the utility room and the bathroom beyond to tend to his injuries.

Nothing was bleeding, which was good. But the swelling was severe. He hadn't had time to get a good look at the man and wouldn't know him again if he saw him, which was daunting. It was always best to know what your enemies looked like. He wondered if the man had gotten a clean look at him and then sighed. It was all up in the air until he found out if the guy was still alive.

He cleaned himself up and then went back to the kitchen to make an ice pack. Bobo was at the back door whining to come in. He opened it enough to let him in and then watched him trot across the floor, leaving water and muddy footprints behind. He thought about their mother's imminent arrival and yelled, "Heel, Bobo!"

Bobo stopped, trotted back across the floor to where Reece was standing and stopped in position.

"Now I have twice as much to clean up," Reece muttered.

He grabbed a towel from the back bathroom and began drying Bobo's feet and fur, then grunted as he bent down to clean up the drips and footprints.

Too many nights of eating and going back to bed were catching up with him. He'd begun buying and selling for himself out of boredom, just for something to do, and everyone, including his mother and Louis, had been surprised at his gift for picking good companies in which to invest. Making money on the computer was so easy that he didn't see the need for breaking a sweat, but he didn't like the idea of being a fat slob, either. Women didn't like a big ass or a sagging belly on a man, and Reece liked women too much to fuck that up.

When he was finished, he tossed the towel in the washing machine, grabbed the ice pack and headed for his bedroom, hoping the swelling would be down by morning.

Mack was already in surgery before Lissa reached the hospital. She sat alone in the waiting room, trying to come to terms with the fact that another member of the Jackson family had been hurt trying to help her. It was beginning to feel like a curse.

One hour passed into the second, and then the third, as she sat with a cup of coffee going cold in her hands and tears drying on her face.

Then Trey Jakes walked in.

She stood immediately, praying for good news.

"Did you catch him?" she asked.

Trey shook his head. "Sorry, the rain destroyed any trail he might have left. The county crime-scene crew is at your house dusting for prints. Unless he was wearing gloves, we should get something, since he handled pretty much everything in your room. Maybe we'll get lucky."

She sat back down with a thump, too dejected to comment.

Trey sat down beside her, struggling with how he was going to get across the seriousness of what he needed to tell her, but when she inadvertently gave him an opening, he jumped on it.

"I shudder to think what he'll try next," she muttered.

"That's something we need to talk about," he said.

Lissa looked up. "What do you mean?"

"I think you need to take a leave of absence from your job until we have this man in custody."

The idea appalled her. She'd worked so hard to develop a rapport with her students. She started to panic, thinking of all the reasons that couldn't happen.

"No! I have a contract to fulfill. I can't just walk out."

"I didn't say quit. I mean step away until he's caught."

"But why?" she asked.

"Because you thwarted him, Lissa. At this point I couldn't predict how far he would go to get you and make you pay. What if he tried to take you out of your classroom? Are you willing to risk a child's life that it won't happen?"

The skin crawled on the back of her neck as she thought of what he'd done to her bedroom.

She began to cry, overwhelmed by the hopelessness of her situation.

"I didn't think. Of course I need to keep them safe. I'll call my principal and hope he understands."

"If he doubts the decision, have him call me," Trey said. "I'll make sure he understands the danger it could create if you stayed."

"I will," she said, swiping away the tears as she pulled out her phone.

"Is there anything you need? Anything we can do for you?" Trey asked.

She slumped. "Just catch him."

"I'll do my best. Call if you need us," he added, as he left the room.

She sat quietly, gathering her thoughts and trying to get her emotions under control before she called her principal. As she was sitting there, she heard footsteps coming down the hall and looked toward the doorway. When the surgeon walked in, she froze.

"Are you here for Mack Jackson?" he asked.

She curled her fingers into fists, bracing herself for the verdict, and nodded.

He smiled and sat down beside her. "Everything went well. He'll be in recovery for the next forty-five minutes or so and then we'll move him to a room. You'll be able to see him then, but he'll be sedated, so don't expect much. The wound on his arm was shallow enough that we didn't have any muscle repair to do, but he has staples, a good number of them. The wound on his back was fairly deep but didn't hit anything vital. He has internal and external stitches, but short of something unexpected, he should regain full range of motion."

"Oh, thank you, thank you so much," Lissa said.

"You're welcome. I'll check on him tomorrow when I make rounds and we'll go from there, okay?"

"Okay," she said. As soon as he left the room she walked to the window that overlooked the parking lot and burst into tears.

It was all good news, and she was crying from relief, but she still had to talk to her principal. She was still choking back sobs as she made the call. It was the middle of the night, but this couldn't be put off. He would have to locate a substitute who could work for an indeterminate length of time. She felt like a failure in so many ways that she couldn't count them. The year had started off so great. Why was this happening? What had she done to draw the attention of someone so deranged?

The phone was ringing and ringing, and just as it was about to go to voice mail, her principal picked up.

"Hello?"

"Mr. Wilson, it's Melissa Sherman. I am so sorry to call you at this time of night, but something has been happening to me that seriously escalated tonight, and it has become imperative that you are informed."

And with that lead-in she began to explain everything, from the first phone calls to what had happened tonight. When she told him what the police chief had recommended, Wilson was understandably shocked.

"He actually believes this stalker could try to get to you at school?"

"Well, the truth is, Chief Jakes said there's no guarantee that he won't, and he advised me it would be putting children's lives at risk to ignore the possibility."

"Oh, dear Lord! Well, I'm so sorry to hear this, and of course we can work with you and the police to everyone's benefit. I assume you have some sick leave?"

She thought of the sick leave she'd given up to come back home to teach and sighed.

"Only what I've accumulated since August," she said.

"Then, you can use that first and if you need longer, we can figure something out. In the meantime, do you have a place to stay?"

She sighed. "Not at the moment, but I'll figure something out. Right now I'm at the hospital. They just brought Mack out of surgery. I'll be here with him until I know he's going to be okay. You have my phone number, and I'll be in touch." Then she hesitated before adding, "I hope you know how upset I am about this, and how bad I feel for putting you in this position. Please don't hold it against me. I love my job and—"

"Miss Sherman...Melissa...your job is safe. Just make sure you stay the same way."

"Thank you, Mr. Wilson, and again, I'm so sorry."

"You have nothing to apologize for. Take care, and hopefully we'll see you soon. Meanwhile, send our best to Mr. Jackson. That was a brave thing for him to do."

"Yes, it was," Lissa said. She added a quick goodbye and hung up the phone.

The sudden silence was overwhelming as she leaned back and closed her eyes.

What in the world was she going to do?

She kept thinking back to what her parents had done. She and Mack should have been able to grieve the loss of their baby together. Instead, her parents had fostered a misunderstanding that tore them apart.

The more she thought about it, the more she understood Mack's shock and his reaction to what he'd overheard. Yes, he should have given her the benefit of the doubt, but she should have called him the moment she came home. They'd both made mistakes. It was time to put the past behind them. Whether or not that led to renewing their relationship, they needed closure on their past.

She was still lost in thought when a nurse came into the waiting room.

"Are you Melissa?" she asked.

"Yes."

The nurse smiled. "I have a patient in room two-twelve who doesn't seem willing to settle down until he finds out if you're okay."

And just like that, Lissa's panic stilled.

"Mack," she said, as emotion welled. "So I can see him now?"

"Yes. Follow me. He's drifting in and out of consciousness, so don't expect much."

Lissa had to run to keep up with the nurse's long strides, and when they reached the room she was taken aback by all the machines around him. Some were beeping, others just registered fluctuating information on his vital signs, but he was alive, and that was enough.

While the nurse was checking the readings, Lissa moved to the side of his bed, which gave her a few moments to look at his near-naked body unobserved.

He'd always been tall, but his body dwarfed the narrow bed. His hair was still thick and dark, his eyebrows and lashes black as coal. He was no longer the boy she remembered. She realized she knew nothing about his personal life and could be completely out of line in even thinking about renewing a relationship with him.

Then he moaned, and when he did, she put a hand on his arm. Almost immediately his eyelids began to flutter.

"Lissa?"

"I'm here, Mack. Just rest."

He exhaled slowly. "Knife… Watch out," he mumbled.

"I know, Mack. I know."

"Tried…to stop."

Lissa put a finger across his lips. "Shh, don't talk. I'm here. I'm safe. I won't leave you."

A tear rolled out from under one closed eyelid and down the side of his face, but he stilled. She knew when he slipped back into unconsciousness, but it didn't change her plans. She'd meant what she'd told him. She wouldn't leave him alone.

Louis woke up just as the alarm began its incessant beeping. He turned it off as he rolled out of bed, then burped and farted as he started toward the bathroom, scratching at his two-day growth of whiskers.

Once there, he glanced at himself in the mirror and frowned. Maybe he should shave. Whiskers made his face look fat. He already had a bit of a belly on him, although he thought Reece's gut was bigger. Still, he didn't want to turn himself into some kind of Santa wannabe. He grabbed the electric razor and shaved his face clean. As he worked, he thought about what it would be like to share a house with his mother again. Some things just couldn't be improved on, and facial hair or no facial hair, he was always going to be "the slow one" in her eyes.

He heard Bobo's toenails clicking on the hardwood floor as the dog trotted into view, his head up and tail wagging, certain of his place in this house. Louis headed for the kitchen and opened the door just enough to let the dog out, then quickly shut it. Last night's rain was over, but the chill was still in the air.

He started a pot of coffee and then went to shower. By the time he got dressed and went back to the kitchen, Bobo was scratching at the back door. Louis grabbed a handful of paper towels before he opened the door and caught the little furball before he could get away.

"You're a mess, boy. Mud all over your feet, and your fur is wet. You can't make messes anymore. Mama is coming for a visit, and while she's here you have to be on your best behavior."

Bobo didn't seem concerned about Mama. He was more interested in the food and water Louis was putting in his bowls.

Louis finished feeding the dog, then washed up and poured a bowl of cereal to go with his coffee, eating it standing up. He winced as he chewed. That jaw tooth without a filling was acting up. He should have had it repaired months ago, but he hated dentists and kept putting off the visit.

When he went to get his phone off the charger, he noticed he had a text. It was from his mother, telling him the bus was due to arrive in Mystic around 5:00 p.m. today, which would be just in time for him to pick her up at the station on his way home. He sighed. This probably meant the end of his evening naps. He wondered how Reece and his weird nocturnal lifestyle were going to play into the visit. Reece was always awake when everyone else was asleep. She wouldn't be happy about that because he was her favorite, but that wasn't Louis's problem.

He was getting ready to leave when he heard Reece's voice.

"Louis! Wait! I need to talk to you," Reece said.

Louis stopped, his shoulders slumping as he turned around and looked down. It was easier listening to his brother than looking at him.

"About what?" Louis asked.

"I, uh…I might have gotten into a little trouble last night and I wanted to prepare you in case—"

That made Louis look up. "What kind of trouble, and what the hell happened to you?"

"I might have killed a man. I know I stabbed him twice."

Louis let out a whimper and then a high keening moan that turned into a shriek. He started turning in circles and hitting the walls with his fists.

"What the fuck is the matter with you? Did anyone see you? Can you be identified? You know we have the same face! You know they'll think it was me!"

Reece was sincerely regretful. Louis was slow, but he was a good guy.

"It was dark. No one saw me," Reece said. "You're safe, Louie… It's okay."

Louis was shaking. "Are you sure? You better be sure or I'll tell Mama. Every time you do this, I have to worry you're going to get caught. We left Florida because too many girls were going missing in our neighborhood because of you, and you know it. I'm not gonna lie for you again."

Reece sighed. "You won't have to, but I have to stay out of sight for a while, so you'll have to do the shopping and take Mama around. I can't show my face because if the guy is still alive he'll tell them we fought, and then the cops will be looking for someone with a bruised-up face."

Louis began pacing the room, trying to find a solution to the mess his brother had dumped in his lap. When he finally stopped, he looked up and saw himself in the mirror, with Reece beside him.

"I'm sorry, Louis," Reece said.

"You did a bad thing again, and they're gonna blame me." Louis's voice was shaking.

"No, they won't," Reece said.

"Why did you hurt the man?" Louis asked.

Reece shrugged. "He just got in the way. I was after the woman."

Louis froze. "What woman? Do I know her? Will she know my face?"

Reece shrugged. "You know her, but she's never seen me, I swear. I've just been courting her a little. She wasn't interested, so I wanted her to pay attention to me. I just went to see her, that's all."

"Who is it?"

"Melissa Sherman."

Louis shrieked, "I work where she works! She'll see me and know!"

"*No!* She's never seen me."

"But you said you were in her house last night, so how can you say that?"

"Because she jumped out the window and ran when she heard my footsteps."

Louis picked up a paperweight from the end table and threw it at the mirror. Glass shattered and fell onto the floor at their feet. He kept his eyes down, determined not to look at his brother again as he read him the riot act.

"You weren't *courting* her. You were *stalking* her. You promised Mama and me you'd never stalk another woman. Last time they almost caught you. You swore you wouldn't do it again," Louis said.

Reece shrugged and then grinned. "Well, my dick had other ideas."

Louis flinched, unable to believe he was even related to someone who could do things like this. "I have to go to work now," he said. He walked out of the house, his steps dragging.

"Sorry!" Reece yelled after him.

Louis kept walking to the truck, then got in and drove away. As he was pulling out of the driveway it occurred to him that he should just withdraw his money from the bank and keep driving. Leave Mama with her favorite son and forget the both of them even existed. But he didn't. Instead, he drove straight to the elementary school and parked.

Ten

Louis saw the principal pulling into his designated parking spot as he got out and started walking toward the building. His stomach was in knots as he saw his boss turn and wave. He ducked his head and waved back, wondering why the man was here so early because it wasn't his usual routine. Still, the principal's job was none of Louis's concern.

He went straight into the building, turned up the thermostat and then began turning on lights as he went from room to room. The day was chilly and wouldn't get any warmer. It was that time of year.

He filled a little cart with rolls of toilet paper and paper towels, and started down the hall toward the bathrooms to refill the paper products. He was trying not to think of the mess Reece had put him in—again—as he reached the boys' bathroom and opened the door. The moment he walked in and realized he was walking in water, he groaned. Something was obviously leaking.

He began moving from toilet stall to toilet stall, trying to find the leak, and then headed to the urinals to check them next. He had just squatted down to check a plumbing joint when he heard a creak, and then something wet fell on his head. He looked up just as the ceiling came crashing down.

Mr. Wilson was on his way to the cafeteria to get a sausage biscuit to have with his coffee when he heard the noise at the far end of the hall and started running. He wasn't sure what had happened, but he could already see water coming out from under the door to the boys' bathroom.

The cooks had also heard the noise and come running from the school cafeteria.

The head cook was a woman they called Miss Eula. When she saw the principal running, she called out, "What was that?"

"I don't know," Wilson said, pushing the bathroom door inward. The first thing he saw was Louis lying on the floor with part of the ceiling on top of him and a huge hole above. He ran back out into the hall. "Call 911!" he yelled. "Part of the ceiling fell in. Louis is pinned beneath it!"

Miss Eula turned and pointed at one of the cooks. "Rhonda, you make the call and wait to lead them in. The rest of you, come with me."

They followed the principal back into the bathroom. They immediately began removing the debris from Louis's body, and Miss Eula got down on her knees and held towels to Louis's bleeding face, while the other cooks tried to mop up the water to keep it from running into nearby classrooms.

Wilson called his secretary to send out an emergency text to the parents and personnel that there would be no school and that it would resume on Monday. Then he contacted the local school superintendent, Will Porter, requesting an electrician and plumber on-site ASAP. All he could tell them was that there was a water leak somewhere up in the ceiling and no way of knowing how many rooms it would impact before it was found and fixed.

He groaned. Friday just kept getting worse.

Louis regained consciousness as they were removing the debris, but when he tried to get up both Mr. Wilson and Miss Eula insisted he was not to move, so he lay as still as possible in the cold water, watching them work. He still wasn't sure what had happened and started fretting about picking Mama up at the bus stop later.

"Am I okay?" he kept asking. "I can't be hurt. Mama is coming to visit me this evening. I have to go get her at the bus stop."

Wilson was on his knees by Louis, trying to keep him from moving.

"I don't know how hurt you are, Louis, but you have to go to the hospital and let them check you out first," he said. "I think your nose might be broken, and there are some cuts on your face."

Louis was in enough shock that the pain was minimal, but things were beginning to burn and sting on his face, and it *was* hard to breathe through his nose.

"Yes, okay," he said, "but I still have to get Mama at five o'clock."

Rhonda ran back into the bathroom.

"Ambulance is here!" she cried, and moments later the small bathroom got even smaller as a half dozen firemen and two EMTs entered.

As soon as the fire department realized there was a leak somewhere above, a couple of the firemen headed back outside to turn the water off at the meter.

"He can move his arms and legs," Wilson said, and then he pointed at the debris piled up against the far wall. "All of that was on top of him when we found him."

"Was he facedown or on his back?" one EMT asked.

"On his back," Wilson said.

They put a collar on Louis to immobilize his head and neck, and began to assess his vitals. A few minutes later they moved him onto the gurney, fastened the straps to keep him stabilized and wheeled him out to the waiting ambulance.

Louis stared up at the ceiling as they passed beneath it, absently counting the number of burned-out fluorescent lightbulbs that needed to be replaced, and wanted to cry. All kinds of stuff was hurting now, his face most of all.

He guessed he was messed up like Reece now, but at least he had an alibi and witnesses as to how he got hurt. They couldn't blame him for attacking that guy. That was on Reece, the stupid bastard.

Lissa's cell phone vibrated in her pocket, signaling a text. She woke abruptly and quickly glanced at Mack, who was still asleep. He'd had a rough night, and now that he was finally resting, she didn't want to disturb him.

Then she read the text and frowned. No school due to a massive water leak. Although it no longer impacted her life, it did give Mr. Wilson more time to find a substitute for her class. She dropped the phone back in her pocket and then slipped out of the room long enough to go to the public bathroom up the hall, where she washed her face and finger combed her hair before heading back.

The shifts were changing, and a fresh batch of nurses were making rounds and assessing the patients' vitals. She grabbed a cup of coffee from the table set up for visitors' convenience and hurried back.

A nurse was already at Mack's bedside checking his IV and taking note of his blood pressure readings, and when she saw Lissa she smiled and introduced herself.

"I'm Jewel. I'll be Mr. Jackson's nurse today."

"I'm Lissa. Does he have a fever? He was very restless all night."

"Just a little. Nothing out of the ordinary for someone just coming out of surgery. I understand he's something of a hero."

Lissa's eyes welled with tears. "He always was."

The nurse left just as Lissa noticed Mack was waking up, and when he reached out, she clasped his hand.

It was the sound of voices that pulled Mack out of the darkness, and when he heard Lissa's voice he remembered. There'd been a fight and a man with a knife who'd been there to hurt her.

"Melissa?"

"I'm here. You're in the hospital. You've had surgery, so you need to lie still."

He exhaled slowly. It hurt to move, but he finally managed to open his eyes. She'd been crying. "You... not hurt?"

"No, I'm not hurt."

He curled his fingers around her wrist.

Lissa couldn't bear to let one more minute go by without making peace between them.

"I need to talk to you, and I don't want you to interrupt me until I've finished, okay?"

Mack was groggy. "Might not remember," he muttered.

"Then, I'll tell you again," she said.

"Deal," he said, and he managed a slight smile.

She threaded her fingers through his and then held on, needing more than just her strength to get through this.

"I know it's not your fault you didn't know about the miscarriage. It's Mom and Dad's fault. They lied to me. Their lies were unfair to both of us, and we fell right into the mess they made for us. I will never know or understand why. But I should have called you the moment I got back to Mystic, and I didn't. You should have asked me about what you heard, but you didn't. We were both so young, and we loved so hard, that the first time we faced a crisis, we broke. I just want you to know how sorry I am. We lost so much. I would give anything to get that back."

Mack's grip tightened around her fingers. "So would I," he said.

The panic she'd been feeling began to fade. It was like getting her best friend ever back in her life. She tried to smile but was so overwhelmed by what was happening between them that all she could do was cry.

"No, Lissa, don't cry. This is all good, okay?"

She nodded as she swiped at the tears, but they just kept coming. "I'm happy and I'm scared and I'm frustrated. Your father was murdered, I'm being stalked, there's a killer among us and no one has the slight-

est idea of where to start looking. I'm not allowed to
go back to my house until the stalker is caught. Chief
Jakes said the man was too dangerous. I even had to
take a leave of absence from school because he also
believes the stalker might try to get to me at school,
and that would put the children's lives in danger. Everything is wonderful *between* us because we've made
peace, and everything's awful about what's happening
to us, and that's why I'm crying."

Mack groaned. He could feel himself fading again.
"You'll be with me. We'll do it…together. Sorry.
Can't…"

And then he was out.

Lissa stumbled backward to the chair where she'd
spent the night and sank into the seat, too numb to
think beyond what he had said. They would be together.

She wasn't alone in the world anymore.

T. J. Silver heard the news about Mack Jackson's
bravery at the coffee shop while he was waiting for
his father. His eyes narrowed angrily as he listened to
the waitress extolling Mack's heroism to the couple at
the table behind him.

"…said she found him covered in blood and hasn't
left his side since," she said.

That alone pissed him off. He'd gone to check on
her and been rebuffed. But Jackson was an old flame,
and his father's death had brought them back together.
Life was an ironic fuckup, and he didn't give a damn
who she liked. He could have his pick of all the girls.
It just pissed him off that she'd been the one to end the

relationship. It was the only failure of his entire life, and he had no idea how to handle it.

He heard the door jingle and looked up to see his father approaching the table. Good. He was ready to get busy with his father's upcoming announcement that he was running for the district's state senate seat. They had almost settled on a campaign manager and needed to set a firm date for the announcement party so things could get under way.

T.J. smiled at his dad as he sat down and handed him a menu.

"I'm having the roast beef sandwich au jus and peach cobbler. What sounds good to you?"

Marcus shrugged. "It doesn't matter."

T.J. frowned. "What's wrong, Dad? Are you feeling okay?"

Marcus glanced around the crowded diner. He knew nearly every face in here and was better off financially than all of them, and yet the excitement was gone from his life. He was bothered by a lot of things and didn't know how to put them into words.

"I'm fine," he said abruptly. "That cobbler sounds good, but I believe I'll have the beans and corn bread today."

T.J. arched an eyebrow. "Beans and corn bread. Eating lowbrow, are you?"

Marcus looked up and frowned at the smirk on his son's face. "I like beans and corn bread, and just because food is cheap to make doesn't mean it's beneath us to eat it."

T.J. caught the glimmer of criticism in the tone of his father's voice and immediately shifted his attitude.

"Oh, no, no, that's not what I meant, Dad. Sorry if

I came across a little snobby. I was just making conversation, that's all."

Marcus shrugged it off. He loved his son, but he'd been spoiled by the good life, something that he had to take the blame for, but he didn't have to tolerate him being a snob.

"So what's on your agenda today?" Marcus asked as he waved the waitress over so they could order.

T.J. leaned forward, excitement in his voice as he said, "Helping you plan your announcement party. Do you still want to do it at Christmas? I think it would be the proper time, but if so, we need to get that guest list finalized, and invitations printed and sent out by Thanksgiving at the latest."

Marcus hesitated. "I guess. Timing is everything, and I don't want to jump the gun before everything else is in place."

T.J. leaned back, accepting his father's decision.

"Whatever you say, Dad. This is your thing, not mine. I just want to do my part to help when you give the word."

Marcus sighed. "You're a good son. I guess I need to go ahead and make that trip to the capitol, hire that campaign manager and then let him do all the work. That's what I'll be paying him for, right?"

"Right. Are you going today?"

"Yes, I'll leave right after we eat."

T.J. was glad the ball was finally rolling on his dad's big dream, and when the waitress arrived at their table, he flashed a broad smile.

"Hello, Jennifer. We're ready to order now." He gave her his order while Marcus stared absently across his son's head to the people beyond.

* * *

It was noon when Louis left the ER with a half dozen staples in his forehead, butterfly bandages on the smaller cuts on his face and wads of gauze stuffed up his nose. His clothing was mostly dry, and he didn't have a concussion or any broken bones, thanks to the fact that the water-soaked ceiling tiles had come apart in soggy pieces on impact. If it hadn't been for the metal grid holding them, which had also fallen, he would have been fine.

However, one eye was swollen shut, and his lips were so puffy it hurt to talk. The bruising on his face was going to be spectacular by tomorrow, the doctor had told him. Louis wasn't quite sure how to take that, but he was very glad tomorrow was Saturday. By the time Monday rolled around, he planned to be back at work. No way was he going to be stuck at home with his mother and Reece for days on end. The weekend would be enough.

An orderly going off duty had offered to drive him home, but Louis asked to be taken back to the school parking lot instead. He needed his truck to go get Mama.

"Man, are you sure you're fit to drive?" the orderly asked as he pulled up behind Louis's truck.

"I can walk and talk and I can see. I can drive myself home," Louis said.

Reece was asleep when Louis walked into the house. It felt strange to be back this time of day. Bobo trotted out to meet him and licked the toe of his work shoe as Louis paused in the hall. When he didn't hear any movement, he went into the kitchen.

He'd missed eating breakfast at school, and he'd

missed lunch, which was also at school. Even though he hurt, he knew he needed to eat something or the pain meds they'd given him would make him sick.

He was prowling through the refrigerator for something easy when his phone signaled a text. It was from the principal, Mr. Wilson, asking if he was okay and if he needed anything.

Louis was touched that his boss had been concerned enough to check on him and sent a quick text back.

I'm okay. Don't need anything.

Bobo whined once as he sniffed at him again. Louis guessed he smelled funny. The hospital had used all kinds of antiseptic stuff on him.

"Yes, it's still me, Bobo. I just hurt. Do you want out?"

Bobo trotted toward the door.

As soon as the dog was outside, Louis opted for something soft and got a leftover bowl of macaroni and cheese, nuked it in the microwave, then sat down at the table with a fork and ate it. When he'd had enough to satisfy the gripe in his belly, he put it back in the refrigerator. He didn't feel like going to the store or doing anything fancy for his mother's visit, so he let the dog in, set the alarm to wake himself up in plenty of time to go pick her up and then went to bed.

It felt strange to be going to bed this early, but he was beginning to ache in every muscle and he wanted to cry. Instead, he pulled up the covers and closed his eyes. Because of the gauze in his nostrils he was going to have to sleep with his mouth open, which would make him snore.

It was not the best day of his life.

* * *

Lissa was sitting cross-legged in the chair near Mack's bed. He talked in his sleep, either from the pain meds or it was a habit she'd known nothing about, but she had heard enough to know he was dreaming, and in the dreams he was young. He kept mumbling his mother's name and telling her he'd fed the puppy. He muttered something about going to his grandparents' house, and then moaned and settled again. He woke briefly and told her that he loved her, and then drifted back to sleep.

She couldn't stop his pain, and she couldn't change the ten years they'd lost, but there was one thing she could do that would mean something to him.

She sent a text to her friend Margaret and then waited. About a half hour later Margaret texted that she was in the second-floor waiting room. Lissa went out to meet her, and her friend greeted her with a tote bag and a smile.

"I am so sorry this happened," Margaret said as she gave Lissa a big hug. "I wish you'd told me about being stalked. I have three really big brothers who don't take well to men abusing women in any way."

"If I'd known about the brothers I sure might have," Lissa said. "Did you find everything?"

Margaret handed her the tote bag.

"Everything, and now I'm going to impose on our friendship and worry about you. What are you going to do when you go home? I can recommend a man who installs security systems."

"I can't go home until the stalker is caught, and the truth is, I dread going back even when I can."

"Why?" Margaret said. "I thought you loved living in the house where you grew up."

Lissa thought again of her parents' betrayal.

"In the past few days, a lot of things have changed my opinion of home. And there's the fact that the stalker did a lot of damage, like a broken window in the back door, broken glass and Mack's blood all over the kitchen floor. They dusted for fingerprints, so there's no telling how much dirt that left, too. And there's my bedroom. He tore it to pieces."

"Melissa! I'm so sorry. Will you let us help? Everyone from school is upset on your behalf. If it's okay with the police, will you let us clean up the house for you?"

"Oh, Margaret, no! It's a horrible mess."

"We don't mind messes, girl. We deal with puke and germs on a daily basis, remember? And since teachers' salaries are less than they should be, cleaning up costs nothing to us but time. It's the perfect way for us to give back."

Lissa heard the sincerity in Margaret's voice and didn't want to deny her friends the right to help. "Then, I accept with gratitude," she said, and dug her house key out of her purse. "Check with Chief Jakes, and if it's okay with him, then it's okay with me, too."

"Great!" Margaret said. Then she glanced at her watch and jumped to her feet. "I need to go. Gotta pick my girls up from basketball practice. I'll get your key back to you soon."

Lissa walked Margaret back to the elevator. "Thanks again for getting this stuff for me," she said, holding up the tote bag.

Margaret smiled. "Can't wait to meet that man," she

said, and then the smile faded. "I'm so sorry about his father. I can't imagine what he must be feeling." Then the elevator arrived, and with one last wave, Margaret was gone.

Lissa took the tote bag back to Mack's room. Since he was still asleep, she slipped into the chair by his bed and began digging through the bag, hoping she wasn't wrong about her surprise. She just wanted to be at peace with the only man she'd ever loved. She wondered where the future would take them.

And then his doctor walked in. "Good afternoon, Melissa. How is our patient today?"

Mack began to rouse as he heard the doctor's voice, and before Lissa could speak, Mack answered for himself. "He's appreciative of being put back together," he said, which made the doctor laugh.

Lissa leaned back in the chair, listening to the doctor question Mack, watching the expressions come and go on Mack's face as he answered, and all the while she kept thinking how close he'd come to dying.

"Have you been up yet?" the doctor asked.

"Once, to walk to the bathroom," Mack said.

"That's good. If you continue to progress without any other issues, you can go home in the morning, provided you have someone who'll be with you."

"I will," Lissa said.

"Yes, I'll have my partner with me," Mack said.

The doctor grinned.

"And a fine-looking partner she is. I'll have written instructions for your care until you come back to get the staples out. In the meantime, move around as much as you feel like, but no lifting. Not anything more than a fork to your mouth, understood?"

Mack nodded. "Understood."

The doctor left, and once again they were alone.

"Come sit beside me," Mack said, patting the side of his bed. "I keep having this need to touch you to remind myself this isn't a dream."

Lissa understood. It was surreal to accept being back together after so many years apart. She lowered the bed rail, then scooted onto the side away from the IV and reached for his hand. His palm was warm and his grip was firm, and when he gave her hand a quick tug, she looked up.

"What?"

"When I leave here we'll go back to Dad's house until after the memorial service, which I have yet to schedule."

"Maybe by then they'll have caught my stalker, and I can go back to my house and back to work," she said.

"I don't want to be apart from you again," Mack said.

Lissa's eyes widened slightly. "What do you mean?"

"We lost ten years. I have no allegiance to anyone. In my heart, you're still my Melissa, just older and prettier. Could we maybe agree to pick up where we left off, and fill in the blanks of what we've missed as we go?"

"Oh, Mack." She leaned forward, very carefully centering her lips on his mouth and closed her eyes.

She heard him groan as she stifled a sob.

It felt the same. The spark between them was immediate. His lips were firm, and she yielded to the hunger when he put a hand behind her head and held her close to lengthen the kiss. When it ended, his eyes were glistening and she couldn't catch a good breath for the lump in her throat.

"So...?"

Lissa sighed. "Except for the fact that you're older and prettier, too, I don't see one reason why we can't make that happen. We'll just have to figure out the logistics because I have to finish out my contract here in Mystic."

"I understand, and if you want to work after we're married maybe you could teach in Summerton, although it's strictly up to you. I have a house waiting for a woman to make it a home, and I make plenty of money if you don't want to work."

She shivered, absorbing the love she heard in his voice. "This feels like the end of a nightmare," she said.

"And a new beginning for us. This is where we were when everything came undone, except then we were broke."

She laughed. "We were sure that, weren't we?"

Mack brushed a thumb across the little mole by her mouth and then eased himself into a more comfortable position.

"And just so you know, when we go back to Dad's house, I'm hiring private security. You won't know they're there, and if the stalker is still hunting, hopefully he won't, either, until it's too late."

She frowned. "But that will cost a lot of money, and it's not fair to you to pay—"

"Hey!"

She stopped talking for a moment, then asked, "What?"

"Two things. Don't worry about money. We're good on that score. And don't forget I have a bone to pick with him, too. I take it personally when someone tries to kill me. Besides, I want to spend the rest of my life with you. I want to make babies and grow old with you, so we need this guy behind bars."

It was the mention of babies that healed the last ache in her heart. Tears rolled.

Mack groaned. "Don't cry."

"Happy tears. Only happy tears," she said.

Eleven

Louis's alarm was going off, but he was having a hard time waking up. Finally it was Reece yelling in his ear that did the trick. He opened his eyes just as Reece disappeared, cursing beneath his breath.

"Yeah, I'm okay. Don't bother to ask what happened to me!" Louis shouted. "I just nearly died today, that's all!"

He threw back the covers and then groaned when he began to move. Every muscle in his body hurt, and as he made his way to the bathroom, he thought too late that he should have put an ice pack on his face before he went to sleep. It might have helped the swelling.

Bobo followed him into the bathroom, then stood with his little ears up, intently watching everything Louis was doing.

"Bobo, I'm going to the bus station to get Mama, so you better be good when we get back, okay?"

The dog snuffed and plopped down on a throw rug in the hall as Louis went to his room to get a jacket and then struggled putting it on. By the time he was ready to leave, he was sweating from the pain and wondering if he should think about suing the school district. If he got a big enough settlement he could quit work, and he and Reece and Mama could move to Florida. It was in the back of his mind as he went out the door and got in the truck.

His phone signaled another text just as he started the engine. It was from Mama.

I'm here.

He sent a text back.

On the way.

Pinky Parsons had gotten through life on her looks, and when they'd begun to fade, she'd utilized the fact that she could give a man a satisfactory blow job in less than two minutes flat. And then she'd lost her front teeth one winter when she'd slipped on ice and fallen face-first onto the steps leading into her apartment, and she'd been without the money to fix them. After that, blow jobs had become harder to come by. It seemed to creep men out that she was missing all four front teeth, although she didn't know why. It should have been a reassuring fact, but there was no accounting for men's tastes.

Now it was her age and her dental problems that had driven her to make this move, and she was not happy about having to come here. The fact that the dog was still around made her even more unhappy.

She was sitting on a bench near the door, watching for her ride while keeping an eye on her things, when she saw a pickup pull up out front. She scooted closer to the edge of her seat, but when she saw the driver get out and close the door, she gasped, and when he walked inside the terminal the first words out of her mouth were "What the fuck happened to you?"

Louis winced. "Had an accident at work today. Are those your things?"

Pinky sighed. "Louis? That *is* you, isn't it?"

Louis frowned and then winced from the pain.

"After all these years you still can't tell me and Reece apart."

She sputtered a bit, but seeing the condition he was in, she grabbed her own bags and started out the door. "Well, you can't blame me for not knowing. I mean, your face looks like shit."

"Yeah, well, his does, too," Louis said, not bothering to help her.

Pinky slung her bags into the truck bed and then glanced at her son again as she got in, feeling bad she'd been so rude. "I'm sorry you got hurt. What happened?"

He started the engine. "Ceiling fell in on me at school."

Pinky frowned. "Well, my goodness, son. That's just awful. Want me to drive?"

"Do you have a license?" he asked.

"No, but—"

"Then, never mind," he said, and drove away.

Pinky sighed and tried to start over. "So, where's Reece?"

"Asleep."

She frowned again.

Louis felt the need to explain. "These days he's only awake at night. That's when he does his stock market stuff."

She rode in silence for a few moments, digesting how that might affect her situation.

"I can't believe that damn dog is still around. Shit. I do not like that little mutt."

"It doesn't matter what you like, Mama. It's his home, not yours, and if anything happens to Bobo, something might happen to you. Reece is a little crazy now."

Pinky gasped and then laughed, certain that was meant as a joke, but when Louis didn't join in, she suddenly shivered. It might have been a mistake to come here. She had to think of something to change the atmosphere or she would never be able to go in the house.

"So you said something happened to Reece's face, too?"

"Yes, and you're not gonna like it."

"What do you mean?"

"He's at it again, Mama."

The knot in Pinky's stomach suddenly got tighter. "What do you mean?"

"He's been stalking another woman. He broke into her house and fought with some man. His face is all messed up, and he said he stabbed the man and thinks he might have killed him."

Pinky screamed and then clasped her hands over her mouth, staring at Louis in disbelief.

"Oh, my God! What did I do to deserve this? How did I give birth to such a monster?"

Louis was somewhat mollified by the fact that for once Mama was more pissed at Reece than she was at him.

"Well, we're home," he said, as he pulled up to the little house and parked.

He got out, unlocked the door and went in without offering to help her. The way he looked at it, she'd invited herself here. The sooner she figured out it wasn't the best idea she'd ever had, the sooner she would leave.

Pinky's hands were shaking as she struggled to get her bags out of the truck bed. Right now, she had nowhere else to go but here, but she wasn't going to waste time before beginning to look for another way out of the predicament she was in.

She dragged her bags into the house, and then shut the door and looked around. It wasn't as messy as she'd expected. She saw the little terrier eyeing her from the throw rug and then looked away. Even the dog didn't want her here.

"Louis!"

He walked out of the kitchen. "What?"

"Where do I sleep?"

He pointed to the sofa.

"You mean you—"

"Unless you want to sleep with Reece."

"A woman needs her privacy," she muttered.

"Reece has money. Tell him to rent you an apartment in town," he said as he walked back into the kitchen.

Pinky's eyes lit up as she followed him. "Reece has money? More money than you?"

Louis looked down as he began measuring coffee into the coffeemaker.

"Yes. He makes a lot of money with his stocks. He's very good at short sales and futurities."

She thought of the dumps she'd been living in for the past five years and started to get mad, then thought better of it.

"So you think you might talk to Reece and tell him I need a place of my own?"

Louis shook his head. "Reece doesn't listen to me. He never did. You know that."

Pinky sighed. "Come on, Louis, you know you—"

"No, Mama! Don't say it!"

She sighed. "Fine. I'll ask Reece myself. When did you say I might expect to see him?"

"He wakes up at night, after I go to bed."

"Fine. I'll talk to him tonight." Then she saw the pain in Louis's face and felt bad again. "Is there anything I can do? I'll make supper if you want to go rest or something."

Louis shrugged. He did want to lie down. He felt like shit.

"I guess you can," he said. "I don't feel so good."

"I'll bet you don't," Pinky said. She headed for the refrigerator. "What do you want me to make?"

"Whatever you can find. There's not much here. I was going to go get groceries and then I got hurt. I'll go tomorrow."

"We'll make do," she said. "It'll be like old times. Mama will find a way to make a yummy meal out of bits and pieces. Remember bits and pieces?" she asked.

Louis was still looking at the floor. "Was that before Daddy hanged himself, or afterward?"

The smile on Pinky's face froze as Louis walked out of the room.

Trey pulled up to his mother's house, then sat for a few moments gathering his thoughts. With the revelation about Paul's murder and the letter from the safety deposit box, it was no longer possible to let his mother off the hook about answering questions. It was his opinion that her life was in danger. Whatever she remembered, no matter how vague, he needed to know, and he was counting on her being more receptive to answering his questions than having someone else interview her for him.

He picked up the video recorder as he got out of the cruiser, noticing as he headed toward the house that Trina was home. He frowned. She didn't usually get off until 4:00 p.m. He hoped nothing had happened to their mom to prompt her early return.

He was on the porch and about to walk in when he remembered the security system and knocked instead.

A few moments later his mother opened the door, which triggered a bell-like sound. It wasn't the alarm indicating a break-in but a warning to let her know the front door had been opened.

"So are you getting used to the security system?"

She rolled her eyes. "I'm making pie," she said as she headed back to the kitchen.

"Why is Trina home? Is she sick?"

Betsy picked up the rolling pin and continued to roll out the pie dough as she talked.

"As I understand it, she and Lee had a horrible fight and broke up. I don't know what prompted it. I don't know what to say to her other than I'm so sorry. She has to cry herself out. It's sad. That's all."

Trey sighed. He knew all too well how it felt to be without the person you loved. Thank God he and Dallas were back together.

"I'm sorry to hear that. I like Lee. I wonder what happened."

"It doesn't really matter what happened when you're

grieving the loss," she said. Then she deftly transferred the piecrust to the fruit-filled pie plate beside her and began crimping the edges of the crusts to keep the juices from bubbling over into the oven.

"I guess you're right about that," Trey said, gauging the expression on her face against why he'd come. "Are you nearly finished?" he asked.

She nodded. "After your last phone call, I suppose you're here on official business."

"Yes."

She slid the pie into the oven, washed her hands and then sat down at the table. "Okay, I'm ready for questioning."

Trey sighed. "Mom, it's—"

She slapped the flat of her hand on the table.

"I know what it is. Just get it over with," she snapped, shoving the gray curls away from her face.

He tried not to take her anger personally and turned on the recorder as he sat, identifying himself for the recording, stating the date and time and the name of the person being interviewed. Then he pulled out a notebook with questions he'd prepared earlier.

"What link do you have to Dick Phillips and Paul Jackson?"

Her right eye twitched, but her voice was calm when she answered, "We went to high school together. I dated Paul Jackson, and we were all in a wreck together the night of our graduation."

"Did anything happen prior to the wreck that would make you think your lives would be in danger?"

"No."

"Did anything happen the night of the wreck that would lead you to believe your lives were in danger?"

"I don't know. None of us remembered anything from that night once we left Mystic after graduation."

"And why was that?"

"Well, we were told we were drunk. And we all had severe head injuries from the wreck. It was a miracle we didn't all die like our friend Connie, who was driving."

"Have any of your memories returned since Dick's and Paul's deaths?"

She hesitated, then looked past his shoulder to the wall behind him.

"I've had dreams. I have no way of knowing what they mean, or *if* they mean anything at all."

Trey reached into his pocket and pulled out a plastic bag containing the bloodstained tassel.

"Does this look familiar to you?"

She looked closer, saw the date on the tiny medal attached and then shuddered.

"It appears to be a tassel from the mortarboard of someone from our graduating class."

"The stains on this tassel were tested. They're blood."

Her eyes widened. "So that brown stuff on the tassel is blood?"

"Yes," Trey said. "Does it look familiar to you?"

"I have no memory of seeing it," she said. She started crying. "Where did it come from?"

He got up to get a box of tissues from the sideboard and shoved it toward her, then sat back down.

"The medical personnel found it on Paul's body when he was unconscious after the wreck. Do you have any idea why Paul Jackson would have it when he stated later that it wasn't his?"

"No."

"Paul said he thought he remembered seeing a body on the ground. Do you remember anything like that?"

She covered her face with both hands, remembering parts of her crazy dreams. "I don't know? Maybe. I'm not sure."

He shifted his line of questioning. "What *do* you know?"

"I've been keeping a journal of my dreams," she said.

"May I see it?" he asked.

She hesitated. "It may mean nothing, and—"

"I can get a search warrant and confiscate it or—"

She lowered her hands and stared at her son as if he was a stranger, then pushed her chair away from the table and got up.

"I'll be right back," she said. She walked out of the kitchen with her head up, leaving Trey feeling like shit amid the tantalizing aroma of her cherry pie.

He heard footsteps and turned around just as Betsy dropped the journal onto the table, then sat back down without a word.

"Do I have your permission to take this as possible evidence in the murder of your two classmates?"

Her shoulders sagged. Put that way, her indignation seemed petty and out of place. "Yes, of course you may," she said softly.

"Thank you," Trey said. "Noted for the record, I'm taking a blue leather journal belonging to Betsy Jakes as evidence."

Betsy was beginning to shake.

Trey feared she was on the verge of an emotional

breakdown, but he couldn't let his personal feelings get in the way.

"In a nutshell, could you explain for the record what the journal contains?"

"Right after Dick Phillips' murder I began having dreams or nightmares or whatever you want to call them. I've been writing them down. Sometimes I think I'm about to remember, and then everything fades. I hope what I've written is helpful in some way."

Trey felt sick to his stomach. This was his mother, and he would have stopped anyone else who was making her this miserable. He couldn't believe this was even happening.

"I have another question. Has there been anyone lately who has given you cause to be afraid?"

"No."

"Do you fear for your life?"

She hesitated again, and then looked straight at him. "Yes."

"Why?"

She took a deep breath and then clasped her hands together in her lap. Tears were rolling down her face, and her voice was shaking when she answered.

"I think we witnessed something bad. I dreamed we saw a body. I think we might have been on our way to report it when we wrecked."

"If that's true, then why would someone wait this long to eliminate witnesses?"

"I don't know. I swear to God, I don't know. I wish I did, but I don't."

Trey glanced down at the notebook. There was one more question he had yet to ask, and he was debating with himself about voicing it. But when it came to doing his duty, he was a lawman first and a son second.

"I have one more question. Has it ever occurred to you that you four could be the ones responsible for the body you mention seeing in your journal?"

Betsy sobbed out loud. "Yes, it's occurred to me."

"Do you think yourself capable of murder?"

"Oh, my God, I don't know, Trey. I don't know! We were eighteen years old and drunk out of our minds. I don't know."

Trey stopped the recorder, circled the table and pulled his mother out of the chair and into his arms.

"I'm sorry. I'm so sorry," he said, his voice thick with tears.

At that point Trina walked into the kitchen, her eyes red and swollen. "What's going on?" she asked.

"I had to officially question Mom about the wreck in case it's connected to Dick Phillips' and Paul Jackson's deaths."

"Why would you do that?" Trina shrieked. "She didn't have anything to do with their murders."

Betsy pulled out of Trey's arms and grabbed Trina by the shoulders, her tears still falling.

"Stop it, Trina! Stop it now! Trey was just doing his job."

"You didn't kill your friends!" Trina shot back.

"Not Dick and Paul, and not Connie. But I'm almost certain someone died before we had the wreck, and I have no idea if we only witnessed it or if we caused it, understand?"

Trina clapped a hand over her mouth, staring at her mother in disbelief, and then came to her senses and threw her arms around her mother's neck.

"I know you didn't cause anyone to die!" Trina cried. "I know you would never hurt a soul! I'm sorry, Mama, I'm sorry for not being more understanding about what you've been going through. I'm here for you. We're all here for you."

Trey walked up behind them, put his arms around both of them and pulled them close.

"We'll get through this, and we'll still be together. I'll find a way to figure this out. I have to. I can't lose either one of you."

Pinky Parsons made a bed for herself on the living room sofa and sidestepped the dog, even though it kept nosing around her things.

Louis had eaten very little, claiming to be in too much pain, and gone to bed over an hour ago. She'd asked him when Reece usually woke up, but he'd answered her with a shrug, saying he had no way of knowing because he was asleep.

She'd bitten her tongue to keep from flying into a fit and was now awaiting Reece's appearance. She glanced at the time and then rolled her eyes as the hour hand moved past 7:00 p.m. It made it past eight and was at less than twenty minutes before nine when she heard a door open down the hall. The dog jumped up from the rug and disappeared.

When she heard the familiar and forceful voice of her favorite son, she stood up, her hands clasped against her belly, ready to welcome him.

He walked into the room with a brash swagger and a smile, which momentarily made her forget she wasn't exactly welcome here. She needed to get him to give her some money, then get out of Mystic before she became too entrenched in what Reece was doing and got arrested for aiding and abetting.

"Mama! It's good to see you."

Pinky knew that was an outright lie, but she managed a smile anyway. "It's good to see you, too, son."

Reece frowned. "Damn, what happened to your teeth?"

She clenched her lips together, but it was too late. "I fell on some ice. They got knocked out."

He frowned. "You need to get them fixed. Makes you look old."

She rolled her eyes. "If I had money for dental work, I would also have money for rent, but I have neither, which is why I'm temporarily on your sofa."

"Yeah, right," Reece said. Then he grinned at Bobo, who was dancing around his feet. "Sorry, Mama. I gotta go let the dog out."

She watched him walk away and then followed him into the kitchen, ready to cater to his needs.

"I made some dinner from what I found in your fridge," she said.

Reece pointed to the pad by the refrigerator. "Louis left me a note."

"Oh, yes. Well…would you like me to heat it up for you? It won't take a minute."

"No, I'm good. My jaw is a little sore right now. Got into a little dustup the other night, but it's nothing serious."

"Louis told me," she said.

He paused, looked at her and then quickly looked away.

"Exactly what did he tell you?" he asked, as he got a bottle of Coke from the refrigerator.

"That you're stalking a woman and might have killed a man."

The Coke slipped from his hands and hit the floor with a bounce. Good thing for plastic bottles. Not a good idea to open it right now. He set it back in the refrigerator and then turned around. "He said all that, did he?"

She nodded. "He also said you had lots of money and would help me get an apartment someplace so I wouldn't be in your way."

A muscle jerked at the side of Reece's right eye as he started walking toward her. If this was anyone but his mother, he would have sworn that she'd mentioned the stalking and the killing so that asking for money next would be a reminder to him of what she knew—and could tell—if he didn't come through. He wanted to wring Louis's neck and break hers, but she was blood, and that kept her breathing.

Pinky wasn't sure whether she should scream or run as he approached because he looked seriously pissed off, and then he took her by the shoulders and pulled her into his arms in a big hug.

"Damn old Louis, but he's right. I do have money, and I'll be thrilled to help you past this rough spot."

Pinky sighed. "Oh, thank you, son."

Reece was still smiling as he cupped her face, but when he began increasing the pressure, she thought her head was going to pop.

"Stop, Reece! You're hurting me."

"It's a reminder, Mother. A reminder to keep your damn toothless mouth shut, okay?"

"Okay," she said, and pushed away, refusing to let him know how much he'd scared her.

"Just so we understand each other," he said. "I'm going to eat a bite, and then I'll give you a check. Maybe Louis can take you to the bank tomorrow to cash it. After that, you're free to go wherever you choose."

"Thank you, Reece."

"You're welcome, Mama."

The dog was scratching at the door to come in.

Reece turned away from her as if she'd just disappeared, and Pinky took advantage of the moment to do just that. She went back into the living room and sat down in the shadows with an eye on the kitchen. She wished Louis would wake up because something had happened to Reece since the last time she'd seen him. She didn't know what it was, but he scared the crap out of her.

Twelve

Pinky sat without moving, listening to Reece talking to the dog and digging through the refrigerator, as normal sounding as anyone, but he had not denied trying to kill a man.

The longer she sat, the tighter the band of muscles across her chest became. She needed to cry but was afraid to show weakness. In an effort to shift focus from her fear, she turned on the television and then lowered the volume. Over time, she became fixated on the screen while purposefully ignoring his presence in the house.

When he walked back through the room a short while later and paused to hand her a check, she quickly muted the volume and stood up to give him a quick kiss on the cheek. When she saw the amount, she was stunned.

"Thank you, son. This is very generous. I'll cash it tomorrow and be out of your way as soon as possible."

"Get your teeth fixed, too," he said.

"I will, oh, I will," she said. She folded the check

and put it in her pocket, then sat back down and resumed her program.

It was time to log some time on the computer, Reece thought, so he left her alone, glad this drama was over. As soon as she had money and a ticket, she would be gone and one less thing for him to worry about. However, he was going to have to talk to Louis. He couldn't have him telling anyone their business. Not even Mama.

Lissa had waited to reveal her surprise until it was close to bedtime. The nurses had already made rounds, and it was quieting down as she turned off the television and closed the door to Mack's room.

He was still finding it hard to believe that she was back in his life, and when she closed the door, he grinned. "Am I about to get lucky?"

"Yes, you are, Mister Man."

He wanted to get turned on. She was so damn cute, but his shoulder hurt like a big dog. He couldn't do anything but watch her curls bounce and appreciate the flash of sexy that came and went without reason.

Lissa was flirting on purpose. It was funny how being loved could make a woman feel.

She straightened his covers, made sure there was a pillow behind his head that would take the pressure off the wound on his back, and then slowly raised the head of his bed just enough so he could swallow without choking.

"First surprise!" she said, and dug a large bag of Peanut M&M's out of the tote bag, tore open the top and put it on the covers where he could easily reach inside.

"Hey, my favorite candy!" he said. He popped a couple into his mouth, enjoying the crunch of the hard candy shell and then the savory taste of the peanut. Meanwhile she poured a glass of water and set it on the table where he could reach it.

She cupped the side of his cheek and then swept a wayward lock of dark hair from his forehead. "Are you comfy, sugar?"

"Yes, I am," he said.

Next she pulled a book out of the tote bag, climbed up onto the bed beside his knee and cleared her throat. Then, with all the ceremony she could muster, she opened it to the first page.

"The Velveteen Rabbit," she announced, just as she would have to her students. Then she began to read.

A wave of emotion swept through Mack so fast that there were tears in his eyes before he knew it. This book was one of the few things he remembered from when his mother was still alive, and the fact that Lissa remembered him telling her that and was reading it now touched his heart.

As a child, he'd been obsessed with it, and his mom had read it to him nightly without complaint. After she died, he'd thought he would never want to hear it again, and now here sat Lissa with the same attention to detail and emotion, telling him the story all over again, and he knew he had been wrong. It was, without doubt, the most thoughtful and loving thing anyone had ever done for him.

So he sat, listening to the story and watching the expressions on her face as she read, thinking about the last thing his father had written to him.

Make peace with Melissa.

This *was* peace, and also love, and the first step in healing the secrets and lies her parents had used to destroy them.

Lissa looked up, saw him watching her and smiled. She paused long enough to shake another candy out of the package for him, waited until he put it in his mouth and then resumed the story.

It occurred to him as she read that if their child had lived, she would already have read this book countless times. But that hadn't happened, so she was reading it to him.

He took a sip of water to stifle unshed tears, and then leaned back and closed his eyes as her voice pulled him back into the story. For the length of the book, time stilled.

It wasn't until he heard her say something about being his own bunny that he opened his eyes. It was over. As her voice faded, a sense of peace washed over him. She'd taken the ugliness out of what had happened and for the space of a few minutes brought his mother to his bedside in the only way she could. He reached for her hand.

"I'll bet you're a remarkable teacher. I can only imagine how much your children love you."

Lissa smiled. "I do love my job. I like watching their faces when they 'get' something new."

"Thank you for the story."

She nodded. "I remembered you telling me once that your mother used to read it to you before you went to bed. I hope—"

"She used to kiss my forehead every night, too," he said, and tugged her closer.

She laid the book aside, and leaned over and kissed him squarely on the lips.

"Just a reminder that I am *not* your mother."

Mack groaned. "Truth is, most of the time I can't remember what she looked like. I just remember things about her. However, you, my love, have haunted me for years. I remember everything about you, from how you always lick the salt off your fingers when you eat fries to the fact that you like cake hot out of the oven with butter melting on it better than cake with icing. I know kissing the back of your neck turns you on, and that your eyelids flutter when you come. I loved you when I was a boy. I cannot wait for you to let me love you as a man does. All I can do is promise that I will never disappoint you again."

Lissa was in tears. "We're really going to do this, aren't we? We're going to be together and—"

"Marry me," he said softly.

It was all she could do to not throw herself into his arms.

"Oh, Mack."

"If we're going to pick up where we left off and fill in the blanks later, that's where we left off."

She started laughing through her tears. "You are a crazy man."

"Not too crazy to marry?"

She sighed. "I will marry you because you've seen me without a stitch of clothes or any makeup and weren't turned off…and because I've seen you without a stitch of clothes and was so turned on."

His eyes darkened. Just the thought of coming home to her every day for the rest of his life seemed surreal.

He kissed the palm of her hand and ached to take her to bed. That, however, would have to wait.

"At least something good is coming out of this chaos, and that's you and me."

A frown darkened her face as she thought about both the murderer and her stalker.

"What if they don't figure out who killed your dad? What if they don't identify my stalker?"

He shook his head. "They will. When I get back to the house tomorrow, I'm calling a security company. I've used them several times before. You aren't going to be unprotected anywhere again."

Her shoulders slumped as she absently rubbed her thumb across the old scar on the back of his hand.

"I was worrying about what a mess my house is in. Last I knew they were dusting for prints. Broken glass and your blood were all over the kitchen floor. A window is out in the back door. Everything is torn up in my bedroom, and the floor was wet from rain getting in…and then my friend Margaret told me she and the other teachers want to help me. They've offered to clean up the house for me, so I won't have to go home to that."

"That's wonderful, darling, but remember, from now on there's nothing we can't do if we're doing it together."

Saturday morning an email went out to the elementary school personnel about the cleanup at Lissa's house. Subsequent messages flew between the teachers as to when they would meet and what they needed to bring. Louis received the email along with everyone else, but he didn't see it first. Reece did.

Reece woke Louis up yelling at the top of his voice, "Get up! Get up, damn it! You have somewhere to be this morning."

Louis glared. "It's Saturday. I don't have to be anywhere."

But Reece kept yelling. "I said, get the fuck up, damn it! The teachers are going to clean up Melissa Sherman's house, and you're going to help because you know how to replace glass and there's a broken window in her back door. Wanna know how I know that? Because I fucking broke it," he crowed. Then he threw back his head and laughed.

"I don't feel good," Louis said.

"Neither do I, but Mama is in the living room driving me crazy, and you have to take her to the bank to cash her check."

Now that he remembered Mama was in the house, Louis began getting dressed. He couldn't go walking around half-naked in front of her.

"You gave Mama money?" he asked.

"Why, yes, I did because my big-mouth brother told her I had a lot of it. He also told her I was stalking a woman and might have killed a man. So now you'd better get up and get out of my sight, or I might have to permanently shut your mouth."

Louis winced as he fingered the staples in his forehead and then felt the gauze pads still stuck up his nose.

"Did you hear me, Louis? I'm talking to you," Reece demanded.

Louis turned around and then began looking for his shoes, muttering as he went. "Yes, I heard you. Do you really think I'm scared? Of you? Really, Reece? Do you?"

Reece was silent, momentarily shocked by Louis's abrupt dismissal of his threats, and then he threw his head back and laughed.

"You are so right, Louie! We're blood. Blood doesn't hurt blood, right, brother? But still…after you take Mama to the bank, you should go help them put Melissa's house back together. Only seems fair, since I'm the one who tore it up."

Now Louis was silent. It aggravated him that Reece's request actually made sense. In a way, it would be an apology from the family.

"Yes, I'll help," Louis said. Then he stumbled off to the bathroom, leaving Reece to consider his sins.

Pinky had dressed and packed before daylight. Now she was waiting at the kitchen table for someone to wake up when she heard the yelling. Her first instinct was to go settle the fuss, as she'd done so many times before, but then she stopped. What went on in that bedroom was best left alone. She just needed a check cashed and a way out of town.

When Louis finally made his way to the kitchen she was horrified by the sight of his poor face. He was a mass of bruising, healing scabs and runny scrapes, even worse than he'd looked yesterday, when the injuries were fresh. The staples just topped it off.

"Oh, Louis! Your poor face," she said. "Can I make you some breakfast? Maybe some oatmeal? That would be easy to eat…not much chewing."

"No, Mama. I'm fine," Louis said, as he poured

himself a cup of coffee from the pot she'd made earlier. He needed it to down a couple of painkillers.

Pinky eyed the long gray ponytail hanging down his back and wanted to suggest that he cut it, but she didn't. Obviously he liked it or it wouldn't be there.

"I heard you yelling," she said.

Louis nodded. "Reece woke me up. I didn't want to get up, but then I did."

"Why?"

He looked at her then, wondering why she always asked the obvious question when she already knew the answer. He wanted to do it, at least in part because no matter how much he talked back, Reece was always in charge. But there was more, too.

"Well, the woman Reece is stalking works at my job, so the employees are going to help clean up the mess he made at her house when he tried to get to her and stabbed the man instead. Reece wants me to go fix the window he broke, so I am."

Pinky's mouth opened but the words wouldn't come. This was so outrageous that she couldn't find a sensible response.

"Can you take me by the bank first?" she asked.

"Yeah, sure, Mama. So Reece came through for you, huh?"

She smiled, revealing the gap in her upper teeth.

"Yes, and there's enough to get my teeth fixed, too."

"That's good. I need to get a few tools to take with me, and then I'll be ready to go."

"Okay," she said, and went back into the living room to wait.

Louis came through a few minutes later carrying a small toolbox and wearing a work jacket. He unlocked the front door and then held it open so she could carry her things out.

"Thanks for the help," she said, sarcasm dripping as she staggered through the doorway with both bags.

"I'm hurt, Mama. It's going to hurt me even more today when I should be in bed. Reece causes trouble and I have to fix it. That's always the way it goes and yet you like him best. If you want help with your bags, ask Reece."

Pinky wouldn't look at him. She just kept moving, dragging one bag and carrying the other. She slung them in the back of the pickup bed again and then got into the cab as Louis eased in behind the wheel with a groan.

At that point she felt sorry for him again. He did look miserable, but this was all too much for her to handle, and the sooner she made her escape the better.

When they got to the bank drive-through, the teller wouldn't cash a check that large from a person who didn't have an account there, which meant Louis had to take her inside and vouch for her.

After a few minutes of explanation about her recent troubles and the fact that her son Reece, who *did* bank there, was giving her money to start over, Pinky left with a couple thousand dollars in cash in her purse and a cashier's check for the rest.

When Louis started to take her back to the house, she stopped him.

"No, no, son. Take me to the bus stop."

"Bus doesn't come through here again until Monday," Louis said.

Pinky moaned. She didn't want to go back to the house. She was afraid of what Reece might do.

"Then, take me to a motel. I'll stay there until Monday, okay?"

Louis didn't care what she did, and shrugged. "Okay."

They rode together for a few minutes in silence, and then, just before Pinky got out, she put a hand on Louis's arm.

"Will you please not tell Reece I'm still in town?"

Louis looked at her then and saw the fear in her eyes. "Okay, Mama. I won't tell."

"Do you swear?"

"Yes, Mama, I swear. Are you scared of him?"

She hesitated a moment and then nodded.

"Don't feel bad," Louis said. "So am I."

Pinky felt like there was more she should say, but Louis would see through it if she lied. "Thank you for the ride," she said.

"You're welcome, Mama. It was nice to see you again."

Pinky sighed. "Thank you, Louis. I'm so sorry you're hurt. I hope you get well soon."

Then she got out of the truck, took her bags from the bed and walked into the motel without looking back.

Louis put the pickup in gear and drove off, her presence already forgotten because that was how it had always been between them.

Lissa pulled up into the driveway of Paul Jackson's house and killed the engine. She hadn't been here since she and Mack were in high school, and for a moment she had that long-ago feeling of anxiety. Could they make love and be back at school by fourth period without anyone knowing what they'd done?

And then she heard Mack groan as he undid the seat belt.

"Oh! Wait a minute," she said, as she jumped out and circled the SUV to help steady his steps as he got out of the car.

"There's nothing wrong with my feet," he said, as she slid an arm around his waist.

"Humor me," she said as they headed toward the house, then up the steps, where she walked him inside.

"Want to lie down in your bed or on the sofa in the living room?"

"Bed, for sure, but I've got this," he said. He kissed her forehead before moving down the hall.

"I'll get our stuff," she said, as she ran back to get her bag and all his paperwork from the hospital.

When she got to the bedroom he was sitting on the edge of the mattress, still in his clothes.

"Okay, it was harder than I thought it would be," Mack said.

She combed her fingers through the thick, spiky length of his hair.

"How about you get into bed and I dig around in the kitchen to make something to eat?"

"I won't argue," he said, as he kicked off his shoes and stood up to take off his pants and shirt.

"I can help," she said.

There was a muscle jerking at the side of Mack's mouth as he eyed the curve of her breasts beneath her sweater and the way the fabric clung to her body, and then he groaned quietly.

"Melissa, if you come any closer we're both gonna be in trouble. I can't make love to you like I want, but

I will damn sure give it a try if you start taking off my clothes."

Lissa's gaze went straight to his crotch and then back up again. "Oh, good grief! You aren't sixteen any longer. Surely you have some control," she muttered, stomping out of the room.

He glared. He would have argued, but she was right. Truth was, he didn't want to be naked in front of her for the first time in years and too helpless to do anything about it.

He got the pants off okay, but getting out of the shirt was harder. He got it unbuttoned, but it was stuck on something on his shoulder and he couldn't figure out why. Frustrated, he just gave it a yank.

"Son of a bitch!" he yelped, as pain shot straight up the back of his neck and out the top of his head.

Lissa was in the kitchen when she heard him yell. She dropped what she was doing and stomped back up the hall, her eyes narrowed and her fingers curled into fists. She entered his room with her head up and her eyes flashing.

"Obviously, hotshot, you *do* need my help, and don't give me that hot-and-bothered excuse because whatever you did to yourself turned you white as a sheet."

"My shirt… I can't get it off," he said.

"Sit back down on the side of the bed and let me see," she said. He sat. "Oh, here's what's wrong. The tape came loose at one end of the bandage and stuck on your shirt. When you pulled, you were pulling the bandage off with it."

"Well, damn," Mack said.

A few moments later she had the shirt off and everything taped back down, then she paused and cupped his face in her hands.

"So this is awkward, but it's still us. Don't think you have to prove anything to me. You have already proved numerous times that you can rock my world, remember?"

He grinned, and then turned his head and kissed the palm of one hand.

"Yes, I remember, and I hear you. Pain is just as good as a cold shower."

She kissed him, softly and then longingly.

"Now rest. Let me do my womanly thing and bang pots in the kitchen."

He sighed. "And she's practical. When did that happen?"

"Twenty-second birthday. I had options. I could pull a double shift at the bakery where I was working or party with some friends, and I chose work. I needed the money."

He let himself look his fill of her face as she talked, thinking how beautiful she had become.

"You know, you still look like the girl I used to know, my Cindy Crawford look-alike, only prettier," he said.

She rolled her eyes as she helped ease him into bed and then pulled up the covers.

"I know love is blind, but I do not now, nor have I ever, looked like Cindy Crawford, except for this little mole by my mouth. She's five-nine and has long dark hair."

"Well, you look like her if she was five-three with curly blond hair."

Lissa laughed. "I'm going to the kitchen now and you're going to rest, confident that I know what I'm doing."

Mack slid a hand behind her neck.

She leaned down, and the magic happened.

The moment their lips connected, she moaned. It would have been so easy to strip naked and crawl into bed beside him.

Mack wanted her. "Lissa?"

She put a finger across his lips. "We have the rest of our lives. Now go to sleep."

The pain meds they'd given him before they left the hospital were pulling him under.

"Is that your teacher voice?" he asked.

"Your eyes are still open."

He closed them.

As she left, Lissa glanced across the hall into his dad's bedroom and felt a moment of such sadness that it was hard to breathe. If she hadn't been so insistent on getting her car back quickly, then he wouldn't have been working late. He would have come home, and he wouldn't be dead. But if he hadn't died, Mack wouldn't have come home and they wouldn't have been thrown together, and the opportunity to fix what her parents had done to them might never have happened. Life was such a mess—such a damned bittersweet mess.

She swallowed past the knot in her throat and went to explore the contents of the refrigerator. When she found a list on the center island of people who'd already brought food to the house, she remembered all the food people had brought to the house when her mama died. People in Mystic took care of their own.

Louis had already been to Melissa Sherman's house to measure the window in the back door so he could replace the broken glass and was back now with the goods to fix what his brother had ruined. Yes, it felt awkward moving around her kitchen, setting the window glass, adding the grout and calmly trimming it out, all the while knowing Reece had stormed through the room like the madman he could be.

He heard the women talking about the condition of her bedroom, and that she wasn't coming back to school until the stalker was apprehended and would be living with her boyfriend, who just happened to be the man Reece had stabbed.

The news that the man was still alive was the best news Louis had heard all day. But he still felt bad for Melissa Sherman because she'd had to take a leave from her job and had been forced to move out of her house temporarily, too afraid to stay alone in her own home.

He'd seen for himself the amount of blood that had been splashed all over the walls and floor. The level of shame he was feeling was so strong he had yet to look up. Even worse, the women kept bragging about him because he'd shown up to help even though he'd been injured. He didn't want them to talk about him. He didn't want anything but to get the job done and leave, and then Margaret Lewis saw him cleaning up the bits of glass and grout, and put her hand on his shoulder to stop him.

"We'll do that, Louis. You replaced the broken glass, and that's the one thing none of us could do. You go home and get some rest, and thank you so much for coming to help. Melissa will be so appreciative."

He could still feel the imprint of Margaret's hand beneath his jacket and struggled with the need to brush it away. He didn't like to be touched.

"Yes, ma'am," he said. He finished gathering up the tools he'd brought with him, and exited the house as fast as his aching muscles would take him, but he didn't want to go home. Reece would start pumping him for information, and he didn't want to talk to him. He'd known about Reece's prior behavior and disapproved, but he'd never personally known one of his brother's victims before, and the personal connection creeped him out. It made Reece seem like a criminal—a real bad-guy criminal who should be behind bars—and not his twin.

This was a terrible day in so many ways, and once again he was thinking about packing up and leaving, but he wasn't sure he could get away. He'd tried it once before and had been on his own for almost three weeks before Reece had just shown up one morning and settled in without an explanation as to how he'd found him. Still, things had changed. Even Mama was scared of Reece now. Reece had changed, and Louis wasn't strong enough to handle the violent stranger his brother had become.

So what to do?

In a rare moment of defiance, Louis drove straight to Charlie's Burgers and went in to eat lunch, choosing the company of strangers instead of home.

He had no more than sat down, accepted a cup of coffee and picked up a menu before he heard someone call out his name. He looked up and saw the principal, Mr. Wilson, waving. He nodded shyly and then looked back down at the menu, but he couldn't see the words for the fear that Wilson would come over and speak. If Louis wasn't taking orders from the man, they had nothing to say to each other. To his relief, the principal left him alone, and when the waitress came back he ordered their homemade vegetable soup and corn bread. It would taste good on this cold day and be easier to eat than something that took a lot of chewing. Now that he'd made the decision, he sat happily in the warmth, listening to the rumble of voices and the occasional outburst of laughter from another table. He couldn't remember laughing, but he remembered when Mama used to laugh. It was a sound without weight, like a feather. Crying was a heavy sound that pressed down on his chest, making it hard to breathe. He liked the sound of laughter better. When the waitress brought his food, she topped off his coffee and then informed him that his food had already been paid for by Mr. Wilson. He felt a little strange that he'd been given a treat and looked up, but Mr. Wilson was gone. Now he would have to remember to thank him when he went back to work on Monday.

Trey searched the back rooms at the precinct for more than two hours before he finally found the old accident report on his mother's wreck, and then he was disappointed by the lack of evidence and the minimal notes from the investigating officer.

He remembered the officer from when he was a kid, but the man had been dead for years, so there was no way to go back and question him.

When he called the hospital where they had been taken, he hit another dead end. The doctor who'd been on duty in the ER that night was in a nursing home suffering from Alzheimer's and had lost his ability to communicate years ago.

Other than the killer, Betsy was the only survivor

that he knew of, and she couldn't remember enough to help. In frustration, he pulled her journal out of evidence and began to read, making notes as he went.

The kitchen in the Jackson house was just as Lissa remembered. The cutlery was still in the same drawer and the dishes in the same place in the cabinets. It was like being in a time warp. Even the curtains were the same, just a little more faded by countless washings over the past ten years. It felt good to be here. She and Mack had made so many good memories in this house. Now she was ready to make some new ones.

She'd settled on reheating a bowl of beef Stroganoff and had noodles cooking on the stove to go with it. She'd taken a peach pie out to reheat and had a fresh pot of coffee brewing.

The day was sunny but cold, and as she worked she thought about her friends cleaning up her house. Until that broken window got fixed, it would be cold inside, and she felt bad they had to work in that.

She had rented a car to drive back and forth to work, but now that she wouldn't be going back for a while, she decided to turn the car back in to the rental agency and gave them a call.

The owner had heard about what had happened to her and was properly horrified on her behalf. After a brief conversation, he offered to pick up the car himself. He and an employee came by a little while later to pick up her check and the car keys, and then left to go to her house to retrieve the car, which was still in the drive.

Lissa was standing at the window, watching them drive away when the timer went off. That meant the pie was ready to take out of the oven. She glanced down the hall on her way to the kitchen, but the door to Mack's room was still closed.

She was getting ready to drain the noodles when she heard a knock at the door. She set them aside and went to answer, quickly recognizing one of her mother's oldest friends.

"Mrs. Sanford! It's so nice to see you. Please come in," Lissa said.

Frieda Sanford smiled as she handed over a plate of cookies and then took a seat on the sofa.

"These look wonderful. Thank you," Lissa said.

"I heard Mack was released from the hospital and wanted to bring a little something. I'm pleasantly surprised to see you here."

Lissa sat down beside her. "He got hurt trying to protect me, and I've been temporarily evicted from my own home because of a stalker. I'm sure you heard all the dirty details."

Frieda's smile faded. "Yes. It's horrible, what's happening to you. I would be terrified out of my mind."

"I was. I will be so grateful when he's caught and jailed."

Frieda nodded, but she'd come for another reason, and she needed to get it said. "You know, your mom and I were best friends."

"Yes, I know. She thought the world of you," Lissa said.

"When she was diagnosed with the brain tumor, she told me first. Of course, you weren't here, and with your father already passed and everything, I guess I was the obvious choice."

"I'm grateful she had you," Lissa said.

Frieda nodded. "Yes, well, about a month before Polly…your mom got to the point where she could no longer speak, she called me over one day. Just to visit, she said, but as soon as I got there, I knew there was more. It didn't take long for her to break down and start crying. She said she'd done a terrible thing to you and Mack right after you graduated, and that she needed to unburden herself before she died."

Lissa froze. All of a sudden she knew she was about to find out why her parents had gone out of their way to break her and Mack up. She took a deep, shaky breath and waited.

"It all had to do with something that happened to her the summer she graduated high school."

Lissa leaned forward, listening intently.

"She was getting ready to go away to college when she found out she was pregnant. She'd already broken up with the boy, so finding out was devastating. When she told him, he denied it—and her. Her parents reacted badly as well, and then made it worse. They sent her away to a home for unwed mothers and then used their religious beliefs as a lever, telling her it would shame their family and stigmatize the child if she raised a bastard. She caved in and put the baby up for adoption."

Lissa was stunned. "Oh, my God! Are you serious? I have a sibling somewhere?"

Frieda's shoulders slumped. "No, and that's part of why she did what she did later to you and Mack."

"What do you mean?" Lissa asked.

"She regretted the adoption almost immediately and tried to change her mind, but the courts wouldn't let her. The baby went to a couple in Miami, Florida, and then died before he was two from child abuse."

Lissa gasped. Her heart was hammering so hard she felt faint.

"Oh, my God, oh, my God," she whispered.

Frieda nodded. "The guilt nearly killed her. She met your dad a couple of years later, and they had a happy marriage and then they had you. She told me she thought she'd moved past all that guilt until you had the miscarriage. She said when they got the call from the hospital that you were losing a baby they didn't even know you were carrying, she freaked out. She said all her guilt and sadness came back, and what was happening to you felt like it was happening to her all over again. Then she felt she had to tell your father about her past, and he gave her a hard time about that. She said she did everything wrong for what she thought were the right reasons, but she knew after you two left for college in two different directions that she'd done you both a disservice."

Lissa was in tears. "I've been back in Mystic almost seven months. Why are you just now telling me this?"

Frieda's expression implored her to understand.

"I guess because I didn't know where to start. For all I knew you'd both moved on, and I didn't want to start something that might turn ugly for one or both of you. Can you understand that?"

"I guess… Yes, I do," Lissa said. "But why now?"

"When I heard that Mack was nearly killed trying to catch your stalker and that you came home from the hospital with him to help nurse him back to health, I knew there had to be something left between you. I'm not betraying your mother's confidence. I'm just telling you what she would have if she was still alive, okay?"

Lissa threw her arms around Frieda's neck and hugged her.

"You've answered a question that neither of us has been able to fathom. They knew we loved each other. I just couldn't understand why they lied."

Frieda patted her heart with relief as Lissa leaned back. "You don't know what a heavy burden this has been to carry. I'm so grateful to get it off my chest."

Lissa's eyes welled again. "My poor mother. What a tragic thing to carry all her life."

"I know it's none of my business, but are you and Mack going to renew your relationship? I know your mother would be pleased if you did," Frieda said.

"We already have," Lissa said.

"Oh, praise the Lord!" Frieda said. She then clapped her hands together as if that task was done and stood abruptly. "I need to be gone, and I'm sure you're busy. You don't know how good I feel now. This is a good day, a very good day."

Lissa got up and walked her to the door. "Thank you for the cookies and for the story. It's explained so much."

"You're welcome," Frieda said. "Be safe, the both of you. Bad things are afoot in Mystic now. I don't know what to make of it. Someone murdering good people, and now a stalker? Our little town has seen too much sadness lately."

Lissa stood in the doorway waving until Frieda Sanford had driven away, and when she turned around, Mack was standing only a few feet behind her wearing a pair of sweats and holding a zip-front hoodie.

"Oh, you're awake! I wish—"

"I heard it…all of it," Mack said. "Are you all right?"

Lissa sighed. "As sad as Mama's story is, I feel better knowing it because I was holding quite a grudge. It was the wrong thing to do, but I guess now I understand why."

Mack held out his good arm and pulled her close.

"I love you, Lissa. We have been given this second chance at happiness, and I will never again put off saying anything that's in my heart."

"I lived ten years without you in my life and grieved about half of that away before I finally accepted I was going to grow old without you."

Mack held her tighter. "I'm sorry, I am so sorry."

"So am I, Mack. Finding out it was my parents who broke us up was shocking. I never thought we would be together again, but I'm forever grateful that we are."

"Dad would be really happy about this," Mack said. "He left a letter for me in a safety deposit box, and the last part of it was about you."

Lissa's eyes widened. "Really? What did he say?"

"Basically, he thought we should make peace with each other. He always thought you were wonderful."

Lissa's eyes filled with tears again. "I love knowing that, but I'm still so sad. I will always hate that it was my car he'd stayed late for when this happened."

Mack wiped the tears off her face.

"No, baby, no. He was murdered on the job. The car could have been anyone's, and if it wasn't that night, it would have been another one. And if Trey Jakes' theory is right, his mother is also in danger."

"What? Why?" Lissa asked.

"I'll tell you about it over lunch, but it has to stay

between us," Mack said. He rubbed a thumb over the little mole above her lips, and then leaned down and kissed it. "For good luck, remember?"

"Yes, I remember…so much," she said softly.

Mack's gut knotted. He wanted her. It was the primal need of a man to claim his mate, but he was already feeling shaky. Damn the timing of all this.

Lissa saw the stress on his face and knew immediately what was wrong.

"You either come sit down in the kitchen or sit down in here. You choose," she said.

"In the kitchen with you," he said.

"Good," she said as she picked up the plate of cookies, and together they moved into the kitchen, where Mack quickly sat.

Lissa helped him get the hoodie on, then zipped it about halfway up.

"How's that?" she asked.

"Perfect."

She continued to chatter as she reheated the Stroganoff and finished draining the noodles. Mack sat in near silence, answering when needed, but mostly he sat and watched while trying to absorb the fact he was actually going to spend the rest of his life with her.

Louis drove home with his belly full of soup and corn bread, but his heart was heavy. Something had to be done about Reece. He sort of wished he'd talked to his mother about that, but she was gone, and he didn't want to go back and drag her into it. He parked and walked into the house in halting steps, just wanting to lie down until he felt better. The pain pills were in his bedroom, but the water was in the kitchen, so he made a detour.

He had the water in hand, ice clinking against the glass as he headed for his bedroom, with no thought in his mind but the pills. He downed them in one gulp, took off his shoes and jacket, and without bothering to undress, just stretched out on top of the bed and closed his eyes.

The silence was bliss, and then Reece started screaming. He could hear him coming, yelling at the top of his voice,

"Mama's gone! Where did you take her? She never even said goodbye. What the fuck kind of woman comes begging for money, then leaves without so much as a thank-you? I'll break her neck. I will break her fucking neck, so help me God!"

Louis groaned. He shouldn't have come home, but it was too late now. He rolled over and sat up on the side of the bed, his hands over his ears, as if trying to block out the noise.

"Don't you do that!" Reece yelled. "Take your damn hands down and listen to me. Where's Mama?"

"Gone. She didn't say where," Louis said.

"Why didn't you—"

"Stop screaming at me, Reece. I don't feel good. I hurt, and I need to rest."

"You were supposed to—"

Louis picked up the water glass and threw it across the room against a wall, splattering water and broken glass all over the floor.

Reece was so shocked, he stopped talking.

"Thank you," Louis said calmly. "I hate when you shout. I have been doing exactly what you told me to do. I helped clean up Melissa Sherman's house, and I want you to know, I have never been so ashamed in my life. The place looked like there was a riot inside. Blood and broken glass everywhere, and you tore up her things. You tore them up like they were nothing. She's a nice lady, and now she won't be teaching or living in her house again until you're arrested and put in jail."

Reece's eyes narrowed angrily. "What do you mean, she's not going back to school or her house?"

"Exactly what I said," Louis snapped. "No one would, you idiot. You've been stalking her, and you tried to kill her boyfriend."

"Boyfriend? She has a boyfriend?"

"Yes, the man you thought you killed—who, by the way you did not, and you better be glad. If you *had* killed him, I would have turned you in myself."

Reece snorted aloud. "Listen to your stupid self. You can't turn me in, and you know it."

Louis's eyes welled. "Go away, Reece. Go away. I don't feel like talking. I need to sleep."

"Fine, I'm leaving, but just remember, you try to fuck me over and I'll kill you first."

"Perfect," Louis muttered. "Go ahead and do it. I'm tired of you. I'm tired of this life. This life hurts."

And just like that, all the rage slid out of Reece's voice. "I'm sorry, Louie. I didn't mean it."

"Yes, you did, because you're bad. You're bad, Reece, and I'm tired. Go away."

Reece left. He couldn't face his brother after what he'd said. He would never kill Louis. They were twins, halves of one whole. Even if Louis didn't like him sometimes, he was the only one who understood him.

* * *

Pinky locked herself in her motel room and turned out the lights. She was in a precarious situation right now, and until she got out of Mystic, she could still wind up in Reece's mess. She took all the money out of her purse except for a hundred dollars in twenties, and hid nine hundred in cash on her person, putting some in her bra, some inside her panty hose and some inside her shoes. She hid the cashier's check and the other thousand in cash inside a small tear in the lining of her coat, and then pinned the tear together with a safety pin. She shoved a chair under the doorknob and then sat in the shadows, trying to figure out a way to get out of town without waiting two days for a bus.

Thirteen

The miracle of Mack and Lissa's reunion was how easily they fell back into the comfort of being in love. They ate their lunch together without worrying about embarrassing themselves as people did on first dates, then ate peach pie à la mode while laughing about the first time they'd made love.

"I didn't even have my pants zipped back up when Dad pulled into the drive," Mack said.

"And my bra was undone in the back, and I had to stuff my panties down the front of my pants because I didn't have time to put them back on."

Mack threw back his head and laughed. "Dad had to know something was up when he walked in, but he never said a thing. What I never told you was that before I went to bed that night he walked into my bedroom, dropped a half dozen condoms in the drawer of my nightstand and walked out without saying a word."

"Oh, my Lord, I would have died," Lissa said.

"You know what bothered me the most? The fact that he had them on hand."

Lissa's eyes widened as she got the implication, and then she burst out laughing.

"I didn't know your dad dated."

"Yeah, neither did I," Mack said, and then lifted his cup of coffee. "To Dad and his secrets. May they all come to light."

Lissa lifted her cup as well, as the seriousness of the moment overcame the earlier mirth. "To your dad." Moments later she set her cup down, reached across the table and took his hand. "They will figure out why this is happening and catch the killer. I have faith."

"God, I hope so," Mack said. "In the meantime, I need to make that call to my security company and get someone over here ASAP. Right now your safety is my top priority."

"I'll get your phone for you. Is it in the bedroom?"

"Yes, on the nightstand."

She left the kitchen in a run and returned moments later with the phone. Before she could hand it over, he grabbed her around the waist with his good arm and pulled her down into his lap.

"Just one knock-my-socks-off kiss and I promise I won't ask for more," he said, as he nuzzled the side of her neck.

"Don't make promises I don't want you to keep," Lissa said as she very carefully slid an arm around his neck and aimed for his mouth, then changed her mind at the last second and bit his lower lip instead. She followed that with a flick of her tongue to temper the nip, and then kissed him full-on while his lips were still parted in shock.

His eyes were still closed when she took his hand off her breast and handed him the phone.

"Love you, Matthew Jackson," she said softly,

Mack shivered as her sweet voice wrapped around his heart. "Love you, too—so much."

There was a lump in her throat as she began clearing off the table. If this was a dream, she didn't want to wake up.

Mack eased himself up from the chair and walked into the living room as Lissa began cleaning up. He sat down, scanned through his contacts until he found Cain's personal number. He got a recording when he made the call.

"This is Cain. Leave a name and number. If I like you, I'll call back."

Mack grinned. "Pick up, you jackass, it's me, Mack Jackson. I need help."

There was a click, and then a deep rumble in his ear. "So whose body did you bury in the cement this time?" Cain Embry asked.

"No one's yet, but if you find this son of a bitch, I'll furnish the cement free," Mack said.

And just like that, the joking was over.

"What's up, boss?"

Mack began to explain in detail because, for Cain, the devil was always in the details.

Cain was silent as Mack spoke, interrupting only when he needed clarification on something.

Then Mack stopped talking.

"Is that it?" Cain asked.

"Yes, it's everything we know."

"I'll be there in a couple of hours. Tell your lady I'll be her shadow, so she can go about her life without concern. I'll have her back."

"Thank you, buddy," Mack said.

"You're more than welcome. I'm sincerely curious to meet the woman who finally took down Summerton's most eligible bachelor."

Mack ended the call, then dropped the phone in the pocket of his hoodie and leaned back in his chair. When he'd first come home, it had hurt to be in this house alone. Now Lissa was in the kitchen doing dishes, the faint odor of his dad's cologne clung to the chair's fabric, reminding him to stand fast against what threatened to break them, and all he could think was that for these few moments, all was right with their world.

Betsy stood on the porch watching her son drive away, and when he was out of sight she went back inside, then stopped at the security panel and set the alarm.

"Are you scared, Mom?" Trina asked.

Betsy glanced over her shoulder, wondering how long Trina had been standing there. It bothered her that there was fear on her daughter's face.

"Oddly enough, now that I've admitted what's been going on with me, not so much."

Trina put her arms around her mother's neck and hugged her close.

"Well, I'm scared for you. I don't want anything to happen to you. You're the hub of our family. You mean everything to us."

"Please don't think like that, baby," Betsy said. "You know me. I fully believe that when it's my time to die, it will happen, no matter what. And I won't mind leaving this earth. I really miss your daddy. It will be wonderful to see him again."

Trina started sobbing, and Betsy knew it had as much to do with her breakup with Lee as it did the fear of losing her mom.

"Come sit down and tell me what's wrong between you and Lee. I thought you two had something special."

"Oh, Mom, so did I," Trina said, and sat down on the sofa beside Betsy. "It all started over nothing, and before I knew it he was accusing me of cheating. I kept trying to explain, but he didn't believe me. He ruined everything with his jealousy. Even if he tries to make up, I don't know if I want him back."

"What happened to make him think that?" Betsy asked.

Trina's shoulders slumped.

"I'm only going to tell you because you're the one person I trust to keep a confidence. One of the employees is stealing at work. My boss, Freddie Miller, has me checking inventory against the daily printouts, trying to find out how the inventory keeps disappearing. Elton, one of the guys at work, is always hitting on me, making jokes about stepping into Lee's shoes and into my bed, and when Lee came in to take me to lunch, he overheard part of what Elton was saying and said something to him. Elton lost his fucking mind and began talking about how good I was in bed. I socked him on the jaw, which was most ladylike, and then walked out of the shop. Lee decided I was angry at Elton for spilling the beans about my cheating and went ballistic. It hurt my feelings that he would believe it. I said stuff to him I shouldn't have said, and it just kept getting worse. I told my boss I was going home and, well…here I am, bawling my head off because men can be so damned stupid."

Betsy put her arm around her daughter's shoulders and pulled her head down into her lap just as she'd done countless times when Trina was small.

Trina wrapped an arm around her mother's knees and cried until she began to hiccup from the stress and strain.

Betsy hurt for her girl, just as she'd hurt for Trey, and just as she still grieved for Sam, her oldest. Of all her children, Sam was the most broken. He'd loved only one woman in his life and then walked away from her because of continuing episodes of PTSD. Betsy hadn't seen him in three years and often thought she was unlikely to see him again before she died. Trey was finally happy. Trina's heart was momentarily broken, but Sam was her failure. She didn't know how to fix him because Sam had stopped communicating.

However, Trina was her immediate concern, and right now there was one thing that Jakes women always did when shit was about to hit the fan. She patted Trina on the back.

"Move a second, honey. I need to get up."

Trina reached for a handful of tissues as she sat up, while Betsy went to the kitchen. A couple of minutes later she came back carrying a partial bottle of Jim Beam and two shot glasses.

She sat back down, poured whiskey to the brim of both glasses, handed one to Trina and picked up the other one.

"To stupid men and the women who love them," Betsy said.

"I'll drink to that," Trina said, smiling through tears as the sound of clinking glasses marked the moment of female camaraderie.

* * *

Cain Embry arrived in Mystic and located the address he'd been given, verifying it by identifying Mack's SUV in the drive. He scouted the neighborhood carefully, mapping the layout in his mind and taking note of unoccupied properties. Then he drove the area again, checking off what would be the most accessible escape routes for a perp.

Once it got dark, Cain noted that all the streetlights in front of the Jackson property were working, ditto the motion-sensor porch lights, and he put a tracking device under Mack's back bumper. It would help him keep track of Melissa when she left the house. The backyard had a six-foot privacy fence, but there was an access gate to the alley, and the lighting there was poor. When he slipped through the gate no lights came on. He got all the way to the back door without calling attention to himself and frowned.

Cain had accessed the DMV database for a picture of Melissa Sherman, so he knew what she looked like, but from the quick glimpse he'd gotten of her a few minutes earlier when she'd taken out the garbage, the photo did not do her justice.

He picked the lock on the door of the garden shed and set up shop right by the single window for the night. If anyone came into the backyard he would see them, and if Melissa Sherman left the house, he would be on her tail.

The late news had come and gone. Mack was propped up in bed struggling with his conscience.

He could hear water running in the bathroom down the hall, well aware Lissa was in there, wet and naked.

And then his thoughts would ricochet to his dad's body, or what was left of it, in some drawer at the morgue, cold and naked.

His emotions were so scattered. He felt such sorrow, and at the same time joy. Lissa was the constant—the anchor to the rest of his life. His dad would be happy about their reunion, which was why he didn't feel guilty for thinking about making love to Lissa in the midst of what should be a grieving period. He could just hear his dad's voice.

The dead have no need for grief. Life is for the living, so live it.

He swiped a shaky hand across his face as he heard the water stop. Fate had thrown them back together and kept him alive when he could have died. They had been given a second chance. Wasting it wasn't an option. But how the hell he was going to make this happen without one or both of them getting hurt again was a whole other story.

Then Lissa walked into the bedroom wearing a bath towel and a smile.

Lissa had seen the want in his eyes all through supper, known he was tracking every step she took with a hungry-hound gaze that made her ache. It had come to her during the shower that there was a way to ease their mutual misery.

"I have an idea," she said.

He groaned. "I had the same idea, but without a solution."

"If you can comfortably lie down on your back without moving, I have your answer," she said.

He eased himself down until the pillow was beneath his head instead of his back.

Her eyes narrowed warningly. "You have to promise not to move."

"Quiet as a mouse here," he said, but his heart was pounding.

"Are there still condoms in that nightstand?" she asked.

"Lord, I hope so," he said.

She sauntered over to the bed and opened the top drawer, then smiled.

"Bingo," she said as she dropped the towel and turned out the light.

"Sweet mercy," Mack whispered as she crawled up onto the bed beside him and pulled off his sweats.

He could see the outline of her body as his eyes adjusted to the dark, and he watched her crawl toward him.

"Remember, don't move," she whispered, and then she proceeded to kiss him senseless.

Her breasts brushed across his chest as she moved back and then straddled his legs. He was already hard, so when she suddenly took him in her hands, and then leaned down and took him in her mouth, he got lost in the sensation of warm and wet. One minute rolled into the next, and then all of a sudden she rose up, unrolled the condom down onto his erection and, without missing a beat, eased down until he was inside her.

Warm and wet turned into tight and hot, and he thought the top of his head was going to explode. He tried to open his eyes, but the pleasure was so intense he got only a glimpse of her head thrown back in ecstasy as she rode him to the climax of his life.

He was already in pieces when she came, but when he heard her moan, he remembered that sound. Seconds later the tremors of her climax rolled around and then through him.

Even after she'd collapsed beside him in a silent, quivering heap, neither of them spoke. His heart was still hammering too hard for him to breathe and talk at the same time, and Lissa was so sated she couldn't move.

"Am I still breathing?" she asked.

He felt the rise and fall of her breasts and groaned. With little coaxing, he could do that all over again.

"You're not only breathing, you're smokin'. That almost made up for the ten years without you."

Lissa threaded her fingers through his hand and then rested it on her belly.

"We have a lot to make up for," she said, and waited for the blood rush of her pulse to settle.

Finally she got up and went back to the bathroom, only to return with a warm wet washcloth. She climbed back on the bed, and proceeded to remove the condom and clean him up.

He watched the intensity on her face without knowing what to say, and then she left again. This time when she came back she was carrying a robe, which she tossed on a chair by the bed.

"I can sleep on the sofa if—"

"No. With me," Mack said, as he scooted over to give her access.

She crawled in and rolled over to face him.

"Do you remember calling me every night after you went to bed?" she asked.

He smiled in the dark. "Yes, baby, I do."

"Remember what you always said?"

He was glad for the shadows that hid sudden tears.

"That I loved you more than all the stars in the sky, and one day I'd say that when you were lying by my side."

"It's taken us a long time to get here, hasn't it?" she asked.

"We were together countless times in bed, but never to sleep, but as long as we draw breath, it's never too late," Mack said. He pulled her hand to his lips and kissed it.

Lissa laid her cheek against his shoulder and closed her eyes. The last thing she thought as she was falling asleep was that she would never sleep afraid again.

The killer was standing at his bedroom window, nursing a nightcap and thinking of how close he was to finishing what should have been done years ago. From where he was standing, he could see the outline of the mountains surrounding Mystic against the backdrop of the night sky. High up on the eastern slope he caught a glimpse of an occasional light flickering through the trees, probably a security light from someone's home.

He knew the general direction of Betsy Jakes' place, but it was on the flatland at the base of the mountain, and there were too many miles and trees in between to see it.

She was the one remaining witness between him and the success of which he dreamed. Something had to be done about her, and soon, but getting to her would require a little finesse. She was bound to be wary now, and while no one had the faintest notion of his identity, it wasn't as if they traveled in the same social circles. At the least, his appearance at her place would be viewed as strange.

He downed the last of his drink, and then took off

his robe and crawled into bed. As he did, he could hear footsteps in the hall outside his room. He wasn't in the mood for conversation, and quickly rolled over and turned out the light. He would figure out some way to make this work. He always did.

Reece waited until Louis was asleep before he slipped the keys out of his brother's pants pocket and sneaked out of the house, for once leaving Bobo behind. Yes, Louis had told him Melissa Sherman was gone, but he wanted to see for himself. He'd gone online and found the address of Paul Jackson's house with the intention of seeing for himself that she was really with Jackson's son.

When he drove past her place and saw the house in darkness and the car missing from the driveway, it made him mad all over again. He thought about a little more vandalism just to make a point and then opted against it. Too risky now that he'd upped his game.

It took him a little longer to find the Jackson residence in the dark, and even though the lights were off inside, the front porch light was on and there were motion-detector lights beyond that. He knew because he saw them come on as a cat ran across the yard.

He frowned as he drove past. This house would be more difficult to get into, and she would no longer be alone. It was only luck that he'd gotten away from that guy the first time, and he wasn't willing to try it again. His best bet would probably be catching her out of the house, but that would entail using the truck in the daytime. Louis would have himself a small fit, but he would get over it.

He certainly wasn't going to let it go. The relationship between him and Melissa Sherman had gone from sexual thrill to payback. She'd made him look bad, gotten away and holed up with another man. He intended to watch her beg and then kill her. Women like her didn't count.

A couple of hours later he was home with a take-out burger and fries from an all-night truck stop a few miles out of town. He let Bobo out and then got a plate and a bottle of ketchup, and sat down with his food. The steel-trap memory for facts and figures that kept him on the high side of investment profits was spinning. He was curious to see how his latest investment was faring and ate quickly.

Bobo began scratching at the door to come in. Reece grabbed a fry as he got up and then tossed it to the dog as he trotted inside.

"All for you, little guy," Reece said, and then laughed when Bobo caught it in midair.

He cleaned off the table, tossed the trash and headed for the computer with the dog at his heels. It was almost 4:00 a.m. He could get in at least two or three hours of good work before Louis woke up, maybe more, since today was Sunday.

"Run, Lissa. Storm's coming. Get in the cellar. Run, baby, run!"

Lissa's feet were flying, barely skimming the ground as she ran, her gaze fixed on her granny, who was standing at the top step of the storm cellar.

Mack was running beside her, shortening his stride so he wouldn't pull ahead.

The wind was blowing so hard. There was so much

debris in the air she could hardly see, but she could hear the terror in her granny's high-pitched voice.

All of a sudden her feet left the ground and she thought it was over, that she was going to die, only to realize Mack had picked her up, trying to save their lives.

He swung her around and into his arms as he lengthened his stride, holding her fast against his chest. Lissa wrapped her legs around his waist for balance and held on for dear life. Moments later they were in the cellar, the door locked fast, and her granny was hugging them both and crying as the tornado's roar was upon them.

"You saved her, son! You saved the both of you!"

"I had to, Ms. Daisy. I can't live without her."

Lissa sat up in bed, her heart pounding, tears running down her face as she looked at the man asleep beside her.

She hadn't thought of that day in years. A picnic at her granny's pond had almost ended in tragedy. It had been her sixteenth birthday, and if it hadn't been for Mack she wouldn't have lived to see her next.

Still rattled by the memory, she slipped quietly out of bed, putting on her robe as she walked down the hall and into the kitchen, then parted the curtains and looked out in the backyard, wondering where the security guard was hidden. Because of the overcast sky there was no visibility between her and heaven, but she knew in her heart her loved ones were there.

"Can you see us, Granny? He did it again. He saved me. Tell Mama and Daddy it's going to be okay. We're figuring it out."

All of a sudden she felt hands around her waist and

for a heartbeat relived that same feeling of weightlessness when she thought the storm had taken her. Then she turned around. "You're awake," she said.

She laid her cheek against the middle of his bare chest as his hands slid beneath her robe.

"I woke up and you were gone," he said.

"I had a dream...no, a nightmare. Remember the picnic at Granny's pond and the tornado?"

She felt him shudder. "Hell yes, I remember," Mack said. "I thought we were both dead."

Lissa leaned back enough to see his face. "You saved my life that day."

He shrugged. "I had no choice. I had promised your daddy I'd bring you home for supper, and my daddy taught me to never go back on my word."

Her eyes welled. "I wish they were still here so I could tell them how special you are."

"As long as you're okay, I'm okay," Mack said. "I'd kiss you right now, but it hurts to bend down."

"For you, I'll grow taller," Lissa said, and pulled him to the kitchen table, then climbed up on a little step stool.

The robe slipped off her shoulders as her breasts flattened against his chest.

When she locked her arms around his neck, he groaned.

"How's this?" she asked.

"As beautiful a thing as I have ever laid eyes on," he whispered, and then centered his mouth across her lips.

Outside, the sky toward the east was beginning to turn from black to a smoky gray. The sun was less than an hour from the horizon. If Mack had been able, he would have carried her back to the bedroom and made love until sunrise.

Lissa heard the catch in his breath and knew it was pain and not passion.

She pulled away from the embrace with one last lingering kiss and jumped down.

"You need your pain pills."

"I need *you*," he said.

"No, you *want* me. You *need* the pills," she said, and got a glass of water, then walked him back to the bedroom.

The room was dark, but the night-light down the hall by the bathroom shed enough light for them to see.

Mack eased down on the side of the bed as she set the water on the nightstand and shook two pain pills into his hand. He downed them gratefully and then stretched out on the bed as she began looking for clothes.

"It's a damn shame to put clothes on anything that beautiful," he said.

She paused and looked up. He was flat on his back with a growing erection.

She pointed. "Are you referring to all that?" she asked. "Or all this?" she added, as she turned to face him.

"Come to bed with me, Lissa."

The deep rumble in his voice made the ache in her belly deepen. She wanted him. There was no question about that.

"Same rules as before?" she asked.

A smile spread across his face. "You work? I watch?"

"Exactly," she said.

"I can do that," he said.

She dropped the underwear from her hand, got into bed with him and then got up on her knees. She stroked him until he was hard and pulsing, and then rolled a condom down onto his erection.

Mack's heart was pounding as he watched her mount him, joining them in one slow, sensuous stroke, then sitting with her head back and her eyes closed as her body adjusted to his girth.

He ran a hand down the length of her leg, wanting so badly to hold her, but she was still motionless. "Lissa?"

"You feel so good," she whispered, and then started to move.

Those words—the same words she'd said to him once before—rolled him backward in time.

Mack was laughing as he pulled her from the creek. She was wet from her hair to the water running out of her shoes.

"Are you okay, honey?" he asked.

She pushed the hair out of her eyes and then pointed at the three flat stepping-stones just beneath the surface of the water.

"Moss. That stuff is slick as snot."

Mack nodded, but he was already noticing the fabric clinging to her curves.

"Yeah, and you have one smokin' hot body under that wet T-shirt, girl."

"Mack," she sputtered as she tried to pull the fabric away from her skin, but to no avail.

"Hey, baby, you don't have to fuss on my account," he said.

He smirked, and that started it. She grabbed the tail

of her T-shirt and pulled it over her head, then unfastened her bra and let it drop at her feet.

The smile died on his face as his nostrils flared.

"Strip and lie down, smart-ass," she said. She gave him a little push in the middle of his chest.

Mack didn't know what was about to happen, but from his standpoint, it couldn't be bad. He stripped out of his clothes in seconds and stretched out on the ground, waiting to see what happened next.

She pulled off the rest of her clothes then knelt, straddling his legs and cupping his penis. It was already hard and straining. When she touched him, he jerked, then shuddered.

She glanced up at him. His eyes were glazed and fixed on her face. They'd never done this before, but he'd wanted to. She leaned down and licked the tip, and when she did, he groaned.

"Not laughing anymore, are you, Jackson?"

He watched as she closed her eyes and just held him. "Lissa?"

She sighed. "You feel so good," she said, and then she shook her head from side to side, water flying from her curls like rain.

When the droplets hit his heated body, he jerked again and moaned.

That was when she bent down and took him in her mouth. The high of being in control of his pleasure was heady. Finally his eyelids fluttered shut and his heartbeat was so fast he was sure she could see it pulsing at the base of his throat. And then she took him up and over so fast he lost his mind. By the time he came down enough to talk, she was sitting cross-legged beside him.

"Still feel like laughing?" she asked.

"All the way to the grave," he drawled, and pulled her into his arms.

Mack was feeling the same blood rush as before, only this time there was no grass beneath him or the bubbling sound of water over rocks, and she was the one in charge.

When he began to feel tiny muscles beginning to contract around him, he knew she was on the verge. He grabbed hold of her waist and pulled her down hard. The jolt shattered his concentration as he closed his eyes and let go.

Every muscle in Lissa's body was coiled and on the verge of a climax when Mack grabbed her around the waist and pulled her down. After that every conscious thought went flying as the climax rolled through her.

Reality hit only moments before she would have fallen on him. She reached out just in time, bracing herself above him with a hand on either side of his shoulders. Face-to-face, beaded in sweat and trembling, she leaned down and brushed a kiss across his lips.

He fisted his hand in her hair and pulled her back, kissing her again, harder and longer.

"I owe you some serious loving," he whispered when he finally let her go.

"I have every confidence you'll pay up," she said.

Fourteen

It was nearing noon, and Lissa had spent most of the morning writing lesson plans for her substitute teacher and emailing them to the school. She hit Send on the last set of plans, and then shoved the chair back from the kitchen table where she'd been working and got up.

She could hear the deep rumble of Mack's voice in the back of the house. He'd been on the phone most of the morning, dealing with work back in Summerton and reassuring his staff that his injuries weren't life threatening. Even though they had reconnected, between a killer and a stalker, their lives were still a mess.

She'd made a grocery list earlier, and started on her way to the bedroom to get her jacket and purse. The clothes she was wearing were comfortable for the fall weather—jeans and a sweater—but she could tell from the way the leaves were blowing out in the front yard that she would need the jacket.

She stopped off in the bathroom to check her makeup, or lack thereof, added a little lipstick and called it good.

Mack walked out of his dad's office as she left the bathroom. The lanky boy he'd been had grown into an imposing figure of a man. It made her a little weak in the knees as he came toward her.

"Going somewhere?" he asked, noticing the lipstick.

"Supermarket. Do you feel like riding along, or would you rather stay here?" she asked.

In the back of his mind he knew Cain Embry would be on her tail regardless of where she went, but he still didn't like the thought of letting her out of his sight.

"I'll ride with you," he said.

She eyed the zip-front hoodie he had on and then zipped it up a little higher. "It's cold outside," she said.

"Thank you, baby," he said, and he kissed the mole above her lips. "For good luck," he added.

She laughed. "You don't have any need for good luck. You just wanted to kiss me."

"Guilty," he said as he followed her out the door.

Louis had been up since before daylight, wrestling with his conscience. He'd had an argument with Reece in the night that had lasted through the wee hours of the morning, and he was scared. Reece had slipped over the edge of reason. He was so fixated on getting even with Melissa Sherman that he seemed oblivious to anything Louis had to say.

Louis knew what it meant to aid and abet in a crime. Mama had told him all about it the last time this had happened. She'd told him that if someone knows about a crime that's going to be committed and does nothing to try to stop it, then they were considered just as guilty as the one who did the deed. The fact that he actually knew Melissa Sherman made it worse. She was a nice woman and a good teacher, and she was always kind to him. He didn't want anything to happen to her, and Reece wanted her dead.

He knew what he had to do and knew it wasn't going to be easy. Reece was still awake. He hadn't gone to sleep in the daytime like usual, and Louis knew in his gut something bad was going to happen, maybe today. In a panic, he sent a text to Pinky. He needed her to understand instead of second-guess why it happened.

Pinky Parsons had slept in, skipped breakfast and was having a pizza for brunch. The delivery boy had just left, and she was halfway through her first slice when her phone signaled a text. She wiped her fingers and then reached for the phone. When she noticed it was a text from Louis she frowned. Louis was never the one who ever initiated contact. And then she read the text and began to shake.

"Damn it all to hell," she mumbled as she quickly called Louis's number. He answered on the first ring, as if he'd known she would call.

"Mama?"

"Yes, Louis, it's me! What do you mean, Reece wants that woman dead?"

"It's what he said. We argued most of the night. I didn't sleep and now he won't. He's going to do something bad to her, and I have to stop him."

Pinky's heart skipped a beat. "What do you mean, you have to stop him? You *can't* stop him. He's—"

"I'm the *only* one who can, Mama, and you know it. I just wanted you to know now instead of trying to figure out what went on later. I know you don't love me, but I know you tried. There's a will in the lockbox in the closet. All of Reece's money will go to you."

Pinky was starting to panic. "Louis, stop! You're talking like—"

"Like Reece and I are going to die? Well, we are, Mama. Both of us."

The disconnect in Pinky's ear was as final as Louis's last sentence.

"Oh, no, no, no," she began mumbling as she called 911.

"911. What is your emergency?" the dispatcher asked.

"My son is crazy and threatening to kill someone."

Louis looked around to make sure Reece was nowhere in sight, and then got his handgun out of the closet and slipped it into the inside pocket of his jacket.

"What are you doing?" Reece shouted.

Louis was so startled by Reece's sudden appearance that he almost stumbled. "Getting a pair of shoes," he said as he grabbed a pair of tennis shoes. He sat down on the side of the bed and began putting them on.

"I need the truck keys," Reece said.

"Why?" Louis asked.

"I just need them, that's why."

"Well, I was already planning to use the truck. We're out of groceries, and I'm going to the supermarket."

"You can buy food anytime. I need it *now*."

Louis tied his last shoe and then stood up. "To do what? Hurt Miss Sherman? No! I won't let you!"

Reece slammed a fist against the wall and screamed,

"This isn't how things work. You don't tell me how to live my life, and I don't tell you how to live yours."

Louis was scared—as scared as he'd ever been in his life—but he stood his ground.

"You're the one who's breaking rules. You sleep in the day and I use the truck, then you use it when I sleep at night."

"But I need it today!" Reece said, starting to whine. "Just this once, Louie. Come on. It's important."

"You just want to hurt Melissa Sherman."

Reece began shaking. "I don't want to, but I have to. She cheated on me. She's shacked up with another man, and I need to make her understand she can't do that."

Louis's eyebrows knit. "You're crazy, Reece. I feel real sad that you've turned into this bad person, but I'm not going to let you hurt her or anyone else again."

Reece was shocked. Louis always gave in. This was the first time he'd ever stood his ground and argued back. He needed to go at him another way.

"Fine. We'll go together. You shop for groceries, and I'll bring you home and use the truck afterward."

Louis shrugged. He couldn't forcibly restrain Reece because his brother was too strong, which only reinforced what he believed he had to do. "So let's go. We need a lot of stuff. I haven't shopped in over a week."

Louis's steps were slow and plodding as he walked out of the house. He paused in the yard and turned around, giving the place one last look. He'd liked his job here in Mystic, and he liked this house. It had been a good place to live—until Reece had messed everything up.

Reece waited impatiently, but he didn't argue. He'd pushed Louis enough for now.

* * *

After receiving the call from the 911 dispatcher, Avery Jones, Trey headed to the Parsonses' residence, with Earl following behind him. The information Pinky Parsons had given Avery was a little sketchy, but when murder was involved, waiting for details could mean the difference between life and death.

They arrived on the scene within minutes of the call, only to find the house empty and the truck gone. Trey ran back to his cruiser to get the rest of the information on the woman who'd called.

Trey got the number and quickly called.

A woman answered. "Hello?"

"This is Police Chief Trey Jakes. Am I speaking to Pinky Parsons?"

Pinky started to shake. "Yes, sir."

"Did you make a phone call to 911 regarding your son Reece Parsons?"

"Yes, I did. Did you find him? Did you stop him?"

"There was no one at the residence. Would you happen to know where he is?"

Pinky started to moan. "Oh, my God, oh, my God."

"Ms. Parsons, I need you to think. Where might he be?"

She choked on a sob. "I heard him talking about a woman. I think he was trying to date her or something, but it was more like stalking her."

Trey stifled a gasp as the hairs rose on the back of his head. He had a sick feeling he was about to find out the identity of Melissa Sherman's stalker.

"Do you know the woman's name?"

"No. Only that she's a teacher here in town."

Shit. "I want to verify that your son Reece Parsons is the person in question. Is that correct?"

"Yes."

"And you have no idea where he might be?"

"None, unless he's gone to find that woman."

"What is he driving?" Trey asked.

"A black pickup truck. I don't know the tag number. It's an older model GM with a silver toolbox against the cab and a big dent in the bumper. That's all I know," Pinky said.

"Thank you. I'll be in touch," Trey said, and disconnected.

Pinky was sick to her stomach. She'd told them all she could, though none of that would help them understand why Reece was made the way he was. She didn't know how to explain what she didn't even understand. Heartsick and terrified of the outcome, she threw herself onto the bed and began to sob.

Trey disconnected as soon as he had all the information Pinky knew.

"We have a problem," he muttered, as he ran the name Louis Parsons and the make and model of the truck through the DMV to get a tag number. As soon as it came back, he had Dispatch relay the info to all deputies on duty and hoped to God someone spotted the vehicle before it was too late. Then he picked up his cell phone. He needed to give Melissa Sherman a heads-up.

Melissa pulled up in front of the supermarket, parked and grabbed her list.

"I won't be long, honey. Will you be okay for a bit?"

"I'm fine," Mack said. "I have some calls to make anyway. Take your time."

She blew him a kiss and jumped out of the SUV.

She was all the way across the parking lot before Mack noticed she'd left her phone. He started to get out and catch up with her, but by the time he looked up she was already inside. Knowing Cain would be somewhere close by, he let it go.

Louis's head was spinning as he drove to the supermarket. He had to find the right moment and the right place to end the chaos without giving Reece the upper hand. This shopping trip would give him time, which he desperately needed. If he pulled the gun out right now and tried to end it, there was nothing to keep Reece from taking it away. He needed Reece to be preoccupied. Maybe Reece would get bored when he went in to buy groceries. Just a few seconds without Reece looking over his shoulder was all the time Louis needed.

He parked near the side entrance and got out, ignoring Reece's presence. His legs were shaking and he felt sick to his stomach, but he had to stay calm or Reece would know something was wrong. Reece was smart like that. Louis knew he was less of a man than his brother, but he wasn't mean, and he wasn't crazy. Today he had to be the hero. Maybe for once Mama would be proud.

He grabbed a shopping cart and began pushing it through the store, up and down aisles, picking up the things they normally used. It was all going to be wasted when they were dead, but that didn't matter.

Two boxes of cereal. Always sugarcoated.

A bag of apples.

A six-pack of Coke for Reece and one of Dr. Pepper for him.

Two pounds of hamburger meat. He could make that tomorrow when…

He paused, then put back the meat because he'd gotten carried away. No tomorrows.

He thought about cheese. He always bought cheese. Reece would wonder why he'd skipped the cheese. He wheeled the cart around and headed toward the back of the store to the dairy department, and the moment he rounded the corner in front of the milk case and saw Melissa Sherman he wanted to cry. He'd tried so hard to save her, and instead he'd delivered Reece into her lap.

"Well, look who's here," Reece drawled.

"No, Reece, you can't—"

"Shut the fuck up, Louis. Go away. Now!"

Reece grabbed the grocery cart and aimed it toward the woman, knowing full well she wouldn't be afraid. She wouldn't run. In her eyes he was Louis, the man who swept the floors where she worked. He was in like Flynn, and she would never see it coming.

He kept moving closer, closer. The blood rush was so strong he felt invincible.

Hot damn, she sees me. She's smiling. I knew it, I knew it. She thinks I'm Louis. Son of a bitch, this is going to be a piece of cake.

Then Reece heard Louis shouting, "Run, Melissa! Run!"

Reece froze. "Louis! Damn it! I told you to get lost!"

Melissa was staring.

Louis gathered every ounce of energy he had left

and began screaming as he ran, "Run! Run! He wants to kill you!"

When Melissa Sherman turned and ran through the double doors leading into the back of the store, Louis felt faint with relief. He'd done it! She was on her own, but she wouldn't be taken unaware.

Reece was running now, past the display aisle with the butter and cheese on sale, shoving aside a shopping cart and the woman pushing it as he went.

"I'm going to catch her, and when I'm done with her, I'm going to kill you, Louis. I swear to God, I am going to kill you!" he screamed.

Cain Embry was on the far side of the dairy section. He appeared to be shopping for yogurt, but in fact his whole focus was on Melissa Sherman. He watched all the people coming and going around her without concern until he saw a stocky, middle-aged man talking to himself, and then all of a sudden he was heading toward her, and something about the way he was moving said trouble.

Then he saw Melissa look up at the man and smile. When she did, he stopped. Then all of a sudden the man started running toward her and screaming. Before he could react, Melissa turned on one heel and shot through the doors behind her with the man only a few yards behind.

What the hell?

Cain ran forward, dodging two aisle displays and three women with shopping carts, hitting the double doors with both hands as he ran.

Mack glanced at his watch and then back up at the front door, willing Lissa to appear when her cell phone rang. He glanced at the screen to see who it was and answered.

"Hey, Trey. This is Mack. Lissa is in the supermarket."

"You need to find her and get her under wraps. We have reason to believe her stalker is after her as we speak, and that's not all. We know who he is."

Mack was already out of the car and hurrying toward the store, ignoring any and all stiffness and pain.

"His name. What's his name?"

"Reece Parsons. All we know is he's average height, middle-aged and stocky, with a long gray ponytail."

"I have private security tailing her, but I'm on my way inside, too. I'll call when I have her home."

Trey started to speak and then stopped. "Hang on. I'm getting info that his truck has been—oh, shit."

Mack was only yards from the entrance. "What's wrong?"

"One of my officers just radioed in that the Parsonses' truck has been located at the supermarket. We're on our way."

Mack dropped the phone in his pocket and started to run. He burst through the front entrance and raced past the checkout stations, looking down each aisle as he passed. He was halfway along when he caught a glimpse of her at the far end of the store and then saw the man running toward her. He took off down the aisle, dodging shoppers and shouting her name as he went.

Lissa was running through the swinging doors into the back of the supermarket, darting past a pallet of produce and screaming, "Help me!" when all of a sudden someone grabbed the back of her jacket and spun her around. She saw a fist coming at her, and then everything went black.

Reece threw her over his shoulder on the run, heading for a door marked Exit about fifty yards away.

A woman opened the door to the public bathroom and was walking out when Reece slammed it back shut on her. He heard her cry out in pain and kept on running.

Then gunshots!

"What the fuck?" he said, and spun.

A big man with a shaved head and a grim expression had a gun pointed straight at them, and there was another man coming up behind him, wearing jeans and a hoodie.

"If you take one step toward me, I'll break her neck. If you shoot, you're going to hit her, too!" Reece shouted. Then he realized the man in the hoodie wasn't stopping.

Mack flew past Cain without hesitation, and when he did, Reece turned and ran with Lissa's limp body still over his shoulder, only she was dead weight, slowing him down. He took a side step toward a wall jutting out to the right and swung Lissa's body like a baseball bat.

"Nooo!" Mack screamed, watching in horror as she hit the wall with a hard, solid thud and slid lifelessly down onto the concrete while Reece disappeared around the corner.

Seconds later Mack was down on both knees, checking for a pulse as Cain skidded to a halt beside him.

"Is she—"

"I have a pulse. Call an ambulance!" Mack said, but

before Cain could get the phone out of his pocket, police were swarming into the area with Trey Jakes leading the pack. He saw Lissa on the floor and stopped as the others ran past him.

"Is she all right?" Trey asked.

"She's breathing. That's all I know," Mack said.

"I'm calling an ambulance," Cain said, and moved away from the noise to make the call.

"Get her out of the line of fire," Trey said. "We have the back doors blocked. He can't get away, but he may be armed."

Mack didn't hesitate as he scooped her up and ran toward a pallet filled with bags of dog food, then ducked down behind it. Cain was right behind him, and as soon as Mack stopped, Cain put himself between them and further danger.

"You okay, boss? Your shoulder is bleeding." With his gun in one hand and a phone in the other, Cain ducked down beside them as the shouting around them got louder.

Mack felt blood running down his back, but it didn't matter. They'd fixed him up before. They could do it again. He just wanted her to wake up.

"It's nothing," he said as he began feeling along the back of Lissa's head. He winced when his fingers came away bloody.

"Oh, God. She's bleeding," he said.

Reece was trying not to panic as he ran. The delivery door was in sight, and he knew the truck was parked at the side of the store, not far away. He would be in it and gone before the cops knew what happened.

And then the delivery door opened.

The moment Reece saw uniformed officers coming in, he skidded to a stop, then started back the other way, only to see more cops coming at him from that direction. He was caught in a narrow hallway with no way out.

"Son of a bitch!" he screamed.

That was when Louis suddenly reappeared.

The cops were yelling at Reece to stop and get down on his knees when Louis pulled the gun out of his inner pocket and began shouting at Reece, too.

The cops froze, uncertain as to what was happening. All of a sudden the man they were after was talking to himself in two different voices. One voice was loud and angry, and the other one was scared and crying. The crying man kept putting the gun up to his head, and then the loud angry man would shout, "No!" and slap it away.

Trey was beginning to realize the man was mentally unbalanced. He was behaving as if he was two different men. Trey wasn't entirely sure what was going on, but he knew the man had a mother and called on that knowledge when he shouted his name.

"Louis! Louis! Put down the gun! Your mama called us. She doesn't want you hurt."

But he didn't respond, and Trey wasn't sure what to do next.

Louis was sobbing and yelling.

Reece spun toward the cops, trying to wrestle mental supremacy from Louis in order to get control of the gun, but Louis wouldn't let go. He was screaming so loudly that Reece thought his eardrums were going to burst.

"Stop it, Reece! Stop it now! I'm not going to let you hurt anyone else. Not ever again!" Louis cried.

Reece was panicked. "Where did you get that gun? How come I didn't know you had a gun?"

Louis kept crying. "You wouldn't listen. I kept telling you it was wrong, but you wouldn't listen."

The employees working in the back of the store and socializing in the break room began opening doors and peering out to see what was going on.

"Get back inside and get down on the floor!" Trey yelled, waving his own gun.

They didn't have to be told twice. They all ducked back inside and shut the doors.

The argument between Louis and Reece was spiraling out of control. It was as if they'd forgotten about everything except themselves.

Reece was begging. "Don't, Louie, don't! You can't kill me, you *can't!*"

Louis took a deep shuddering breath. "Yes, I can, Reece, because *you* killed *me.*"

And then Louis put the gun to his temple and pulled the trigger.

The bullet blew through his head, shattering bone, and scattering blood and brains onto the wall behind him.

Trey felt sick as he turned away. There'd been no stopping this.

Fifteen

Lissa was still unconscious when they reached the ER. Mack was scared, as scared as the day he'd driven to her house to ask if she'd had an abortion, and he felt the same horrible uncertainty now.

He already knew he was going to have nightmares about watching her body hit that wall and not being able to get to her fast enough to save her. And now that the shock and adrenaline were fading, he was starting to feel the pain of what he'd done to himself.

As they were assessing Lissa's injuries, one of the nurses saw the fresh blood on his hoodie, and before he knew what was happening they'd taken him into the next bay and removed the hoodie he was wearing. Once they saw the evidence of recent surgery, and despite his argument that he needed to be with Lissa, they set out to repair the reopened shoulder wound.

"Just tell me what's going on next door," he begged.

"They're still examining her," the doctor said.

"Is she still unconscious? Just tell me that much."

"In a few minutes you can go see for yourself," the doctor countered.

Mack was heartsick. He'd hired security to keep her safe, but even that hadn't been enough to stop a madman. He took a deep breath and closed his eyes as the doctor began working on his shoulder. A few minutes in, he got a one-word text from Cain.

Sorry.

"Damn it," he muttered, swallowing past the lump in his throat. Not being able to keep her safe was troubling Cain as much as it was him.

"Bad news?" the doctor asked.

"The only bad news I'm dealing with is what happened to my girl."

"She had a stalker, I hear?"

"Yeah."

"Did they catch him?"

Mack thought about what Trey had told him while they were waiting for the ambulance.

"He killed himself," Mack said, then he turned his head, trying to see what the doctor was doing. "Are you about finished?"

The doctor nodded. "As soon as the nurse redresses this you'll be good to go. You can fill in the pertinent information as you sign out."

The moment the nurse finished putting a bandage over the wound, Mack grabbed his hoodie and stood up. She tried to hand him a clipboard, but he shook his head.

"Uh-uh. You already have my pertinent information from a couple of days ago when they brought me in here with this same wound. Nothing has changed. I need to get back to Lissa."

He walked out of one bay and back into the other as a tech and a portable X-ray machine came out. The doctor who had been working on her was gone, and a nurse was adjusting a drip.

The obvious change was that she now had an IV, was wearing a hospital gown instead of her clothes and had a couple of blankets pulled up to her waist.

He threaded his fingers through hers as he glanced up at the blood pressure reading. "Did she wake up yet?"

Lissa's fingers tightened on his as he spoke.

The nurse smiled and nodded, and relief rushed through him as he looked down. "Lissa? Honey?"

Her eyelids fluttered. "Mack?"

He felt like crying. "Yes, baby, I'm here."

"I hurt."

He looked up at the nurse. "Her head was bleeding. Did it need stitches?"

"No. It was a small cut. We glued it, and now we're waiting on X-rays."

Mack rubbed the knuckle of her thumb. "I'm sorry. I thought I could protect you," he said.

Tears rolled from under her eyelids. "I worked with him every day, and he stalked me every night."

"I'm sorry, honey," Mack said, and then he bit his lip as a wave of pain rolled across his back.

The nurse glanced at him, and then pushed a chair up behind him and pointed.

Grateful that she was so observant, he sat.

Lissa continued slipping in and out of consciousness, which kept him somewhere north of panic. It was almost an hour before the doctor returned.

Mack stood.

"Mr. Jackson, right?"

"Yes. What can you tell me about Melissa's injuries?"

"We x-rayed her head and her spine. Everything is intact, and there are no broken bones."

"Oh, thank God," Mack said.

"But she has a concussion, so I want to keep her overnight." The doctor eyed the blood on Mack's hoodie. "What about you?"

"I just pulled a couple of staples loose. I'm good."

"You already had staples?"

Mack sighed. "It's a long story."

The doctor frowned. "Then, I suggest you go home and rest. She's not going to know whether you're here or not."

"But I'll know," Mack said.

The doctor's frown deepened. "Look, we don't have many patients right now. I'll have them put her in a room with two beds. I assume you were taking meds?"

"At home."

"What are you taking?"

Mack told him what the doctor had prescribed.

"I'll check with your doctor and see if he'll okay us to dispense them while you're here with her, and if you use one of the beds, I won't argue with your decision."

"Deal," Mack said.

"They'll move her shortly. In the meantime, get off your feet."

Mack scooted the chair closer to the bed and then eased down and leaned back. It was going to be a long night.

Pinky was still in her room staring at the door, dreading the inevitable knock. She'd heard the police and ambulance sirens, and suspected the worst. They could be responding to a totally unrelated incident, but she guessed they'd found the truck.

She didn't know how to feel, and it had been too many years since she'd prayed. In her heart, she feared Reece would prevail, which meant he would either kill the woman he was after, then get caught and go to jail, or get away and live to cause chaos elsewhere. On the other hand, if Louis did what he'd said he would do, she would have one more child to bury. It hurt to breathe and she was too scared to cry, so she waited.

One hour passed, and then a second hour. It was nearing midafternoon, and she had finally fallen asleep from exhaustion when someone knocked. At first she thought she was dreaming, and then they knocked again and she heard them saying, "Mrs. Parsons. Mrs. Parsons, are you there?"

She scrambled out of bed and stumbled to the door, oblivious of the mashed-flat side of her hair where she'd been lying and the mascara smudged beneath one eye.

Trey Jakes saw the fear on her face. "Mrs. Parsons, I'm Chief Jakes. We spoke earlier. May I come in?"

She stepped aside, then shut the door behind him as he entered.

"So did you find him?" she asked.

Trey sighed. "Yes, ma'am, and I want you to know that your call saved a woman's life."

Pinky's belly knotted. "Did you arrest him?" she asked.

Trey shook his head. "No, Mrs. Parsons. I'm sorry to inform you that your son took his own life."

Pinky thought she'd been prepared for those words,

but when she heard them she moaned and staggered backward.

Trey caught her before she fell and settled her down onto the side of the bed.

"I can't believe Louis actually did it. I thought for sure Reece would win out."

Trey didn't know how to begin, so he just launched in. "Look, it became obvious to all of us that your son had some kind of mental illness. He kept yelling and crying and arguing with himself. Was he schizophrenic?"

She reached for a tissue and blew her nose, glanced up at the cop and then down at a bare spot on the rug.

"Forty-two years ago I gave birth to twin boys. Reece and Louis. Reece was oldest by five minutes, and strongest. Louis was weak and sickly. When they were eight, Reece came in one day and told me Louis wasn't breathing. I ran out and found him facedown on the ground, his face mashed into the mud. His death was ruled an accident, but my husband said different. He said Reece had the sickness—the bad blood that ran in his family. He said Reece had killed Louis, and then he went into the garage and hanged himself."

Trey was shocked. "Your husband… Lord. Did you believe him?"

She drew a deep, shaky breath.

"Not at first, but then, as the years went by… When Reece was thirteen, he came into the house one day, talking. I thought he was talking to me, but he said no, he was talking to Louis, and then this other voice came out of his mouth and it was Louis to a T. I didn't know what to make of it and didn't have the money to take him to any doctors, so over time it became the three of us instead of the two of us. Reece began to develop an obsession with women and Louis was afraid of them, and that's how they've been all these years." Silent tears rolled down Pinky's cheeks. "So now I bury him."

"Louis's truck was in the supermarket parking lot. I had one of my deputies drive it here for you." He dropped the ring of keys into her hand. "It wasn't part of the crime scene, and neither is his house. I believe he was renting that place, so you're free to remove his personal effects. I wouldn't wait too long. The land-lord will be doing it for you if you don't."

Her fingers curled around the keys as she remem-bered Louis's words. *There's a will in the lockbox in the closet. All of Reece's money will go to you.*

She didn't know how she felt right now, but happy about coming into money wasn't part of it. She looked up, seeking some kind of absolution for her family.

"I don't know how to feel. My son tried to murder someone and now he's dead, but there was a small part of him that struggled to be good." She wiped away the tears and, in true Pinky fashion, got down to business. "Will I be notified when his body is released?"

"Yes. I gave the authorities your contact informa-tion."

She fingered the key ring, glad the cop hadn't asked her if she had a license. "Thank you for bringing me his truck."

"You're welcome. I'm sorry for your loss, and I'll let myself out," Trey said.

Pinky followed him to the door and turned the dead bolt after he left, then faced the room. She'd come to Mystic for a handout and instead had become the catalyst for her son's death. Fate could be a cruel bitch. Pinky knew that better than most.

Her heart was pounding and her belly rolling as she felt the food coming back up her throat. She staggered to the bathroom and threw up until she could no longer stand, then dropped to her knees and held on to the toilet bowl until her belly was as empty as her soul.

Mack's sleep was restless. The nurses kept coming into the room every few hours to wake Lissa. It was part of the process of caring for a concussion by making sure the victim hadn't slipped into a coma.

The thought of that even being a possibility kept him so anxious he couldn't relax. He was lying on his side facing her bed so that he could see her face as she slept, and the sight was a vivid reminder of what she'd endured.

A dark bruise had appeared on the side of her forehead, and her lower lip was swollen and cut. The sight made him sick to his stomach, and yet he couldn't turn away. Then his eyes grew heavy and without intending to he fell asleep. He woke abruptly to the sound of Lissa crying.

He rolled out of bed so fast he forgot he was hurt. Pain ripped across his shoulder as he stumbled toward her just in time to hear what she was saying.

"Call Mack, Mama. Call Mack."

Oh, hell, she's dreaming about the miscarriage!

"It hurts, Mama."

He took her hand and leaned a little closer. "I'm here, baby."

But Lissa was still locked into the dream. "Mama, did you call him?"

The tears were killing him. He turned loose of her hand and cupped her face.

"I'm here, Lissa, I'm here. Open your eyes, baby. See me. See my face."

Lissa gasped as if she'd been drowning and just reached the surface. Her eyes were open, but he didn't think she saw him.

He bent over and kissed the mole above her lip. "For good luck, baby."

She shuddered. "For good luck," she whispered, and then she blinked, saw his face and sighed. "You came."

Blaming her confusion on the concussion and pain, he saw no need to challenge where her thoughts had gone. She just needed to know he was there.

"Yes, I'm here."

Her features twisted from the emotional agony of where she'd been. "The baby…"

"I know, sweetheart, I know. There will be others. Just rest and get well."

"So sorry," she whispered as her eyelids fluttered shut.

He stood for a few moments to make sure she'd moved past that dream, feeling shattered by the brief glimpse of what she'd endured without him.

A couple of minutes passed, and then a nurse came in on her rounds and saw him standing at Lissa's bedside. "Is everything okay? How is her pain level?"

"She woke up. She was having a bad dream," he said.

The nurse nodded. "After what she went through, I'd be having bad dreams, too. If you'll step back a bit I'll just check her vitals and be out of your way."

Sleep was over for Mack, so he went up the hall to

the waiting area to get a cold drink from one of the vending machines, looking for something with caffeine. The last time he and Lissa had eaten was at breakfast, so he got a Pepsi and a packaged sweet roll, and headed back to the room.

The nurse was gone. The night-light was on in the adjoining bathroom, and Lissa seemed at peace as she slept. He walked to the window and opened the shades enough to see out as he ate. When he'd finished, he threw away his trash and pulled a chair up near her bed.

It was nearly four in the morning.

His eyes were burning from lack of sleep. His shoulder was one miserable ache. But none of it would matter if Lissa woke up on the good side of getting well.

Lissa was dreaming that she was falling, tumbling head over heels down a steep, rocky slope. She grabbed at a bush, but it slipped through her fingers, and then she reached for an embedded rock that came loose in her hands. She knew there was a precipice at the bottom, and when she reached it she would fall over the edge and die. No one knew where she was. No one knew she was falling to her death. They would never find her. She was lost. And when she tumbled over the edge and out into space, she threw back her head and screamed.

Mack came up out of the chair so fast it took a couple of seconds for him to remember where he was. Lissa was kicking beneath the covers and clawing at the air when he grabbed hold of her arms.

"Lissa! Wake up! You're okay. You're okay. It's just a bad dream."

Lissa opened her eyes with a gasp, expecting to see the ground coming up to meet her. When she saw Mack instead, she began to shake.

"I was falling! I thought I was going to die!"

"Easy, honey, calm down. You're pulling all the tubes out of your arms," he said.

A nurse came through the door on the run, turning on lights as she went.

"What happened?" she cried.

"Another bad dream," Mack said.

An alarm was going off on one machine, and another was registering off the charts.

Lissa was trembling. The dream was still so vivid she was having trouble grasping the fact that it wasn't real. "I'm sorry. I thought I was falling off a mountain," she said, and then looked at Mack for reassurance.

"Well, bless your heart," the nurse said, as she began checking Lissa's IV and then resetting the systems.

"Did I mess stuff up?" Lissa asked, watching as the nurse began untangling wires and hooking them back up.

Mack shook his head. "No, baby. You didn't mess up anything that can't be fixed."

"That's right," the nurse said as she added a new piece of tape to the IV line. "There. I think you're good to go."

"I'm thirsty. Can I have some water?" Lissa asked.

"I'll check the orders," the nurse said. "Be right back."

Lissa looked at Mack. "Tell me it's over. Tell me the stalker is behind bars."

"What do you remember?" he asked.

"Seeing Louis and then watching him turn into a madman. I ran away."

"The only thing you need to know is that he's dead. He killed himself. We'll worry about filling in the blanks later, okay?"

She sighed. "Between the ten years we were apart and now this, we're going to have a whole lot of blanks to fill in."

"And a lifetime to do it," he said as he leaned over and kissed her.

She eased back onto the pillow and then licked her lips. "You taste sweet...like a honey bun."

He chuckled. "You're correct. Want one? We can ask the nurse."

"I want water most," she said.

He gently pushed straggling curls away from her forehead. "It feels good to know you're no longer in danger," he said. "I won't worry about you now whenever you're out of sight."

"As soon as I feel better, I can go back to work. With him dead, there's no longer a danger to the children."

"I know."

The nurse came back into the room, carrying a pitcher of ice water and a cup.

"Here you go, honey. Ring if you need to get up."

"If someone was to come in here with a honey bun, I don't suppose there would be any reason for me to turn down a bite if it was offered?" Lissa asked.

The nurse laughed. "Technically you're not on a restricted diet."

Lissa looked at Mack.

"I'll be right back," he drawled, and headed back to the vending machines with a lighter step. If she was hungry, that meant she was on the mend. Good news. Very good news.

By the time he returned, she'd fallen back to sleep, so he set the sweet roll aside and crawled into the other bed. Morning was already here. He just needed a little sunshine to go with it.

Sixteen

Marcus Silver was in the library going over invitation samples. He needed to pick one, and have them printed and ready when it came time to invite the necessary bigwigs to his announcement party. Running for senate was no small feat, and he wanted all the backing he could get. He'd talked to his cook, who'd already volunteered to give over her kitchen to a catering company for the night, and he was debating about which florist to use to decorate the mansion when he heard footsteps outside the doorway. He looked up just as T.J. walked in.

"Hey, Dad, what are you doing?" T.J. asked.

"Picking out the invitation for the party."

"Cool, can I see?"

"As far as I'm concerned, you can make the final decision. I like any of these four here. You choose and then drop it off at the printers, will you? I need to find out if they've released Paul Jackson's body, and if so, see if his son has set a date and time for the services."

"Are you planning something kind of like you did for Dick Phillips?" T.J. asked. "You know, where all the classmates who come get up and say something personal about him?"

Marcus sighed. "I was thinking we should. I mean, we did it once, so it seems like we'd be slighting Paul if we didn't do it for him, too."

T.J. nodded. "That's kind of how I see it. Do you need any help making calls?"

"No," Marcus said. "But thanks for asking."

"I could actually drop by the hospital and talk to Mack myself, if you like," T.J. offered.

"The hospital? Why is he at the hospital again?"

T.J. frowned. "You mean to tell me you didn't hear about what happened at the supermarket yesterday?"

"If you'll remember, I left town after we ate lunch yesterday," Marcus said.

"That's right, you did. Well, long story short, someone's been stalking Melissa Sherman, and yesterday he tried to abduct her from the supermarket. He wound up killing himself when he couldn't get away, but she was injured. Mack is at the hospital with her."

"She and Mack Jackson are a thing?" Marcus asked.

T.J. rolled his eyes. "Evidently."

"You dated her for a while. You don't mind talking to him for me?

"Of course not. It was just a couple of casual dates when she first moved back. I haven't taken her out in months."

"Well, in that case, yes, that would be helpful, son. See what Mack says about us doing something like that. If he doesn't like it, then of course we won't."

"I'll go right now," T.J. said, leaving the room as quickly as he'd entered.

T.J. knew he would most likely see Lissa, which

was the main reason he'd been so willing to help out. He knew she wouldn't like it, but if the boyfriend took offense at his presence and it caused a little trouble between them, he wouldn't care. In fact, he would like it.

Lissa sat up in bed long enough to eat a little of the breakfast on her tray and part of the honey bun Mack had bought for her last night, but before long she gave up and quit. Sitting up made her dizzy, and her head was throbbing with every beat of her heart. As she lay there with her eyes closed, willing the bed to stop spinning, she thought of all the years and all the pro football games she'd watched. She couldn't remember how many times she'd heard an announcer say something offhand about a player being pulled from the game because of a concussion, and never once had she thought about what that actually meant. Now she knew.

She could hear Mack in her bathroom and knew he was changing clothes. Earlier he'd called Cain and asked him to bring clean clothes from the house. Now Cain was on his way back to Summerton, and Mack was within the sound of her voice. There wasn't anything left for her to worry about but getting well.

"Well, Liss, you do get yourself into the damnedest situations. That bruise looks downright miserable. Is there anything I can get you?"

Lissa refused to open her eyes. "T.J.?"

"Yes, it's me, hon."

"Why, yes, there *is* something I need. Would you please go into the bathroom and bring me a wet cloth for my head?"

T.J. blinked, a little startled that she was actually being cordial, and his Southern gentleman manners kicked right in.

"I'd be happy to," he said.

Three steps to the left and the doorknob was in his hand. He thought he heard something on the other side, but by the time it registered that someone was in there, he'd already opened the door. "Uh…"

Dressed, Mack was an imposing man. Bare chested and somewhat pissed off, he was nearly scary, especially to T.J., whose daddy always settled his debts and troubles.

Mack picked up a shirt and walked out of the bathroom, giving T.J. a clear view of the staples in his arm and shoulder.

T.J. shuddered, and then followed Mack back into the room.

"What do you want here?" Mack asked.

The fact was not lost on T.J. that Mack was standing in front of Lissa's bed like a guard dog. It was time for him to behave himself.

"Mack, I apologize if my appearance here seems like I'm overstepping my bounds, but I assure you I mean no harm. I'm actually here to speak to you at my father's request."

Mack's eyes narrowed. T.J. was a couple of years younger than he was, but they'd never liked each other as kids, and getting older hadn't changed things in any way. "If your father needed to speak to me, why didn't he come himself?"

T.J. could feel this whole visit slipping away, and he also realized that Lissa had delivered him to the guard dog without a qualm. Even hurt, she was still a bitch.

T.J. smiled. "Well, I knew he was busy and I offered—"

Mack's eyes narrowed even farther. "When he gets un-busy, tell him to give me a call."

T.J. shrugged. "Look, all he wanted to know was if you'd like him to organize your father's classmates to speak at the funeral services like they did for Dick Phillips' funeral."

A chill ran up Mack's spine. The fact that the two men had been classmates was most likely what had made their murderer target them.

"I'll be in charge of Dad's services, but you can thank your father for the offer."

T.J. reeled like he'd been punched in the face. It took him a couple of seconds to realize no one had moved and he hadn't been touched.

"Yes, of course. I'll pass the message on, and you have my sincerest condolences on the loss of your father. Liss, I hope you get well real soon. Y'all take care now."

T.J. smiled at Mack and walked out, resisting the urge to run.

Mack followed the man far enough to shut the door behind him, then walked back to the bed.

"Liss? He called you Liss?"

She opened her eyes. "That was a blank we just filled in. He asked me out. Three dates. Didn't like him. Dumped his ass."

Mack grinned. "That's my girl. You always did have good taste."

Lissa started to laugh, and then grabbed her head with both hands and groaned. "Lord, that hurt."

"Sorry, baby," Mack said. "Do you still want that wet cloth?"

She laughed again and then moaned. "You heard that, too?"

"I wasn't sure who it was you were talking to, but since you were sending him straight to me, I guessed you wanted him gone."

Lissa shuddered. "He gives me the creeps."

"He's just a rich daddy's boy. You take it easy, honey. I need to finish dressing before your doctor comes by," he said before going back into the bathroom.

Pinky's Monday morning was far different from what she'd planned when Louis had dropped her off at the motel. Instead of taking a bus out of town, she was driving her son's truck back to his house. There was a key to the front door on the ring, and when she went in, she was startled to see the little dog standing in the hall.

"Oh, hell. Bobo. I know you need out."

The little dog made a beeline for the back door. She let him out, and then grabbed a handful of paper towels and went through the house, certain she would find dog pee or poop everywhere, but there was just one little puddle beside the bed.

She wiped it up, then dug around in the kitchen until she found his kibble, and filled his food and water bowls before letting him in.

Bobo came bouncing in, then sniffed the air with a hopeful look in his eyes.

Pinky guessed what that meant. Tears welled. "He's not coming back, dog. Sorry."

Bobo looked at her, then walked over to his bowl, lapped up a little water and lay down beside the food with his chin on his paws.

She could tell he was sad. Well, so was she.

She headed for the bedroom where Louis had said the will would be located and dug through a conglomeration of boxes before she found the lockbox. She was a little stunned by the thoroughness with which Reece had covered his bases. She didn't even notice that she was still thinking of them as separate people.

The will would have to go through probate before she could claim Reece's estate, even though she was named as sole heir, and she would have to bury his body. But the more she thought about it, the more she decided not to bury him at all. She would have him cremated. She would figure out later how to dispose of the ashes. All she knew was that she wasn't taking him back to where her husband and little boy were buried. She didn't think her little Louis would appreciate spending eternity beside the person who'd killed him.

She found the computer and nearby a copy of the lease, and she was sitting on the side of the bed reading it—relieved to see that the rent had already been paid for the next couple of weeks—when Bobo trotted in. She saw movement from the corner of her eye and looked over just as the little dog plopped down beside her. Its long, heartfelt sigh broke her heart. The poor little thing was grieving. She leaned down and tentatively patted the top of its head, and was surprised by how soft the fur was beneath her fingertips.

"I guess you're not so bad," she mumbled, and then she got up and started going through the dresser drawers, making sure she didn't leave anything important behind when she left.

When she found an extra set of car keys she dropped them in her pocket. As she did, it occurred to her that she needed to get another driver's license. She hadn't had a car in so long that she'd just let it lapse, but she still used her old one for a photo ID. Might as well find out what she needed to do to get a new one while she was here.

By the time noon rolled around she was in the kitchen making a meal from more leftovers.

"Bits and pieces," she said, trying not to cry as she stirred some peas and carrots into leftover gravy, chopped up a piece of cold fried chicken she'd found, stirred it into the mix, scooped some mashed potatoes out of a storage container and spread them on top for a crust and put it in the oven to heat. "Shepherd's pie, but with chicken not beef. Louis would have liked it," she added. Then she set a timer and went into the living room to wait.

She turned on the TV and then stared absently at the screen without registering what was playing. She heard a thump, and noticed Bobo had jumped up on the sofa and was sitting on the cushion at the far end, watching her intently. She had to admit the terrier's fuzzy face was sort of cute, and when she looked closer, she imagined his dark beady eyes were full of tears.

"Well, come on over if you want," she said. "I won't hurt you."

Bobo flopped down on his belly and watched her.

She shrugged and then turned her attention back to the TV. The next time she sensed movement he was belly crawling toward her with his head down and his ears flat. She pretended not to see him as he crawled all the way to her leg and then stopped.

Pinky sighed. "Oh, what the hell. At least I won't be talking to myself anymore," she said, and she reached down and gently stroked the top of his head.

Within minutes he was in her lap, licking her fingers, and she was sobbing. Reece had left her more than money, as it turned out.

And in the past hour she'd come to another decision. She was leaving town. The fewer people who knew her connection to a madman, the better off she would be.

She would get the will to the lawyer, but since it would probably take ages for it to go through probate, she would send him her new contact information once she relocated, and they could go from there. She could leave orders for Reece's body to be sent to the local funeral home for cremation. Thanks to him, she had the money to pay for that before she left, but what she wasn't going to tell them was what she'd decided to do with the ashes, which was nothing. They could sit on a shelf at the funeral home for eternity and it would be all right with her because she didn't ever want to be close to that much evil again.

She looked down at the dog in her lap and patted his head. "You and me, Bobo. What do you say? Think we can get along?"

Bobo whined and laid his head against her breasts. It was ironic that the only living thing left on this planet that was going to mourn Reece Parsons' death was a dog.

* * *

It had taken a bit of doing and a couple of phone calls to the two men who used to work for his dad, but Mack finally got his SUV moved from the parking lot of the supermarket to the hospital. He thanked them profusely and took the opportunity to offer both of them jobs at his lumberyard if they were interested. To his surprise, Everett, the older employee, told Mack he was interested in buying the station if the price was right. The thought of someone local carrying on at the place his dad built made him happy, and he assured Everett that he would make sure the price was right.

He walked back into the hospital with a lighter heart. Lots of details still had to be worked out and the place had to be appraised, but it felt right.

He hurried down the hall to the elevator, ready to be free of this place, and walked up on a woman already waiting for it to arrive. When she turned and saw him, she broke into a wide smile.

"Mack Jackson! It's been ages." Then the smile shifted to an expression of sympathy. "I'm so sorry about your father's passing. He was a good man."

"Thanks," Mack said, trying not to stare.

She smiled again. "You don't know who I am, do you?"

"No, I'm sorry but—"

"Jessica York…used to be Jessica Shayne. We were in the same graduating class, remember?"

His eyes narrowed and then he looked away. "Yes, I remember."

"I'll bet you're on the way to visit the same person I'm going to see. Melissa Sherman?"

"No, you aren't going to visit her. She isn't going to want to see you," he snapped.

Jessica gasped at the insult. "I know you two were a thing years ago, but I'm certain you don't speak for her."

"We're still a thing, and the reason I know she isn't going to want to see you is because she told me only a few days ago that it was you who started the rumor about her having an abortion back in high school, when you knew all along it was a miscarriage. It hurt her in more ways than you will ever imagine."

An angry red flush swept up Jessica's throat and face. "Why, I never—"

Mack poked a finger in her face, stopping only inches away from her nose.

"Yes, you did, and if you ever start another ugly lie about her, I will make you sorry. Do we understand each other?"

Her face went from red to a pale, pasty white as she turned on one heel and started walking toward the exit. Her stride was hurried. And she kept looking over her shoulder every few seconds, as if fearing he was on the attack.

The elevator doors opened.

Mack walked in, punched the number to the floor and watched Jessica York until the doors completely closed. The last glimpse he had of the woman, she was running.

It was midafternoon by the time Lissa was released from the hospital, and now she was waiting for Mack to come get her. He'd gone down to the parking lot a short while ago to meet some men who were bringing his car. She couldn't wait to get home. It felt like she'd been gone for days instead of twenty-four hours.

They'd cut off her clothes in the ER, so they'd found a pair of hospital scrubs for her to wear home. She was stiff and sore in almost every muscle and still battling a horrible headache, but she was no longer seeing double and had lost the need to fall asleep every ten minutes. The restrictions on what she could and could not do were enough for her to know she still couldn't go back to the classroom, but as Mack kept telling her, they would figure all that out later.

When she heard footsteps coming down the hall, she rolled over and sat up on the side of the bed. She would know that stride anywhere. Mack was back.

"Hey, baby! Did you miss me?" he asked, and then gave her a quick kiss. "Nice duds," he added.

"I just want to go home," she said.

"Me, too. The nurse is coming with the wheelchair. I have all your paperwork, so we're good to go."

They both turned as the sound of footsteps neared the open doorway, and were surprised when it was Chief Jakes who walked in and not the nurse.

"Hey, Melissa. It's good to see you up and smiling," Trey said, and then he gave her the sack he was holding. "It's your purse. It was still in your cart at the supermarket. One of the shoppers turned it in to the manager, and he brought it to the police department this morning."

Lissa sighed. "I hadn't even thought of it, which tells you how rattled my head has been. Thank you so much."

Trey smiled. "Happy to help."

"Hey, Trey, I don't suppose you have anything new on Dad's death?" Mack asked.

The smile disappeared. "I'm sorry to say I don't. I sent that tassel to the state crime lab with a rush request, but I haven't heard anything."

"I had to ask," Mack said.

"So where are you headed from here?" Trey asked.

"Back to Dad's house," Mack said. "There's still the memorial service to get through."

"If either of you needs anything, all you have to do is ask," Trey said. He left just as a nurse pushed a wheelchair into the room.

"There's your ride," Mack said as he helped Lissa down from the bed.

"You go bring the car up to the door while I wheel her down," the nurse said.

"Yes, ma'am," Mack said, and headed for the elevator as the nurse settled Lissa into the wheelchair.

His shoulder was aching and the staples in his arm were beginning to pull, but he felt like he was walking on water.

The danger to Lissa was over, and their life together was about to begin.

The drive home was anticlimactic. Knowing Mack was beside her and her life was no longer in jeopardy was a gift. The simple pleasure of sunlight coming in through the windshield and someone waving at them as they passed put a smile on Lissa's face.

Mack went by the drive-through pharmacy and picked up a prescription that had been called in for her. The lady at the window had to take the time to tell

Lissa that she'd heard all about her ordeal and wished her well before they could leave.

Lissa was smiling as they drove away, but it did occur to her that she was once again without a car.

"I hate to bring this up, but I need to make a decision about my car," Lissa said.

"I don't know when Trey is going to release it," Mack said.

"Whenever he does, I'm going to trade it in and get a new one."

"Are you sure you—"

Lissa held up a finger to make her point, just as she would have had done in the classroom. "I'm positive. I do not ever want to sit in that car again."

He nodded. "I totally understand. Look, if it's okay with you, you can drive this SUV and I'll drive Dad's truck until we can arrange something else. That way we won't be under any pressure to hurry."

"That sounds like a good idea, thank you," she said.

There was a lump in Lissa's throat the size of her fist. She blew him a kiss and quickly looked away.

Mack saw the tears in her eyes and knew what she was thinking. They would never get back the years that they'd lost, and they'd almost died before getting their second chance. It was enough to make anyone cry.

He took the next left and fixed his eyes on the third house on the right.

"And we're here," he said, as he pulled up into the driveway and parked beneath the carport.

Lissa got out without saying much, but she clasped

his hand tightly as he walked her up the steps and then to the door.

The click of a turning lock had never sounded so good.

Mack felt blessed. The familiarity of comfortable surroundings and the woman at his side gave him a sense of peace. He hadn't felt this at ease since he'd gotten the call about his father's death.

Lissa was just as relieved to still be alive and was grateful for Mack's presence.

"I just want to lie down," she said.

"Sure thing, honey," he said, and he helped her to the bedroom. He pulled back the covers as she kicked off her shoes and eased down onto the mattress.

"Oh, dear God, every muscle in my body aches," she whispered, then rolled over and closed her eyes. The pillow was cool against her cheek as Mack pulled up the covers.

"You need to rest, too," she said.

"Don't worry about me, honey. I'm a couple of days ahead of you on healing. I'll be back shortly. I just have a few phone calls to make."

Mack's steps were long and measured as he headed for his dad's office. It was time to make arrangements for the memorial service. He sat down at the desk, and as he did, he felt his father's presence so strongly it made him ache.

"I miss you," he said, then he called Pastor Farley.

The church secretary answered, then transferred his call. Pastor Farley answered immediately.

"Pastor Farley speaking," he said.

"It's me, sir. Mack Jackson. You told me to give

you a call when I was ready to schedule the memorial service."

"Yes. Of course," the pastor said. "What did you have in mind?"

Mack went through the list of things he wanted to include. After a brief discussion regarding dates and times, they settled on the day after next at 2:00 p.m.

"Wednesday at two," Pastor Farley repeated. "I'll have my secretary get it in the daily paper, and we'll need a eulogy from you."

Mack sighed. "I'll get it to you tomorrow. I just got Melissa home from the hospital, and we're both beat."

"Is there anything I can do for you? Do you want flowers at the church?"

Mack sighed. "Yes. I forgot about that. I'll call them now." He disconnected, then found the number and called the florist.

A few minutes later he hung up again and got up to take his pain meds. There were other things he probably should do, like check in at the lumberyard. Maybe get one of the casseroles from the church ladies out of the freezer. Check to see if he had any messages. But all he could think about was getting to his bedroom and lying down beside the woman he loved. He'd lost her ten years ago and by the grace of God had her back. He would tend to business later.

He downed the meds and headed back to his bedroom, where he stopped in the doorway. All he could see was the back of her head and a tangle of honey-colored curls. She looked so small beneath the covers, but her heart and courage made up for her lack of height.

He stripped off clothes as he went until he was down to undershorts and a T-shirt, and then he eased into bed, being careful not to jostle her awake.

Thick golden eyelashes rested lightly on the bruise around her eye. The bruise would fade, but his love never would. He leaned over just far enough to kiss her cheek, then stretched out beside her and closed his eyes.

Seventeen

Lissa woke up to the sound of rain on the roof. The first thought that went through her head was that the students wouldn't be allowed to go out at recess, which meant she would be penned in with a room full of antsy six-year-olds.

And then she remembered and rolled over.

Mack was asleep beside her, still *her* Mack, just a little older and a whole lot sexier. He wore maturity well, but he looked as battered as she felt. There were so many staples in his left arm it looked like he had a zipper, and she knew his back was bandaged again because the doctor had needed to repair what he'd done to himself in getting her to safety. They were both wrecks, but still here and still together. It was enough.

She slipped out of bed and then hobbled her way to the bathroom. She came out a few minutes later feeling better for having slept and slightly surprised it was only a little after 5:00 p.m. She'd thought she'd slept all night, not just through the afternoon.

When she got back to the bedroom she changed out of the scrubs she'd come home in and into sweatpants and a long-sleeved T-shirt. After pulling the shirt over her head, she reached up to finger comb her curls back into place and, as she did, accidentally touched the cut the doctors had fixed.

Then she wondered if her hair was bloody and had to go back to the bathroom to look. To her surprise, it wasn't, and she could only assume that when they flushed the cut to clean it, they must have rinsed the blood from her hair, as well. What she did see was a small circle about the size of a half-dollar that had been shaved before they had glued the edges of the cut back together again. But when she fluffed the curls back around the spot, it disappeared. So there was a reason for thick, curly hair after all.

She put on a pair of warm socks and some slippers, and headed for the kitchen. She was hungry and thirsty, and guessed Mack would wake up the same way.

She got a drink and then started to dig through the refrigerator before she remembered the donated food he'd put in the freezer. She looked until she found a casserole full of meat and vegetables, then put it in the oven to heat. A little too hungry to wait for it to be ready, she got a couple of Frieda Sanford's cookies and sat down at the kitchen table with those and a glass of milk.

She had just taken the first bite of her last cookie when she heard Mack's footsteps.

"There you are," he said, and leaned down to give her a quick kiss. "Mmm, you taste like cookies."

"Open wide," she said, and when he did, she poked the rest of her cookie in his mouth. "Some of Frieda Sanford's cookies," she said. "I was starving, so I got a casserole out of the freezer and put it in the oven. It should be ready in about an hour or so."

He got a bottle of pop from the refrigerator and then sat down at the table with her.

"I talked to Pastor Farley while you were asleep. I've set Dad's memorial service for Wednesday afternoon at 2:00 p.m. When they finally release his body, we'll do a graveside burial without a need for ceremony."

Lissa circled the table, sat down in his lap and kissed him.

"It's a little daunting to know you're in the world without another soul who shares your blood, isn't it?"

He nuzzled a spot behind her ear and then hugged her, taking care not to squeeze too tight.

"It would be hell except for you. We *are* family, Melissa, even though the ceremony has yet to happen. We belong—you to me and me to you."

"And the babies to come," she added.

He was still smiling, but there were tears in his voice when he said, "Yes…and the babies to come."

The next morning dawned damp and cold, and they were both trying to find comfortable clothes for the day. Mack was digging through the clothes he'd brought with him from home, looking for something to wear that would still be comfortable on his shoulder and arm, when he realized tomorrow was the memorial service and everything he needed was at his house in Summerton.

"Well, hell," he muttered, as he shoved a dresser drawer shut.

Lissa had on a pair of jeans and a sweater, and was

looking for a clean pair of socks to wear with her boots, when she heard him slam the drawer shut with a curse.

"What's wrong?"

"Tomorrow is the memorial service, and the clothes I need are back at my house in Summerton."

"Oh, you're right! Mine aren't here, either, but at least my house is closer than yours. I don't think Louis…er, Reece or…whoever…got to that part of my closet, although he did tear up a lot of stuff."

Mack frowned. "We'll go check at your house first, and if you can't find anything you want, we can go shopping in Summerton."

"I'm sure I can find something. My winter clothes were actually still packed away in another room, so he didn't even get to them. I'll be fine." Then she eyed the frown on his face. "Are you up to driving that far? We could probably get someone to take us if—"

"No, of course I can do it," he said. "Do you feel like riding that far?"

"Yes, I'll be fine. Besides, I want to see your home."

"Soon to be *our* home," he said.

"Then, why the frown?" she asked, as she traced a finger down the line between his eyebrows.

"I dread the service. I have to drop the eulogy off at the church. Getting the right clothes together is one more thing. It's not an issue. I just made it a roadblock when it didn't need to be."

Lissa slid her arms around his waist and laid her cheek against the middle of his chest. The steady thump of his heartbeat always had the power to center her world, and today was no different.

"It will be okay because we'll do it together, remember?"

He exhaled slowly as he pulled her close. "God, I am so grateful for you. I hope one day you realize how much I love you."

She cupped his face. "You always were my hero, even before you saved my life."

And just like that, all the tension he was feeling faded.

"So, my sweet lady, are you ready to go see your new home?"

"Yes, yes, yes," Lissa said. "But first I need shoes."

She moved out of his arms to finish dressing, leaving him with a slight, but heartfelt, smile on his face.

A short while later they pulled into her driveway.

Lissa shivered. "I haven't been back since the…"

Mack frowned. "That's over, Lissa. Don't let that part of your life color how you feel about the house you grew up in."

"Right," she said, and she got out with purpose in her step.

Mack thought he was following for moral support, but even so, the hair stood up on the back of his neck when he walked into the house. Bad things had gone down in here. This house needed people and laughter in it again to heal the energy.

"Oh, my teacher friends did such a great job," Lissa said, as she went into the kitchen.

The last time she'd been here, Mack had been bloody and unconscious. She traced the caulking on the new window glass with a finger, then moved out of the kitchen and down the hall to her bedroom with Mack right behind her.

"Here goes nothing," she said, and walked in.

The chaos she'd seen the night of the attack might

never have happened. The broken glass, the torn clothing, even the broken night-light that had been the last link to her childhood…all gone.

"Oh, wow," she said softly, moving to the closet and turning on the light.

Her clothes were back on hangers, her shoes back on the rack.

She opened the drawers in the dresser at the far end of the closet and sighed at the sight of everything clean, folded and back in place.

"They put everything back together again."

Mack walked up behind her and took her by the shoulders. "Good friends are worth their weight in gold, right, honey?"

"Yes, they are," she said. "Now give me a few minutes to find something suitable and we'll be out of here."

Mack gave her a quick pat on the butt and then sat down on the side of the bed to watch. She flipped through the hangers for a couple of minutes before she zeroed in on one outfit, and promptly took it out of the closet and slipped it into a garment bag. Then she chose shoes to go with it.

"I'm ready," she said just as Mack took everything out of her hands.

"You lead the way and lock the door behind us. I've got this."

After dropping off the eulogy at the church, they were finally on their way to Summerton.

Lissa pulled the visor down to use the mirror on the back, looked at her reflection and groaned.

"Just look at me. Black eye, bruise over half my

forehead and a busted lip. What on earth are people going to think?"

"That you won the fight?"

She grinned. "Really?"

Mack shook his head. "I am in so much trouble, aren't I?"

"No. I like you. I won't ever hurt you, I promise."

He eyed the little blonde sitting beside him and burst into laughter. "Like I'm scared," he drawled.

"Well, you're not and we both know it, but I love you for not minding being seen with a girl with a smashed-up face."

She flipped the visor back into place, smiled when he winked at her and settled in for the ride.

After Trey's interrogation, Betsy Jakes had been feeling less scattered. Maybe it was turning her dream journal over to the police that made the difference, as if she'd given up the responsibility of trying to figure it out to someone else.

Trina's breakup with Lee Daniels had also helped shift her focus. Trina's heartache had turned on Betsy's mother mode. She was still having nightmares, but now she was able to let go of them more easily on waking.

Still, she couldn't get rid of the feeling that she'd lost a limb and was just pretending she still walked and talked like everyone else, knowing any minute they would see her for the fake she was. And when the reveal finally happened, which she knew was inevitable, she would never get back up again. She'd even come to terms with the fear of dying. After all, Connie had been dead for years. The rest of them had gotten a free pass from that wreck. Despite how this was playing out, maybe it was just God's way of putting out that final call.

The killer was on a mission, reconnoitering. Everything he'd been working toward was almost finished. Only one more to get rid of and he would be home free, with no one the wiser.

According to today's paper, Paul Jackson's memorial service was going to be held tomorrow afternoon. Everyone in town would be there, including him. He couldn't afford to be visibly absent, but he intended to take advantage of everyone being out of place when it was over. It would take a bit of luck, a little finesse and a good aim, but he'd always managed to land on his feet in life and expected nothing less now.

He was almost at the Jakeses' place now. All he needed was to remind himself of the layout and see if his plan would hold water; if not, he would take care of things somewhere else.

He could see the mailbox in the distance, and of all things, there was Betsy herself getting the mail. If only he'd brought his weapon, everything would be over. But he hadn't, and maybe there was a reason. As he neared the mailbox she turned and disappeared. That was when he realized how dense that stand of trees was on the north side of the drive. It might be a good place to hide out until he could get inside.

As he drew closer he saw a small blue metal sign fastened to her mailbox post. A security company! Hell, her house was probably wired to the hilt, which entailed a change of plans. He would not be taking her out inside her own home. Then he saw her about twenty yards down the drive and, on a whim, honked and waved. When she turned and waved back, he took it as a sign.

She thought she'd just said hello, but he knew it was goodbye.

The closer Mack got to Summerton, the more anxious he became. Lissa had been asleep for half an hour, but he was going to wake her up because they would drive right past his lumberyard and he wanted her to see his name on it. He was proud of what he'd accomplished. He wanted her to see his business and his neighborhood and the street where he lived. He wanted Lissa to love his home as much as he did. He wanted her to walk in and feel like she'd lived there forever. He hoped he wasn't wanting too much.

As soon as he reached the city limits, he reached over and touched her arm. "Lissa, honey? We're here. We're in Summerton."

Her eyelids fluttered, and then she raised her seat back to a sitting position, and began fluffing at her hair and looking around.

"I'm ashamed to say I haven't been here once since I moved home, although I didn't really have a need."

"Well, you're here now, and I wanted to show you something as we pass."

She smiled. "Okay. What should I look for?"

He pointed up at a huge warehouse-style building spread out over the entire block, and then to the name over the wide porch at the front door.

"Jackson Lumber Company," she said, and then gasped. "Oh! Jackson! Your company! Oh, my gosh! Oh, Mack! It's huge. It's amazing."

"Yeah, do you want to see inside? If you don't feel like it yet I totally understand. We're a little short on time anyway, so—"

"Yes, I want to see inside. I feel fine. If you don't mind introducing me looking like this," she added, and pointed at her face.

"Baby, trust me, they already know I got hurt and why. They already know you nearly died. You're going to come across as one tough survivor, okay?"

She nodded, already getting nervous as he pulled into the parking area and then drove around back.

"This is where I always park," he said, and before he even got out, someone had already spotted his SUV and was pointing. "Well, no sneaking in for us. We've been made. Are you ready?"

"I feel like I'm about to meet your family for the first time," she said.

He paused, touched by what she'd said. "In a way, I guess you are."

He circled the truck to help her out. By the time she had both feet on the ground, at least a dozen men had surrounded them.

"Wow, boss, it's good to see you up and around," one man said, and then he grinned at Lissa. "So here's the little lady who just took Summerton's most eligible bachelor off the market. She's sure a pretty thing."

Lissa grinned. "Most eligible bachelor?"

Mack couldn't have wiped the smile off his face if he'd tried. "Just filled in one of my blanks there," he said. Then he introduced her. "Everyone, this is Melissa Sherman, the girl I should have married ten years ago and didn't, but that's about to change. Melissa, these are the best employees in town. The old guy is Mark. The one with the Mohawk is Charlie. The bald guy with the beard is Andy. He grows hair on his face because it won't grow on his head."

And so it went as he introduced one after the other, all the men laughing at how he singled them out. By the time he was through, Lissa had forgotten about her face and everything else but how absolutely perfect the rest of her life was going to be.

"It's great to meet all of you, but I still have one heck of a concussion and just quit seeing double. So if I forget your names next time I see you, I hope you'll understand."

And with that admission, she sealed herself as all right with every man there. She'd seen them like Mack saw them—as equals, not the hired help, which was part of why Mack Jackson's business thrived.

"You guys get back to work," Mack said then. "I've gotta take her in to meet the real boss or I'll never hear the end of it."

They all laughed as they went back to their jobs, knowing just who Mack was referring to.

As they walked through the lumber barn, Lissa was properly impressed with the size of the area where the lumber was sorted and stored.

"Are you up for the stairs?" Mack asked, pointing to a flight with a dozen steps that led into the back of the building, where the offices were located and then it opened out into the shopping area up front.

"Yes, if I go slow," she said.

"I can carry you," he offered.

"No, you can't, because the last time you did that it made you bleed, so just give me time and I'll be fine."

He grinned at her bossy attitude and followed that

sweet little ass all the way up and then inside the building.

"My office is four doors up the hall on the left," he said. "My secretary's office is up one from mine."

"Well, your 'brothers' out there were fun, but now I'm meeting 'Mother' and it's making me nervous."

He took her by the hand. "Honey, no matter what I said out there, I *am* the boss. I can assure you if I love you, they'll love you, too."

They had only gone a few steps when a skinny middle-aged woman came flying out of the office he'd said belonged to his secretary, and when she saw them, she threw up her hands and headed their way.

"It *is* true! They said you were here, but I didn't believe them." She kept talking as she walked, waving her hands and wiping away tears. "Oh, Mack Jackson, it is so good to see you in one piece. When we heard what happened, I can tell you there were some prayers sent up. And this must be Melissa. My sister works at the hospital in Mystic. I already know the whole awful story about what happened to you, and I can't tell you how thrilled we are that this ridiculously handsome boss of ours is finally going to settle down and get married."

Lissa laughed. She couldn't help it. The woman was adorable, and she'd actually made Mack blush, something she'd never seen happen before.

Mack just shook his head. "Melissa, this is Bella Garfield. She's not just my secretary, she also knows where all the bodies are hidden around here. I couldn't do this without her. Bella, this is my girl, Melissa Sherman, but everyone calls her Lissa."

Bella was beaming as she took Lissa's hand, and

patted it over and over. "I'd hug you, but I know you're hurt. And I know Mack probably wants to show you off to everyone else. It's a joy to meet you, and I know you're going to have a long and happy life with our own James Bond."

Lissa frowned. "James Bond?"

Bella giggled. "Yes! We all think he looks like Daniel Craig. You know, the actor who plays James Bond."

Mack stifled a snort. "Except I'm taller, not blond or British and my eyes aren't blue. Except for all that, sure I do," Mack muttered. "Damned embarrassing, if you ask me."

"Makes as much sense as you claiming I look like Cindy Crawford," Lissa said.

Bella stared at Lissa, and then squealed and clapped her hands. "Oh! You *do*! My goodness, you sure do, with that cute little mole by your lips and all!"

Lissa rolled her eyes. "Oh, sure, except that I don't have long dark hair, I'm half a foot shorter and the only similarity between my face and hers is a mole."

"Then, we're a pair of misfits, girl," Mack said. "Bella, go back to work. Lissa, come with me. There are people to meet, and we have places to be."

Bella giggled and flew back to her office, and for the next thirty minutes Lissa was introduced to so many people who blatantly adored Mack that her head was spinning. By the time they were back in the car and on their way to his house, she was exhausted and he was wired.

"After you see the house and I get my clothes, we need to eat some lunch. I don't know about you, but I'm hungry already," he said. "If it's okay with you, we can get takeout and eat on the way back to Mystic."

Lissa agreed. "That would be wonderful. I think I'm all talked out for now, but this morning has been an eye-opener for me in so many ways. I've always believed that everything happens for a reason, and, Mack, if we had gotten married and had a baby ten years ago, there's no telling how our lives would have turned out. The one sure thing is that we would be two different people than the ones we are now, so just for the record, I admire the man you became without me."

Mack thought about what she'd said.

"I never thought about it like that, but you're right. Even if I regret losing those ten years with you, we have so much to be thankful for now. You're one hell of a woman, Melissa, and however you got to be the warrior woman that you are, I'm grateful you're mine."

She was still smiling when he turned a corner and pointed down the street.

"There's the house, the white two-story with the stained glass. It's been completely remodeled since I bought it, but if there are things you don't like we can always change—"

Lissa held up her teacher finger to indicate silence.

"No, that is not an option. I do not come into your world and change it, just as you do not come into my world and change me. We're filling in blanks, not redoing lives. I already loved everything about you before. We're picking up where we left off, which means I already love your house because I love *you*."

Mack grabbed that teacher finger and kissed it, then pulled up into the driveway and stopped beneath the portico.

"There's also a three-car garage in the back, but I rarely use it," he said.

"Oh, Mack, this place is breathtaking. I can't believe this is going to be my home."

He grinned, excited that she was so obviously pleased.

"Come inside and prowl around to your heart's content while I get some clothes, okay?"

"You don't want to give me the grand tour?" she asked.

"I don't think I could stand the suspense," he said. "I'd rather you poke about and pretend it's a house you're thinking about buying."

She laughed. "That sounds like fun. I think I'd like that."

"So take the grand tour on your own, m'lady. Your castle awaits."

Eighteen

Lissa's mouth dropped as they entered the foyer.

"Mack! Oh, my Lord!"

"You like it?" he asked, trying to see the house anew through her eyes, from the white marble flooring to the two-story entryway with the spiral staircase in the center and the massive chandelier dangling overhead.

"It's stunning. And this spiral staircase is straight out of a movie."

He grinned, thrilled that she was as entranced with the old girl as he was.

"That staircase was a huge selling point for me when I bought it. My bedroom is upstairs, first door on the right. You explore down here and I'll be down soon. If you want to go upstairs, wait and I'll take you up in the elevator."

"You have an elevator?" she asked.

"The old woman who lived here before I bought it had it put in. She was crippled with arthritis, so the stairs had become an issue for her, but she refused to move her bedroom downstairs. The elevator was her solution. It's safe. I've used it before."

Lissa was listening, but already itching to see more, and Mack could tell it.

"Go," he said. "I'll be down in a few minutes. The library and office are that way. The kitchen and dining room are over there. The living room is straight in front of you. There's a guest bath just before the library, and a bathroom inside the utility room off the kitchen."

Lissa turned left, a little intimidated by the sound of her footsteps echoing on the marble, and poked her head in the guest bathroom. She was enchanted by the Old World decor mixed with state-of-the-art bath fixtures. She went from there to the library and was immediately hooked by his collection of books. She moved up for a closer look at the shelves, running her fingers along the spines, checking titles and authors.

The large overstuffed chairs scattered around the room had been situated near the best natural lighting, and the thought of whiling away long hours curled up in one of those chairs with a good book and a blanket seemed like heaven.

The office was decorated much like the library— walnut stain on the wide-plank flooring, soft-as-butter leather in a dark oxblood color and the most up-to-date office equipment anyone could need. The computer system alone was awe inspiring, considering the fact that hers consisted of a laptop and a cheap printer.

She was imagining this house decorated at Christmas, with seven-foot tall trees and garlands hanging from the doorways, as she backtracked and found the dining room. When she saw the length and breadth of the room, she gasped, then, on impulse, sat down in the chair at the head of the table, folded her hands in her lap and gazed down the length of the cherrywood table with seating for twelve. The chandelier hanging midway above the table was obviously an antique that had been wired for electricity, although it had once been made for candles. She closed her eyes, picturing the chairs filling up with family—multiple generations all linked by blood and marriage. She could hear the faint sound of footsteps overhead and knew Mack was still up there gathering what he needed. It seemed a bit sinful to be so happy in the midst of such sadness, but that was how she felt.

The thought of the kitchen beckoned, and she moved quickly from the dining area straight into the kitchen just by crossing a hallway.

A massive expanse of white cabinetry hung on two entire sides of the room, with a long working island in the center. The countertops were white granite with swirls of gray, highlighted by a black-and-silver back-splash. She found a pantry the size of her little kitchen back home and a door leading down into a huge basement. The commercial stove and adjoining convection oven and grill were complemented by a massive side-by-side refrigerator-freezer. After a little more poking into what she thought was another refrigerator, she quickly realized it was a commercial-size cooler. Mack obviously had no reason for keeping it full, but it held an assortment of cold drinks and fresh produce. She imagined a holiday's worth of baking lining the shelves and did a happy dance as she moved through a generously sized utility room with a large washer and dryer to the bathroom beyond, pleased by all she was seeing.

The only thing left to see on the first floor was the living room, so she returned to the two-story foyer and circled the spiral staircase, opening the floor-to-ceiling double doors behind it, only to find the room that felt most like home.

Despite its massive size, the overstuffed furniture looked inviting. There was a fireplace at the end of the room, and French doors on the wall to her right that exited onto a large covered verandah. She could see the entire scope of the grounds behind the house as well as a ten-foot-high privacy fence made of huge chunks of gray stone. Except for the big-screen TV and the up-to-date technology elsewhere in the house, the place was straight out of the late nineteenth century. She couldn't believe this would be home for the rest of her life.

She walked back into the foyer just as Mack came down the stairs carrying a garment bag and a small duffel.

"So what do you think?" he asked, as he hung the garment bag over the stairs and pulled her into his arms.

"This doesn't feel real. It's so elegant and so comfortably inviting that I keep thinking I'm going to wake up and find out it was just a dream."

"No dream, just me making dreams come true. I always loved this era of architecture. It was a job bringing this house up to a contemporary level of comfort without ruining the aesthetic of it."

"I love it, I love your taste in decorating and I love you."

"Good," he said. He kissed her soundly. "Now let me show you where the real loving happens."

"You mean the bedrooms," Lissa said.

He just smiled and pointed to a door on the east wall.

"The elevator," he said.

Her steps were hurried as she followed him, and when he opened the door, she was immediately enchanted with the decor of the elevator car.

"It's all mirrors," she said.

"With silver-plated handrails," he added, pointing to the panel. "Up and down buttons. You can't get lost."

And up they went. The door opened to reveal a hallway, and a few steps farther along was the master bedroom. Mack opened the door and then walked her in.

Lissa's eyes widened as she saw the elaborately carved polished-wood headboard. The dark burgundy bedspread and the burgundy-and-gold draperies at the windows added to the feeling of a bygone era. There was a wide-screen TV on the wall opposite the bed, a separate dressing area with two large walk-in closets and, beyond, a very elegant en suite bath.

Lissa walked around examining everything, listening to him talk about how he'd found the antiques and how they tied in with the decor, and she realized how many blanks she needed to fill in with this man compared to the young man he'd been.

"Are those cherubs on the headboard?" she asked as she moved closer.

"For fertility, I was told."

"Said the most eligible bachelor in town," she said, unaware she'd spoken out loud.

Mack suddenly sensed her insecurity.

"You're the first woman who's been in this bedroom, Melissa. I did all my entertaining downstairs."

She turned and walked into his arms and buried her face against his chest.

"You don't have to explain. You don't have to say

anything. Thanks to my mother, our allegiance to each other ended ten years ago. What happened between then and now doesn't matter to me except that you've become an amazing person because of it."

He tilted her chin until he could see her face, then looked beyond the bruises and the swollen lip to the woman he loved.

"All the time I was working on the house, people kept asking me who the woman was who would hold court here. I never could answer because every time I closed my eyes and imagined a woman at my side, I always saw your face. When my shoulder is well, I'm going to carry you across the threshold to seal the deal, but, Melissa, my love, for all intents and purposes, welcome home."

They sealed the moment with a long, heartfelt kiss that made the massive bed that much more inviting, but that was for later, when they could both move without pain.

Lissa was overwhelmed and bubbling with excitement as they finally started home with a bag of burgers and fries between them and two cold drinks in the cup holders in the console.

They ate as they went, looking forward to their future, but at the same time still cognizant of the memorial service to get through before that future could officially begin.

Lissa needed to check in with her principal, and as soon as they got back to Mystic, she asked Mack to drop her off at the elementary school.

When he pulled up to the curb, she patted his knee.

"I'll call you as soon as I'm through, and you can pick me up, okay?"

"Absolutely," he said. "I need to drop by the church. I got a text from Pastor Farley while I was gathering up my clothes. He said the ladies at the church want to serve desserts and coffee after the memorial service. He said it won't take any planning on my part, just an okay. What do you think?"

"I think it's the perfect way to end the service. You and your dad's friends all coming together is a good thing, and you know how he loved his sweets."

Mack pushed a tumble of curls back off her forehead with the tip of his finger, smiling absently at the way the curls wound back around it, ensnaring his finger just as she had his heart.

"He sure did like his sweets, and you're right. It's a thoughtful thing they've offered to do. I'll give him the green light when I get there. You call when you're ready and I'll be right back, okay?"

"Yes, all right," she said. Then she eased across the seat and quickly kissed him. "For good luck," she said softly, and then she was out the door.

He waited, watching until she was all the way inside the building before he left.

Lissa sniffed the air as she walked in the front door. There was something about the scent of a schoolhouse that was unmistakable. It had to do with lots of children, huge amounts of food cooking in a cafeteria and books—books that had been handled by generations of little hands. She felt at home here, and yet she was torn by what was happening in her life. She wanted so badly to make a home with Mack and live the life they'd meant to have, raise the babies they were meant to raise and just be. But there was this business of a contract to fulfill and half a year of school yet to teach. Either she stayed here to teach and saw Mack only on weekends, or she moved into the house in Summerton straightaway and drove almost an hour to work and an hour home every day.

But like Mack said, they would figure it out, and right now she needed to let Mr. Wilson know that she still hadn't been cleared for work.

She walked into the office and was greeted by the secretary's squeals of surprise and joy at seeing her back. There was a teacher there who had to have a hug, which brought the principal out of his office to see what all the fuss was about.

When Wilson saw Melissa's face, he tried without success to hide his dismay.

"Melissa! Good Lord. Are you all right to be up and about?"

She smiled. "For short stints, yes."

He nodded, pleased that she seemed to be in good spirits. "What a nice surprise to see you walking around. Is there anything you need?"

"Yes. Do you have time to talk with me a bit?" she asked.

"Of course I do. Come in, come in," he said, leading the way back into his office.

Lissa sat down, folded her hands in her lap and then got right to the point.

"As you know, my stalker problem is over. What you don't know is that I'm getting married soon and moving to Summerton, or living here through the week and going there on weekends. We haven't worked that part out yet, but I want you to know I fully intend to honor my contract and finish out the year."

Wilson had a knack for hearing more than what was being said. "Congratulations! As for coming back to work, I have no doubt of your sense of professional responsibility."

Lissa nodded. "Thank you, but you should know that while I am up and moving around some, I haven't been released to come back to work yet. I hope that's not a problem."

"Not at all. In fact, the woman we hired as your substitute is doing a great job. It seems this job came along at the perfect time for her. She's recently divorced and the mother of two young ones. They've been living with her mother, but she said it's causing a bit of tension, and the sooner she can save up to get her own place, the better."

As Lissa was listening to the story, a whole scenario was opening up inside her head.

"I take it she's certified to teach?"

"Yes, fortunately for us," Wilson said.

"Does she want a permanent teaching job?" Lissa asked.

"Oh, yes, she already had a résumé on file here, hoping something would open up for the fall semester."

Lissa saw a solution to two problems instead of one, but she needed Wilson's approval to make it happen.

"Mr. Wilson, I have a suggestion that might solve both her problem and mine. I would gratefully turn in my resignation now due to a family move if she could be hired in my place. It would give her the steady job she needs, and me the freedom to move and live with my husband. It's just a suggestion, and I'm not trying to tell you how to do your job, but…"

Wilson smiled. "No, no, I see the wisdom in the suggestion. However, we couldn't offer her a job until we receive your resignation."

Lissa's heart skipped a beat. "Can I give it to you now, handwritten?"

Wilson was a little surprised, but he nodded in agreement. "I don't see why not. Would you like a pen and paper?"

Lissa was stifling an urge to giggle. "Yes, please."

The principal handed her a piece of school letterhead and a pen. "I'll just give you a couple of minutes on your own," he said as he left the room.

Lissa's hands were shaking as she began to write, but by the time the principal returned with a young woman behind him, her note was finished and lying on his desk.

Lissa saw them walk in and guessed the woman must be the substitute because she knew everyone else at the school. When Mr. Wilson introduced them, she knew she'd been right.

"Have a seat here, Carly. I want you to meet Melissa Sherman. It's her class you've been subbing with. Melissa, this is Carly Vance."

Carly smiled while clearly trying not to stare at the bruises on Melissa's face. "It's nice to meet you, and even better to know the danger to your life is over." Her hands began trembling as she glanced back at the principal. "So is this about terminating the sub job?"

"In a manner of speaking," Wilson said. "Miss Sherman has tendered her resignation due to a family move out of the district, so I thought it prudent to let you know that your presence will still be needed here until we can hire a full-time teacher to finish out the year. I hope you can accommodate us in this manner?"

Lissa saw hope flash across Carly's face. "Oh, yes, sir! No problem. No problem at all, and I hope you'll consider my résumé when you make your decision."

"Of course," Mr. Wilson said. "I'll make sure that happens. Everything takes time."

Carly was still arguing her cause. "Before my divorce I worked for the federal government and had a high security clearance. My girls and I are in need of stability, and this would make all the difference in the world to us."

And just like that, Lissa realized she'd found the perfect family for her little house. "You have two girls?" she asked.

Carly nodded. "They're three and almost five. My oldest goes to pre-K here."

"In case you're interested in moving, I'm going to have an empty two-bedroom house when I leave Mystic," Lissa said. "I was going to sell, but I'd happily rent it with intent to sell if you're interested."

Carly burst into tears. "I came in here expecting to be told I wasn't needed anymore and instead found out my job's been extended *and* there's a permanent opening. If I get the job, I can pay rent."

The principal's smile widened. He picked up Melissa's letter of resignation and stamped it with the date.

"So, Carly, I think for now we're done."

Lissa got a piece of paper out of her purse, wrote down her cell phone number and address and handed it to Carly. "If everything works out for you and you're interested, just give me a call. I can always drive back to Mystic to show you the house."

"Thank you. Thank you so much. Both of you," Carly said. She left the office with a bounce in her step.

Lissa knew how she felt.

"Thank you, Mr. Wilson. I've loved working here, and I appreciate your understanding in what's been a very traumatic time in my life. I'm ready for some good days."

"Perfect," Wilson said. "I'll notify Superintendent Porter of your resignation, but I don't expect any problems, since she's already doing a fine job in the position. And your resignation in the middle of a contract won't affect my willingness to give you a glowing recommendation, given the circumstances."

"So we're good?" Lissa asked.

"We're good," he said. And when they stood up, he shook her hand and then showed her out.

Her friend Margaret Lewis was in the office waiting to see her, and she was properly horrified by Lissa's injuries, and she even cried a little when she learned Lissa was leaving.

"Don't get me wrong. I'm happy for you," Margaret said. "Just a little sad for myself that I won't see you again."

"We'll see each other, for sure," Lissa said. "But I know a new substitute teacher who's shy on friends right now, too."

Margaret nodded and gave her a careful hug. "We'll still have to do Saturday lunch now and then, even if you *are* going to be living in Summerton."

Lissa thought of her beautiful new home and what fun it was going to be to show it off. "You'll have to come visit me for the first lunch, just so you'll know where I live."

"It's a deal," Margaret said. Then she glanced at her watch. "Gotta go. My planning period is over. I love you, girl, and I wish you the best."

Lissa waved. "I'm going to miss hanging out with you daily, but I promise we won't lose touch."

They left the office together, and Lissa texted Mack as she walked toward the exit. He was going to be so excited, and as much as she would miss her kids, she wanted a life with Mack even more.

She sat down on a bench at the curb, waiting for him to come get her and marveled at how quickly life could change—this time for the better.

Her phone signaled a text, and she read it smiling.

On my way.

She leaned back against the bench and sighed. The memorial service was one more hard thing to get through, although this would never truly be behind them until Paul Jackson's murder was solved.

Within minutes, Mack pulled up at the curb and got out.

"Hi, baby. Ready to go home?"

"Yes, please," she said. She waited until they were on their way before she gave him the good news. "Hey, Mack, guess what?"

"What, honey?"

"I found out the substitute teacher in my class is looking for a full-time job, and I took it as the answer to a prayer. Mr. Wilson let me turn in my resignation, and I can pretty much guarantee she'll get the job. As of fifteen minutes ago, I'm unemployed."

Mack let out a whoop of joy.

"This is wonderful. Are you okay with it? You didn't do it just for me? I don't want you unhappy and missing your work."

"I did it for both of us, but mostly for me. I had a drive to face every day, or a long five days without you and only weekends together until summer. I wasn't looking forward to either one. This was the perfect solution."

"What a great way to end the day," Mack said. "I'm so happy for us. I wish Dad was here to see this happening."

Lissa sighed. "So do I. He could have walked me down the aisle."

Mack slid a hand across the seat and patted her leg.

"I'll walk you down the aisle…all the way to the preacher. You're no longer alone here, honey. Remember that."

Lissa's eyes lit up at the idea of walking down the aisle with Mack, and the longer she thought about it, the more perfect it seemed.

"We're here," he said as he pulled up beneath the carport, then handed her the keys. "You go unlock the door. I'll get our things."

Lissa didn't argue. The day had worn her out, and her steps were suddenly dragging.

By the time they got everything hung up and Mack had gone into the other room to start answering messages, she had fallen asleep on the bed, shoes and all.

Mack breathed a sigh of exhaustion as he returned the last call, which was from Trey Jakes.

"Trey, this is Mack. I saw I missed your call. Lissa and I have been in Summerton, and I didn't hear the phone. Sorry."

"No problem," Trey said. "I wanted to run something by you, and if it seems inappropriate, or it offends you, please don't hesitate to say so, and that will be the end of it."

Mack frowned. "That sounds ominous. What's wrong?"

"What's wrong is that we have absolutely no suspects, no witnesses, not a freaking clue as to where to start looking for the killer beyond the fact that because of that bloody tassel, I'm beginning to believe he was either a member of your dad's graduating class or someone he grew up with. I know at first I didn't want to alert the killer that we had connected him to the wreck, but I've discussed this with a police psychologist and alerted Mom. I need to start a fire, and I thought your dad's memorial service might be the place to do it."

Mack frowned. He'd already denied Marcus Silver's offer of getting his dad's classmates together to speak at the service. "What did you have in mind?"

"I want a few minutes of time at the pulpit after the preacher is through and before the congregation is dismissed."

"To say what?" Mack asked.

"To say that the police are aware that the person who killed your dad and Dick Phillips was a classmate, or at the least a schoolmate, and that I believe someone in Mystic knows why this is happening. I want to announce that a hotline has been set up that will keep callers anonymous, and that ten thousand dollars has been donated by a national agency to be given to any person with information that leads to the arrest and conviction of the killer."

Mack took a deep breath. On the surface, his father's memorial service didn't seem like the proper place for this to happen, but the longer he thought about it, the more certain he became that it was actually the perfect place. Nearly everyone in Mystic would be there. What better place to spread the word than when they were sitting among people they'd known all their lives, suddenly having to face the fact that one of them was most likely a killer.

Trey waited and got nothing but silence. He sighed. It had been a wild shot, and it hadn't worked. No loss, no foul.

"It's okay, Mack. I completely understand your reluctance to—"

"Do it," Mack said. "Do it."

"Thank you. Thank you, Mack."

"No, the thanks will go to you when you find the bastard who's doing this," Mack said, and then he disconnected.

He walked back to his bedroom in silence, thinking about what a bombshell that would be, and then found Lissa asleep on the bed, still fully dressed.

Poor baby. Today really kicked her ass.

He slipped the shoes off her feet and covered her with a blanket, then kicked off his own shoes and lay down beside her. Two more nights in this house, the final goodbye to his father tomorrow, and then they could go home.

Nineteen

The urns of green ferns on either side of the pulpit and the large arrangement of fall-colored flowers in front of it were reminders that this was essentially a funeral, even though there was no casket. Paul Jackson's body was still in cold storage in a drawer at the county morgue and in no shape to be viewed, not now and not ever.

To Mack, who was already seated in the front row with Melissa at his side, the absence of a coffin was an ugly reminder of what had happened to his dad, and how truly alone he and Melissa were in this world, with no extended family members to gather on the pew in mutual grief.

The church was not just full but overflowing, and the staff had even added metal folding chairs along the walls and out into the foyer for extra seating. The citizens of Mystic were there both to offer up their condolences and partly out of curiosity at how this funeral would match up to the one held for Dick Phillips. Everyone noticed Mack Jackson and Melissa Sherman sitting alone on the front pew, which made the service that much more poignant. Reuniting and resuming an old love affair in the midst of such sadness had captured every woman's heart in Mystic, except maybe Jessica York, who had taken it upon herself to be out of town.

Lissa knew her facial bruises were a source of discussion, but not in a mean way, and Mack's careful movements were a reminder that he'd nearly died in an effort to catch her stalker. She felt battered and sore, and today she also felt grief. She remembered the day she'd buried her mother and how alone in the world it had left her feeling.

She glanced up at Mack, and he seemed to sense her scrutiny because he looked down, saw tears glistening in her eyes and frowned.

"What, honey? Are you okay? Do you need to get out of here?" he asked.

"No, nothing like that," she whispered, as she gave his hand a quick squeeze. "I'm just so sad for you today."

His belly knotted a little bit tighter. Sympathy was going to be hard to deal with today.

"Thank you, baby," he said softly.

She leaned her head against his shoulder and kept hold of his hand, and that was the way they were sitting when the service began.

Mack noticed more about Pastor Farley's clothing than he did what the man was saying. The moment the pastor had approached the pulpit, Mack's mind had gone blank. He kept staring at the stained-glass window above the choir loft, noticing how the sunlight coming through the colored panes painted the walls and floor and the top of the preacher's bald head.

This was a travesty, an awful nightmare that wouldn't come to an end.

When Lissa began to weep, his focus shifted to the sadness on her face, and he knew she was remembering all over again that it had been her car. Even if a killer had pushed the button, her car had been his weapon.

The knot in his throat grew tighter as he pulled her close. Even when the preacher stopped talking and someone started singing, Mack felt emotionally raw. He barely remembered his mother's funeral, but he would never forget today. This one shouldn't have happened. Not now. Not like this.

Pastor Farley stood after the end of the song. He'd already been forewarned that the police chief wanted to speak, but not told why. He had one last thing on his agenda, and then he would turn the podium over to Trey Jakes.

"I have two announcements to make before we adjourn. One is that the ladies of our church have dessert and coffee waiting in the dining area. Mack and Melissa will join you for a short time, but as you can see, they are both still healing from their own ordeal. And now the last thing of note. Chief Jakes of the Mystic Police Department has something to announce. Chief, the podium is yours."

Lissa quickly realized Mack was not surprised, although from the murmurs of the congregation behind her, they certainly were. This was definitely out of the norm.

Trey walked down the middle aisle of the church with long, steady strides. His uniform was spotless, and the Stetson he habitually wore was in his hand.

When he stepped up to the podium, he looked first at Mack and then out across the congregation.

"Mack has given me permission to make this announcement at his father's service because he and my fiancée, Dallas Phillips, are still waiting for justice for their fathers' deaths. So this is what we now believe— a killer sits among you."

The uproar that followed was instantaneous and full of righteous indignation, but Trey kept speaking and they wanted to hear the rest, so silence quickly fell as he continued.

"Someone in this town, maybe more than one of you, knows something they're afraid to tell. Or maybe you don't even realize that what you know could possibly matter. What some of you don't know, and others may have forgotten, is that the night of the 1980 high school graduation, four of the graduates were in a deadly wreck. One girl died at the scene. To this day, the three survivors have no memory of why the car they were in was going over a hundred miles an hour when it hit a tree. They have no memory of anything that night after they stepped off that stage at graduation.

"And then there are two men, good men and our friends, who have been murdered within weeks of each other here in Mystic. Is it any coincidence that Dick Phillips and Paul Jackson were two of the three survivors of that wreck? Does their killer think we are stupid and naive enough to overlook that fact? To assume it's not connected?

"Someone in here knows something more about that night and they're not telling. Mack and Dallas have lost their fathers because of your silence. So if you don't have the guts to come forward in person, you might be compelled to come forward now that a national victims and survivors group has donated ten thousand dollars to be given to the person with information that leads to the arrest and conviction of the killer. There's a hotline you can call. It won't record your identity or location. You can remain anonymous if you choose.

"So before you go eat your cake and drink your coffee, think back, and think hard. What did you see that night? What do you know? What gossip did you hear? The phone number is on a sign posted on the church bulletin board, and it will be in the newspaper, as well. Please call before it's too late."

Trey was about to walk away when someone from the congregation called out, "Who was the other survivor? Who was the girl who didn't die?"

A muscle ticked at the side of Trey's mouth, but he didn't hesitate to answer. "My mother, Betsy Jakes."

Silence enveloped the room as he stepped down from the pulpit and exited the church. Everyone got the implication. If she was the only one left alive, then she was the killer's next target. The hush was palpable.

Pastor Farley walked back up to the microphone.

"Dessert is being served in the dining hall. Please join me in giving Mack and Melissa our condolences."

Then the pastor whisked Mack and Melissa through a door just off to the side of the pulpit and into the dining hall before the congregation could get there, and got them seated.

"Mack, I think that was a brave and gutsy thing to do. I hope it pays off," he said.

"So do I," Mack said.

"You knew ahead of time, didn't you?" Lissa asked.

"I didn't see the message from Trey until we got home, and by the time I read it you'd fallen asleep. And then this morning, there was just so much going on that—"

"Oh, it doesn't matter whether I knew beforehand or not," she said. "I'm just hopeful the shock factor knocks at someone's memory."

"Yeah, that and the ten thousand dollars," Mack added.

Lissa sighed. "True. Money talks."

And then she heard the rumble of a crowd and turned toward the door. "Here they come. Are you okay?"

Mack leaned over and lightly kissed her on the cheek. "Yes, and thank you."

"For what?"

"For forgiving me for breaking your heart and still loving me anyway," he said softly. Then he stood as the first wave of people approached. After that, time seemed to fly.

Someone brought Lissa a piece of pie and, at her request, a glass of iced tea. She ate a few bites and then handed the rest to Mack when there was a lull.

He ate standing up, but with an eye on her pale face. "Are you okay?"

"I think I need to lie down," she said.

"Then, we're out of here," he said, setting the plate aside. He waved the pastor down as he gathered up her purse and took her by the arm. "Lissa needs to rest. Please give everyone our apologies."

"Absolutely," Farley said, and he patted Lissa's arm. "I wish both of you the best."

"Thank you for everything," she said.

Mack wound his way through the crowded dining hall, saying goodbyes, nodding and smiling, all without pausing. Lissa's exhaustion was evident. What wasn't bruised and purple on her face was ghostly white.

Mack got her in the SUV and then headed home.

"You should have said something sooner, honey."

"No, it wasn't that. It sort of hit me all at once," she said. "I'm sure I'll feel better once we get back to the house. I already feel better just being away from that noise."

Mack reached for her hand and held it all the way home.

Once inside, he paused in the living room to see what she might need.

"Do you need a cold drink or anything?"

"No, sweetheart. I just want to lie down. Will you help me out of this dress? My arms feel like lead."

He hurried her down the hall, and then had her undressed and in bed within minutes.

As soon as she was comfortable, he began to change out of his suit, talking to her as she watched him.

"Tomorrow we go home. When you feel like it, we'll get a moving crew to your house and pack up everything you want to bring with you."

"I'm leaving all the furnishings with the house. There are some keepsakes I want, some of the dishes and such, but all I'll really need are my clothes and laptop."

"You want to sell the place?" he asked. "If you do, we'll list it when we list this one. I don't have any desire to keep it without Dad in it."

"No," she said as she rolled the pillow beneath her neck and shifted to a more comfortable position. "The substitute teacher who's handling my class is probably going to be hired in my place. She needs a house for herself and her two girls. I offered to rent her mine if she was interested."

Mack paused and then smiled at her. "That was very generous of you."

Lissa shrugged. "She needs something that I have and no longer need. It seemed the logical thing to do." She watched him for a few moments longer, thinking to herself how blessed she was that he was back in her life. "Hey, Mack?"

"Yeah?" he said, as he began hanging up the suit.

"Do you want a big wedding?"

He stopped. "I want what you want."

"We don't have any family. We have friends, but that's not the same thing."

"Agreed," he said.

"How would you feel if we just got married one morning by a justice of the peace and then went about our day as if nothing had changed?"

He smiled. "No honeymoon, either?"

She yawned. "We couldn't afford one the first time, and I don't feel much like a honeymoon while your Dad's murder remains unsolved."

Mack sat down on the side of the bed and then scooped her up and into his arms.

"You're going to hurt yourself!" Lissa cried.

"But I didn't," he said. "I just had to hold you. You are, without doubt, the most precious thing in my life. We always were on the same page. It's nice to know some things never change."

Then he leaned down and kissed her, first on the lips until he heard her groan, and then the top of her head where the curls were the thickest, taking care not to get too close to the healing wound.

"One of these days, when we no longer have staples or sores, or scabs or black eyes, I am going to take you to bed for a week. Think you can handle that?"

"I look forward to the experience," she drawled.

Mack threw back his head and laughed, and then was shocked at the joy in his heart on this saddest of days.

"We're going to live a long and happy life," he said.

"Just as we always planned," she added.

He shrugged. "Better now than never?"

She cupped a hand against his cheek as she watched the expressions changing on his face.

"We got our chance, Matthew...our second chance. We owe it to ourselves to live it to the fullest."

He kissed her again, this time longer. Reluctantly, he finally stopped.

"Rest now. We'll pack in the morning and sleep in our own bed tomorrow night."

She grinned. "That bed with all the fertility cherubs?"

"That's the one."

"I can hardly wait," she said softly. When he pulled the covers up over her shoulders, she was still smiling as she closed her eyes.

The killer grabbed a piece of cake and began forking small bites into his mouth as he moved among the people. He was still reeling from the shock of the chief's announcement and feeling just the tiniest bit vulnerable. Instead of leaving right away as he'd planned, now he wanted people to remember he was there if the need for an alibi ever arose.

One of the first people he saw was Betsy Jakes, and then he noticed her daughter, Trina, just a short distance away. Betsy was being inundated with people who were both curious and concerned on her behalf. She must have known that announcement was coming, he thought, which meant she had been forewarned, as well. Now there would be all kinds of people helping keep watch on her. He had to act quickly, while everyone was still absorbing the shock.

He casually strolled up close to where she was standing, eating his cake and smiling at people passing by, but listening carefully to everything Betsy said.

Then he heard his name being called and scanned the crowd. When he saw an old friend waving, he headed toward him to visit while keeping an eye on the time. As soon as he'd circled the room at least twice and spoken to a goodly number of the people who were there, he set down his plate, nodded at Mack and Melissa, who were already on their way out, and slipped out of the church by a back door and left town.

He needed to be in place when Betsy and her daughter drove home. It was unfortunate they were together. He had no desire to kill Trina Jakes, but leaving her alive as a witness wasn't happening.

Betsy saw Mack leaving and noticed the pallor of Melissa's face and felt sorry for their misery. They weren't only grieving a loss, but were trying to heal from their nearly fatal experiences. Another fifteen minutes passed before Betsy began looking around for her daughter. With Mack gone, the other guests had gravitated to her and quickly overwhelmed her with their concern, until she was ready to get away.

When she finally spotted Trina, she was surprised to see her over in a corner talking to Lee, which made her hesitate. If they were trying to work things out, she didn't want to be the one to mess up a good thing. But she couldn't leave without letting Trina know and decided she would just text her. It was be less problematic all around.

Trina was in tears and trying not to break down. The last thing she had expected was for Lee to approach her in public and try to make up, although she should have expected something, since she'd been refusing to answer his calls and texts.

Lee was heartsick. He had known within minutes of their fight that he'd made the biggest mistake of his life, and he desperately wanted her back. He was willing to do anything she asked to make that happen.

"Please, Trina. Can't we just go get a Coke together? We can sit together and talk. No pressure, and I'll take you home anytime you say. I made a mistake flying off the handle like that. My jealousy is an ugly fault, and I've been working on it all my life. You know my story. You know my mom left my dad for another man when my three brothers and I were just babies. I should have trusted you. I shouldn't have let that asshole get to me, but I did. I'm sorry. I am *so* sorry."

It was everything she'd wanted to hear, but she didn't know if it was wise to trust him again.

"How can I believe this won't happen over and over throughout our lives? I work with the public. I interact with people on a daily basis, and I enjoy spending time with my friends. I was trying to tell you that he was just pissed off at me because I kept turning him down. He wanted to hurt me, so he lied to you. You don't even know him. You *do* know me. You believed the ranting of a man you barely know by name, but not the woman you're supposed to love. I don't intend to live my entire life being afraid of making you mad. Just let it be, Lee."

Lee groaned. "Please don't let this be the end. Give it more time. I'm good with that. I'll wait. I'll wait as long as you need."

She wanted to say yes. She loved him. God help her, she loved him to distraction, but she was afraid.

"I don't know. Maybe," she said.

Relief surged through Lee so fast his knees nearly buckled.

"Thank you, Trina! Thank you. I swear on my daddy's grave that I will never let you down again."

She frowned. "I didn't say yes. I said maybe."

"I know, and I'll take a maybe any day. I love you. You're all that matters to me."

Trina's phone began signaling a text. She glanced down, then saw it was from her mom and read it.

"That was from Mom. She's ready to go home. Look, call me tomorrow evening after I get off work. We'll talk, okay?"

"Yes, yes," Lee said, and then he took her by both hands and kissed them, one after the other. "I love you, Trina. Thank you for giving me a second chance."

She sighed. "I love you, too, Lee. That's why it hurt so much."

She pulled her hands away and left him standing, but it was more than he'd hoped for when he had come here today. He took a long shaky breath, and then left the church and headed for his car.

Trina went over to her mother, slid a hand across her shoulders and gave her a quick hug. "You've had quite an afternoon. So you're ready to get out of here, huh?"

"Yes, but I saw you talking to Lee, and if you'd rather stay and spend some time with him, feel free. I just didn't want to leave without letting you know I was going."

Trina shook her head. "No, I'm ready to leave, too. I told him to call me tomorrow after I get home from work. I said I'd talk."

Betsy smiled. "If you love him, this is good. Forgiveness is a powerful thing, and no one's perfect."

Trina smiled. "I know, Mama, but I've given him all the time he deserves today. Let's go. I'm ready to get out of these shoes."

"Then, we're gone," Betsy said.

She got in the car, sent Trey a text that they were going home and buckled up.

A few minutes later she and Trina passed the city-limit sign on their way out of town. The drive home usually took around fifteen minutes, and they were eager to get back. They were both talked out and rode in comfortable silence, each locked into her own memories of the day.

It wasn't until Betsy topped the hill leading down to their drive that she noticed a car stalled on the side of the road. The hood was up, but she couldn't see the driver. "Looks like someone is having car trouble," she said.

Trina sat up, and then straightened the seat belt over

her breasts. "I'm sure they used their cell to call for help," she said.

"Most likely, but I can hardly drive by without checking. We don't have to get out, okay?"

Trina frowned. "Mama, your life is in danger."

Betsy sighed. "Sweetheart, you cannot hide from life and then say you're living. Understand?"

Trina rolled her eyes. "I hear you, but I don't have to agree."

Betsy laughed and began to brake as they approached. Then the driver stepped out from behind the raised hood, and Betsy snorted as she put the car in Park.

"See. Hardly the big bad wolf. Roll your window down a second. We'll make sure help is on the way."

"Hey!" Betsy said as the man bent down to look in the window. "Looks like you're having a little car trouble. Do you need any help?"

"Not a bit," he said. Then he raised the handgun and shot Trina point-blank in the chest and Betsy before she had time to scream.

Then he went back to his car, lowered the hood and drove away, leaving the women's car idling and the two of them dead where they sat.

It was the squawk of a crow sitting on a nearby fence that Trina heard first, then she heard herself moan as she fought her way back to consciousness. She didn't know where she was or what was happening, but her chest felt like it was on fire.

"Mama, Mama, I'm sick," she mumbled, and was grabbing at her breasts as she opened her eyes.

Then she saw where they were and the blood—God, the blood. Her mother was slumped over the steering wheel with a hole in the side of her face, and Trina knew she was dead. The pain of that loss was beyond measure. She wanted to scream, but she had no breath to spare, and in that moment she knew if she didn't do something, she was going to be dead, too.

She was struggling to stay conscious when she felt something in her hand. Her phone! It was her phone. She managed to punch in 911. She was trying to stay conscious, but by the time the call was answered she was slumped sideways, her head hanging partway out the window.

When the call first came in, dispatcher Avery Jones got no answer, but he kept repeating, "911, what is your emergency? Hello! This is 911. What is your emergency, please?"

Trey was standing in the hallway outside his office when he heard the dispatcher repeating himself and walked over.

"Got a hang-up?" he asked.

"I don't think so," Avery said. "I can hear an engine running, like a car. The line is still open. I think someone called and passed out. It's a cell phone, so it's not registering an address."

Trey frowned. "Give me the number. I'll see if we can triangulate from the location."

Even before the dispatcher was through reading out the last two digits of the number, every muscle in Trey's body had turned to stone. His ears were roaring, and he felt like he was going to throw up.

"Did you get it?" the dispatcher asked. "Want me to read it out to you again?"

"No need," Trey said. "That's my sister's number. She and Mom were on their way home from the church."

His hands were shaking as he tried his mother's cell, but the call rang unanswered, then went to voice mail. He tried Trina's number, but just as he'd expected, it went straight to voice mail.

"I'm going out to the farm. Get an ambulance en route to the farm."

"Yes, sir," Avery said. "Do you want company? Earl is on patrol."

"I'll let you know."

Trey ran for his patrol car, and left town with lights and sirens blasting. He wanted to pray, but the only words that would come to mind were *No, please, please, no.*

The miles flew past so fast that the roadside was a blur, and then he topped the hill just above the driveway to their farm and his heart dropped. Betsy's car was idling in the middle of the blacktop only a few yards away from the mailbox. He could see someone's head hanging partway out of the passenger side window, and he started to scream.

"No, damn it, no!"

He slammed the patrol car into Park as soon as he was close and got out on the run.

The driver's-side window was covered in blood and brain matter, and he was struggling with the need to vomit as he opened the door and slid a hand along his mother's neck checking for a pulse that he already knew wasn't there.

"Jesus, Mary and Joseph," he sobbed, staggering around to the other side of the car with tears rolling down his face and a pain he couldn't describe in his chest.

Trina's head was lying partway out the window, and it was quickly obvious that she'd been shot in the chest. When he saw the phone in her hand, he thought about how scared she must have been to call for help.

He ran his hand down the side of her neck, feeling desperately for a pulse, and when it kicked faintly beneath his fingertips he was so shocked he almost forgot what to do.

"Shit! She's alive," he mumbled, and ran back to his patrol car to call it in.

"This is Chief Jakes. Radio the ambulance en route to 19929 West Covell Road that I have a live one. Gunshot wound to the chest. Then contact the coroner's office and dispatch him to the same address. Then contact the county sheriff and get him here ASAP. I need all available deputies at this site."

"Yes, sir. Dispatching, sir."

Trey threw the mike down, popped the trunk for the first-aid kit and then ran back to the car. Within seconds he had made pressure bandages out of some disposable towels and was holding them on both Trina's entrance and exit wounds, trying to stop the bleeding. He couldn't look at his mother because he knew he would lose his mind. There was still a chance, albeit a slim one, to save his sister's life, and he wasn't going to fail her if he could help it.

And so he stood in the road, engulfed by the scent of blood and exhaust fumes, his sister's body sandwiched between the two pressure bandages he was holding, unaware that he was sobbing. The blood continued to ooze between his fingers as he prayed.

He didn't think about the fact that every local with a scanner had heard his broadcast, or that a good number of listeners would recognize the address of the Jakes farm, but it was apparent to everyone who'd heard him that his call for help at the church earlier had come too late. Someone was dead, and someone else was probably dying. They'd all seen Betsy and her daughter together. Which one of them was still alive?

The killer heard the news as he was gassing up his car and nearly dropped the hose. The chief had requested an ambulance and the coroner. That couldn't happen. That couldn't be true. He'd completed kill shots to the both of them. One in the heart. One in the head. What the fuck had gone wrong?

* * * * *

Don't miss
DARK HEARTS,
the final book in
New York Times *bestselling author*
Sharon Sala's
SECRETS AND LIES *trilogy.*

Discover the next spine-tingling *Krewe of Hunters*
story from *New York Times* bestselling author and
queen of paranormal suspense

HEATHER GRAHAM

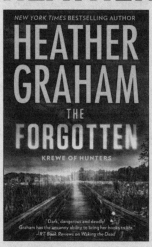

Was Maria Gomez murdered by
her husband? A man presumed
dead—slain by a crime boss? FBI
agent Brett Cody can't believe
it; dead or alive, the man had
loved his wife. Then, at a
dolphin research facility just a
few miles away, new employee
Lara Mayhew discovers a piece
of evidence that proves Brett
right. *A human hand*. A hand
from the dismembered corpse
of Miguel Gomez.

As rumors of crazed zombies
abound in the Miami media,
Brett and Lara find themselves
working closely with the FBI's elite unit of paranormal
investigators, the Krewe of Hunters. An elderly crime boss who's
losing his memory seems to be key to solving this case, but…
there's no motive. Unless Brett and Lara can uncover one in
the Miami underworld. And that means they have to protect
themselves. *And each other*.

Available now, wherever books are sold!

Be sure to connect with us at:
Harlequin.com/Newsletters
Facebook.com/HarlequinBooks
Twitter.com/HarlequinBooks

MIRA®

www.MIRABooks.com

MHG1789

Discover the captivating new psychological thriller
from national bestselling author

MARY KUBICA

A simple act of kindness can have
unintended consequences...

She sees the teenage girl on the train platform, standing in the pouring rain, clutching an infant in her arms. She boards a train and is whisked away. But she can't get the girl out of her head...

Heidi Wood has always been a charitable woman. Still, her husband and daughter are horrified when Heidi returns home one day with a young woman named Willow and her four-month-old baby in tow. Disheveled and apparently homeless, this girl could be a criminal—or worse. Despite her family's objections, Heidi invites Willow and the baby to take refuge in their home.

Heidi spends the next few days helping Willow get back on her feet, but as clues into Willow's past begin to surface, Heidi is soon forced to decide just how far she'd be willing to go to help a stranger.

Available now, wherever books are sold!